Confidant

Scott Hamill

Prologue

'I just don't know how to thank you,' Lorraine said with moistening eyes, 'I just feel like everything's falling into place.'

'I'm glad to hear it,' James replied, leaning back in his padded rocking chair.

Lorraine reached forward to grab a tissue from a box on the adjacent bookshelf. As she did so the old grey sofa creaked under her. James made a mental note for the hundredth time to replace the junky old thing when he had the chance.

James simply watched with his hands clasped over his knee as Loraine wiped a single escaping tear from her face and crumpled the tissue into the pocket of her jeans that were far too big for her.

'I think I'll go talk to Travis,' She said after a few ugly sniffs.

'Do you think it'll be all right, have all the doubts gone?' James said, making as much eye contact as he could.

'Yeah. We can make this work. I haven't really believed that in a while.' Lorraine sniffed again as she smiled an overly toothy smile.

'Well my door's always open if that's not the case, Lorraine,' James smiled warmly. Lorraine simply nodded in response. Another sniff, wetter this time.

'I should go talk to him,' She checked her phone.

'Good idea,' James replied, resting his smile as she looked away. He tried not to sound too absent minded. He wasn't uncaring, but he knew his tone could make it sound as though he were. Though he couldn't escape the feeling that he had lost more interest than he would admit out loud.

As he walked with Lorraine down the hall towards the front door she was quietly saying things that could have either been practice conversations for Travis or more thank yous directed in James' direction. He didn't appreciate gratitude as much as he should, and in his line of work a lot of people tended to go over the top.

He really didn't feel like he was doing that much.

As James held the heavy door Lorraine held up her head and thanked him once again. He pretended to be happy to hear it.

The hallway housed the lift, the stairwell exit that no one ever took from his floor, and the entrance to the flat across the way which had been vacant since James moved in.

After Lorraine thanked him one last time he watched her get into the lift and waved a happy goodbye. As the doors closed and she went out of sight James recognised the fact that he would likely never see her again.

It didn't bother him so much that time.

The minimally furnished living room always felt emptier than usual after a patient had left. For most people guests left their presence in the form of crumbs, coffee stains or the faint smell of whatever fragrance they had been wearing. To James it was more of a tangible vacancy, a hollow soundlessness that made his footsteps echo and his own home feel like the unknown quarters of a distant stranger.

With a calm sigh James loosened the tie he didn't have to wear and poured himself a generous snifter of whisky from the globe in the corner before taking a seat in his rocking chair and looking for a moment at where Lorraine had been sitting, where many others had and would sit.

He wondered if he would miss her. Their friendship was different from most he had experienced, it had started out casually when they had been sat next to each other in a GCSE maths class nine years before. It had been a slow burn, the odd conversation, the half-hearted invitation for coffee, nothing serious for months though they considered each other friends.

It only really kicked off after a year when Lorraine's parents had kicked her out of the house at seventeen, James could still remember the phone call he received at two in the morning when she was outside his door, seven miles from her own.

After that they had gotten much closer, they had even toyed with the idea of a romantic relationship, though it didn't last longer than a few months. She began seeing Travis at eighteen and they were engaged within a month of knowing each other. From then on Lorraine stopped speaking to James. It was not a slow process.

Six years later her marriage began to face some serious issues, only then did she reach out to her old friend. It had been a year since then. Lorraine had been visiting James on the worst days, after something bad had happened. She had messaged ahead most of the time, a rare enough courtesy which James appreciated.

She came to him for advice and insight because she felt she could trust him. James took her in with no hard feelings, he found it hard to hold grudges.

In recent weeks Lorraine had seemed more herself – at least as far as James knew. She was happier, calmer, she had been reaching for the tissues less and less. James had known before she came that evening that it would probably be the last time he would see her. It was just the way things went.

James had a degree in psychology but had worked as a barista after university before the death of his father, who had left him a sizeable inheritance that shocked the entire family, James included.

He had bought his penthouse – it wasn't actually a penthouse, that was just what the appraiser had said and James liked to run with it – and had enough money to live comfortably for the foreseeable future so long as he didn't make any overly extravagant purchases.

He was not a psychiatrist, much less employed, but he had regular visits from people of various stages of familiarity. It had reached the point where James had placed some of his lesser used folding chairs in the hallway outside his flat to simulate a doctor's waiting room. He had only done so because he considered it funny, but found that a few of his visitors who were less familiar with his sense of humour had taken the gesture somewhat too literally.

James was considering topping off his whisky when he heard his phone vibrate on the windowsill by his chair, its movements muffled by the books it sat on. It was a message from Charlotte asking if he wanted to go for a few drinks at The Regal. It didn't take any more than a few seconds for James to come to the conclusion that, yes, he did in fact want to go for a few drinks at The Regal.

1.

Charlotte sat at her favourite booth directly behind the main service area of The Regal. Upon arrival, two all too familiar thoughts entered James' mind. The first was why Charlotte always chose to sit at the only table out of sight of the bar staff where they couldn't get direct service. The second was why Charlotte, a woman proud of her ability to flirt with just about anyone, always chose to drink with James in the only gay pub for miles.

'Hey there hot stuff,' Charlotte beamed when she saw him. A pint sat in front of her, it was obviously not her first. A second pint of something light sat on a paper bar mat across from her.

'Long day?' James asked as he sat down and took his first sip. Charlotte had good taste in beer.

'Surprised you came,' she smiled.

'No you're not,' James returned her smile.

'You got me,' Charlotte threw her arms into the air.

'Why do you always choose this place?' James said after thanking her for the drink. 'And why always this seat?'

'Something wrong with The Regal?' She asked insincerely, knowing what he was getting at. 'And don't tell me the nostalgia's lost to you already. Don't you remember it was at this seat, out of sight, where you-'

'I remember what happened,' James glared. Charlotte was definitely a few pints in already.

'Even ignoring that, what about us? This is where we went.' Charlotte winked, 'We met here, remember?'

'No we didn't,' James couldn't help but smile, the dates he and Charlotte had gone on in that bar was the source of many of their jokes.

'Well we had our first drink together here. I consider that to be more a first meeting.'

'I'll drink to that I suppose,' James said, taking a larger swig than he normally did as he acknowledged he needed to catch up to his friend.

'So, what about us?' Charlotte winked.

'You already said that.'

'I mean *us*.' she said playfully.

'That was a long time ago,' James sighed.

'Two years isn't that long'

'No argument. Still no. You wanna pick up men then go to a straight bar.' The two of them laughed heartily.

James lived for the quiet nights with good company. He had always hated the clubs and live music venues that made conversation almost impossible. He had not drank with Charlotte in a few weeks, though it could have only been days. It warmed him to sit opposite a good friend without having to give advice or try to tiptoe around his words.

Once James had finished his beer he let out a quiet belch and got up to get another round, keeping in mind to make sure his drink was stronger than Charlotte's.

'You know,' Charlotte said when he returned, 'for a psychiatrist you're pretty dismissive.'

'I'm not a psychiatrist,' James said the words that had long since become something of a catchphrase.

'You basically are,' Charlotte's voice was marked with a hint of sadness, her words were not slurred.

'Am I being dismissive?' James said, the accusation stinging him slightly.

'No. I just. I don't know.'

'So how's Andy?' James asked, a smug smirk appearing on his face as he lifted the glass to his lips.

'How did you know?'

'Lucky guess.'

'Bullshit,' Charlotte leaned back. 'It's never a lucky guess with you.'

'So how is he?'

'He's fine. Got a new guy.'

'Already?' James tried to not sound too surprised, 'What happened to Gregg?'

'Didn't work out. Turns out Gregg wasn't happy that Andy used to sleep with his psychiatrist.'

'I'm not a-'

'I know, I know.' Charlotte waved her hand in the air as though shooing James' words away. 'Andy wanted to come when I mentioned I was gonna meet you.'

'Why didn't he?'

'I told him not to. Figured you wouldn't want him here.'

'You could have asked me, you know?' James said, though he didn't really mean it. Charlotte knew him too well and he didn't want to see Andy so soon, they both knew Charlotte had neglected to ask him to save James the guilt of saying no.

***

James wasn't as drunk as he had hoped to be when he returned to his building, but the lift still jostled him more than he would have liked. He knew he needed sleep, but he also knew he had beers in the fridge.

As the lift reached the top floor and the doors opened at his hallway waiting room James smelled something familiar that was different from the scented powder the cleaners spread over the carpet. It was an aftershave hastily and amply applied to cover the smell of sweat as one would do before a nervous first date or job interview.

James turned the corner after stepping out of the lift and greeted his guest before even looking at him.

'Hello Andy,' he tried not to sound inconvenienced.

'You're late,' Andy folded his arms.

'For... what? You knew I was out with Charlotte.'

'You didn't keep my time slot open?' Andy approached the door to James' flat, clearly looking to invite himself in.

'I'm not a-'

'Can we talk or not?' Andy interrupted.

'I've had a bit to drink,' James said.

'Good. Me too.'

'You're not going to leave, are you?' James turned around as Andy took his first step into the hallway.

'Not without a fight,' Andy smiled.

'You know where to sit.'

'Been a while since I sat here,' Andy bounced slightly on the sofa. 'Still not replaced this old thing, huh?'

'It's been six months,' James said as he brought in two opened bottles of beer. He was beginning to see Charlotte's point about being dismissive, though being half drunk was not the best time to start thinking about self-improvement.

'Been counting?'

'No,' James said sternly as he sat in his rocking chair.

'How's living alone?'

'Pretty good once I got used to it.'

'Have you been-'

'Why are you here, Andy?' James looked to him with tired eyes.

'Touchy,' Andy looked offended.

'Why are you here?' James repeated.

'Can't a guy stop in on an old friend?' Andy leant back, trying to lighten the mood.

'He can,' James nodded then looked to the floor, 'but it is one in the morning so at least respect my scepticism a little, huh?' James knew he was being a little wordy, that he often sounded more like an intellectual when he was just the right amount of smashed. Alcohol affected his judgement, but rarely his speech.

'I was in the neighbourhood and that I'd drop in. Nothing nefarious, I swear,' he threw his arms into the air, almost spilling his beer. 'So how's Charlotte?'

'Why are you asking me?' James flashed a knowing look, a smug expression that made Andy look away. Andy had always hated that about James, his attentiveness made it impossible to sneak anything by him.

'What is it with you, man?' Andy dropped his joviality a little too quickly, 'Why do you treat me like I cheated on you?'

'I never used that word.'

'Wronged you, then,' Andy rolled his eyes more than he meant to.

'It's history,' James said half-heartedly as he looked out the window. His building was the tallest for miles and he could see out to the North Sea on a good day. Now he only saw the sparkling lights of the city and distant towns across the water. A cruise ship moved slowly across the water, its glowing orange radiance danced on the water's darkness.

'How's the new beau?' James asked without looking back.

'I knew it,' Andy beamed, something of a triumphant grin appeared on his face.

'What?' James looked away from the window and back towards his guest.

'You wanna know if he's better than you, don't you?' Andy chuckled.

'I was thinking you'd start with his name,' James glared jokingly.

'People call him The Wraith.'

'The Wraith?' James scrunched up his face at the ugly nickname.

'A nickname he got in halls, he's a moaner.'

'Wraiths don't moan,' James said with uncertainty, 'they scream.'

'You're thinking of banshees,' Andy replied confidently. 'Well either way he does both.'

James noticed it then, in the last sentence Andy averted his gaze and his playfulness dissolved entirely. He knew then why Andy had seen fit to come to his door that evening, or at least one of the reasons.

'Or so you've heard,' James said coldly. It was not a question, though he did his best to not sound insulting.

'Come on, man,' Andy sank into the sofa, he held his beer with both hands and began to pick at the label.

'You don't have to say it,' James tried to reassure him.

They spent some time in silence as they drank. Andy collected his scattered thoughts and stewed in the words he knew he had come to say but ultimately didn't really want to. James knew to give his friend the space he needed, when it came time to offer another drink Andy accepted with no hesitation.

James had become accustomed to silences and had learned that they were necessary in his line of pseudo-work. Andy had brought up the nickname and revealed an insecurity with little to no prompting. Social calls for James were never really that social.

'Was I...' Andy spoke hesitantly, 'Was I good? Y'know, with you?'

'Why is that important?' James said, knowing the deflection would be noted.

'That's a no,' Andy rubbed the back of his neck.

'It's an 'it doesn't matter',' James said reassuringly. 'Look, if I answered that question, be it good or bad, would that help you at all? What would you get out of it?'

Andy took a moment to think. 'Nothing, I guess,' he admitted.

'So why ask?'

'I don't know, man.' Andy set his beer on the floor and clasped his hands behind his head, he exhaled loudly before picking the bottle back up. His movements were erratic as though he had forgotten how to relax. 'How much beer have you got?' He asked.

'Enough,' James smiled.

***

James could hear Andy's snoring while he mixed himself a hangover remedy from crushed up painkillers and a red berry smoothie. His hangover consisted of little more than a dull headache thanks to how slowly he'd been drinking in the three hours he and Andy had been talking.

Andy had never been good at handling his alcohol, which made drinking with him occasionally problematic. James knew he would likely be incapable of speech upon waking.

James was half way towards concluding the decision of whether or not a coffee would compliment his smoothie when a too-loud knock at his front door made him forget what he was thinking about. The noise instead shook a memory loose from the night before, something Andy had said to him that James was not prepared to hear.

'You're never going to be able to find someone unless you get over-'

Someone knocked again, louder this time. James walked down the hallway, smoothie in hand, and opened the door to see the postman, his expression far too happy to match how loudly and impatiently he had knocked. James was relieved to see him as morning visits often offered people frantically panicking about what they had drunkenly done the night before, normally when James himself was too hungover to want to deal with any of it.

James signed for the package despite not remembering ordering anything, bid the postman a farewell and walked into the living room to see Andy still unconscious on the sofa. James set the package down on the coffee table too heavily and Andy stirred awake.

'What? What?' Andy groaned as his mind slowly returned to whatever reality his hangover would allow.

'Time to wake up,' James said coldly.

'Man,' Andy rubbed his head as he sat up. 'The sofa? You couldn't even give me the spare room?'

'You passed out before I could offer,' James walked out of the room, remembering his thoughts before the postman had interrupted. He filled the kettle and poured some instant coffee into a cup. A loud yawn sounded from the doorway as Andy made his way into the kitchen.

'Hey, man,' Andy began, the usual hungover melancholy in his voice, 'about what I said lat nig-'

'Don't worry about it,' James said quickly without looking at him.

'But I said some real-'

'Don't worry about it,' James said slightly louder, giving Andy a look this time that told him he needed to shut up. 'Coffee?' He offered.

'What? God no,' Andy recoiled. 'That shit dehydrates you. Why would you drink it with a hangover?'

'Because it wakes you up,' James said plainly.

'Nah thanks. I'm meeting someone for lunch today, anyway. That reminds me, can I use your shower?' Andy said, James ignored how much Andy seemed to stumble over referring to it as *his* shower.

'Go ahead.' James replied, unsure as to what was said that had reminded Andy that he needed to take a shower.

Without another word Andy marched into the bathroom, leaving James to go back to the living room and inspect the package on the coffee table. He didn't remember ordering anything and wasn't expecting any gifts. Though he was occasionally in the habit of buying unnecessary things while drunk, he could normally recall doing so.

He lifted the package and checked it, it was not a professionally wrapped parcel from any credible online store and his address had been written in pen. He flipped the box upside down and found the return address in small print on the upper corner of the base. It was an address in Manchester, one he recognised immediately. He set the package back on the coffee table and turned from it, its contents were a mystery he would leave to a later time when his brain didn't feel quite so fragile.

James heard singing then, the discordant voice muffled by water and the glass partition which separated the shower from the rest of the bathroom. It was familiar, something Andy always did when he was hungover. James had not missed it.

2.

It would be almost a week before James found any time to himself, time to just sit on his sofa and relax without feeling like he either needed to listen out for the door or go to bed.

James looked at his phone for the tenth time in three minutes. He had heard nothing from Lorraine, though he knew it would be two to three weeks before he could bank on their sessions, and likely their friendship, to be at an end. Depressing as it seemed, James wasn't unhappy at the prospect. He had done and said everything he could and knew that as long as she was happy then he had done his duty and had no right to complain. He felt sad, of course, but only in a way he found too selfish to really acknowledge.

He had been checking his phone out of curiosity more than anything else, with the occasionally twinge of something he felt was just short of apathy, and not just about Lorraine. He was bored and he knew it, once again being reminded of the irritating cycle he had found himself caught in, knowing he spent most of his time either wishing he had nothing to do and wanting to find something to do.

James had a hundred ways to deal with boredom. Out of all his videogames, books, phone apps and other indulgences that would pass the time, he sometimes found himself feeling like all of his pastimes amounted to exactly nothing, making him feel more like a spoiled child than a directionless adult. He was alone with his thoughts, something James knew could be dangerous when sober.

An epiphany came to him then. He was sober. That could be easily fixed.

James hadn't seen Charlotte since the night Andy had come to visit. He knew she was normally as up for a drink as he was and while he wasn't above drinking alone, the company of a proven friend was always preferable.

To James' surprise his message was received and replied to with a haste and gusto that was enthusiastic even by Charlotte's standards. With her response the essence of a plan was made, and with it came a certain anxiety that began to sneak through the valleys of James' indecisive mind. This uncertain feeling echoed without sound in his brain just as the air of emptiness did in his living room right after someone left.

The absence of sobbing help-seeker or patient seemed more noticeable to James than that of a smiling friend. It was that distinction that he always felt but rarely spoke about.

He would flood the valley with alcohol knowing that it wasn't the healthiest decision, but also knowing than in the grander scheme of things nothing was really wrong with his life. James was happy, and he knew he was happy, but he still needed a hobby to fill a nameless void left in him. A void that had always been there but only recently became noticeable, void that his own amateur psychiatry had been unable to fill.

James replied to Charlotte, a simple text saying he was on his way even though he wouldn't be for another ten or fifteen minutes.

***

'So how's Lorraine?' Charlotte asked after pretending to listen to James' complaints about her choice of seat once again. She had told him that if he wanted to chose then he should arrive on time for once. James couldn't argue.

'No idea. I assume fine.' He replied.

'Another one bites the dust, huh? Must be tough.'

'It's not so bad,' James said truthfully, 'It's not like we were close.'

'You were, though.' Charlotte looked confused.

'And how many high school friends are you close to?' James raised his eyebrows dramatically, as he normally did when proving a point.

'Fair enough,' Charlotte admitted, 'I still think you could use a better hobby, though.'

'You know I was just thinking that myself.'

'What about Doctor Noore?' Charlotte said quickly, as though she had it on her mind from before James had sat down.

'The See-All? What about her?'

'She still cites your dissertation in her lectures, you know.'

'So?'

'So maybe she'd like to hear from you, maybe take her under your wing. I hear she's been looking to mentor again.' Charlotte tried to act aloof, it was not working.

'You've been asking around for me, haven't you?'

'I'm just worried about you, man.' Charlotte was quick to accept being caught out, 'It's not healthy being stuck in that flat and dealing with everyone else's shit. You need to get out, and not just to drink.'

'You're one to talk,' James chuckled, 'But you've got a point. Maybe I'll send an e-mail out tomorrow or something. Thanks.'

'No need to thank me,' Charlotte winked, 'Though I have a few ideas if you want to show me appreciation.'

'So how do you know the whispers around the psychology department, anyway?' James asked, ignoring Charlotte's insinuation.

'I do have friends outside of my own course, you know.' Charlotte pretended to take offense.

'Friends?' James raised an eyebrow in as exaggerated a way as he could, 'Or *friends*?'

'Very funny,' Charlotte smiled, lowering her voice. 'Speaking of, there's a guy a few tables behind you who's been staring at you since you sat down.'

'It is a gay pub,' James shrugged, 'Maybe he's checking me out?' He joked.

'Oh yeah,' Charlotte folded her arms over the table. 'I'm sure the back of your head is *so* sexy.'

'Who knows what these randos are in to?'

'Why don't you find out?'

'Nah thanks.' James held his head up with his arm and began slowly rotating his glass on the table, the circles of condensation forming a large spiral pattern.

'You used to be such a player,' Charlotte appeared to sulk.

'You really don't understand the concept of not being in the mood, do you?' James laughed.

'Don't slut shame me, boy.'

'You started it,' James lifted his glass to his lips, 'Besides, is it really shaming if you're proud of it?'

'It can be,' Charlotte glared, her eyes showed anger but her smile betrayed otherwise.

'What are friends for if not to mercilessly mock?' James held up his glass.

'You got that right, for sure.' Charlotte also held up her glass and they clinked merrily. 'Drink up,' she said after downing the remainder of her beer, 'You've got another round coming.'

'You're probably right about Doctor Noore.' James said several rounds and many tangents later.

'I'm probably right about most things.' Charlotte lifted her fifth pint in her hand and began to twirl it slowly as though it were an expensive brandy.

James promised to himself to get in touch with his old teacher, though it was a half-assed promise. A question had been on his mind since before he had gone out to meet Charlotte, a question which had raised the anxiety within his mind yet seemed too dull to ask even to him. He hadn't cared enough at the time, but the alcohol had begun to make him care.

'Hey, Charlotte.' He said plainly, 'Since when are you free at last notice on a Friday night?'

'Hey,' Charlotte turned the word into four syllables, 'I'm not just some party girl.'

'Everyone else had plans, huh?'

'Yeah. Andy's been going on dates with this new guy if you can believe it. Actual fucking *dates*.' She sounded disgusted at the idea, 'And I can't get a hold of Gregg to save my life. Fuck knows what that mopey twat's been doing.'

'What about your uni friends?' James didn't make the same joke twice.

'Studying like I should be. Honestly I was about to turn in when I got your text.'

And there it was, the answer James had been anticipating from the moment the question entered his head. He knew better than to dwell, pessimistic brooding rarely made for good company, especially when he was the one who had done the inviting.

James had no right to be offended, or so he told himself, that Charlotte hadn't been hadn't considered him before giving up on plans. To allow oneself to feel bad about such things was nothing short of petty, pointless at the least and embarrassing to admit out loud.

'Hope I didn't interrupt your all important sleeping plans,' was all James could bring himself to say. He tried to make it sound like a joke.

'Sleep is for the week,' Charlotte replied. James didn't need to ask which word she meant.

***

Tuesday afternoon seemed to have snuck up on James as he found himself knocking on the familiar office door with almost no idea of what to say.

Doctor Dahlia Noore was the head of the psychology department of Lothian University, known jokingly by most of her students as some kind of highly intelligent witch or psychic. She had an impeccable ability to have a perfect and eloquently worded response to every sentence in every conversation and an unarguable answer to any question one could think to ask.

It was this peculiar feature of hers that had most of her colleagues and students wonder if she could somehow see the future and prepare her lines in advance like an actress with a particularly perfect memory. In time she had earned the moniker of 'The See-All'.

Dahlia was a psychiatrist, psychologist, novelist, lecturer and occasionally a friend. Her legacy was an extensive one, all members of the Noore family were renowned in every scientific and medical field there was, between them there were hundreds of accolades, awards, books and chapters dedicated to their works and contributions to humanity.

Dahlia seemed to live both with and up to her intimidating lineage with little effort, making her one of the most terrifying people to be alone with if you in any way doubted your own intelligence. James had found himself occasionally stressing out just being in her presence, though he hoped his ability to hide such stress had not rusted on him in the years since his graduation. He had somewhat gotten used to what she said and the way she acted, he even had a crush on her for a while.

James was not surprised at Doctor Noore's lack of surprise at receiving his e-mail, though the speed with which she got back to him was something of a shock. Dahlia was not a woman who was known for having a wealth of free time.

'Mister Steele,' she greeted him with a smile that looked as real as it did rehearsed. In her late forties, Dahlia showed not a single wrinkle on her kind face nor gray hair in her golden locks.

'Doctor Noore,' James returned her smile before following her into the office and closing the door behind him.

'Can I offer you a drink?' Dahlia asked as she walked to a drinks stand by her desk, she poured herself a whisky.

'Please,' James hung up his coat. Drink in hand, James was directed to one of the Lawson chairs sitting by the large window on the far side of the office. Dahlia took a seat in her identical chair, facing James, and set her drink on the coffee table which sat between them.

The layout was perfect, they were just the right distance apart to be comfortable regardless of their relationship, but close enough to give an air of comfort. James was impressed, but far from surprised, he had used similar methods in decorating his own flat.

The office itself was a large glass reconstruction built into the corner of the three storey psychology building. The window by James overlooked the university library and its surrounding gardens, while the view behind Dahlia offered a look at the large field and the duck pond by the university's main entrance.

'I call you 'Mister Steele' with a level of disappointment, James,' she crossed her legs knee over knee, the same way James did when talking to a patient. 'I had rather hoped you'd be well on your way to Doctor by now.'

'Maybe someday,' James sipped on his whisky, it had a familiar flavour though he was unable to place it. The honesty of his statement was debateable, even to him.

'I'd like to believe that this request to shadow me is a step in continuing your studies, albeit an unorthodox one.'

'I guess we'll see how it goes,' James smiled into his glass. He wasn't used to drinking whisky without ice.

'Let's start with what you've been doing these past three years,' Dahlia said, making just enough eye contact to be effective without making James uncomfortable. 'I must admit I was sorry to hear about the passing of your father, but I understand that the resulting windfall was an unexpected boon to your free time.'

'Charlotte's a talker, huh?' James grimaced as he turned his head to peer out the window.

'I hear you've used this time to become something of a full-time psychiatrist,' Dahlia didn't hide a smirk. 'While I know you better than to use the word 'amateur', I believe 'underqualified' remains apt.'

'It's not like I'm charging people, much less asking for them,' James exhaled deeply. 'Besides, it's not like it's a new trend. People have always come to me with their messes, the only difference now is that I have the time to deal with it all.'

'You speak about it so flippantly for someone with a waiting room in their hallway,' Dahlia didn't miss a beat in her responses, she never did. She leaned forward, the smirk still gracing her face. Not once since James had met her had she ever been wrong about anything.

'That started out as a joke,' he blushed slightly.

'Started out,' Dahlia held up her index finger as though she was pointing to the words as they came out of James' mouth. 'But thanks to it you now see your own living space as an office of ill fates. Your home has become a tributary through which wander the trifles of people's lives like fish who misjudged the current.'

James sipped slowly at his whisky, feeling as he did so that the crystal made smash in his grip. Dahlia's assessment had come out of nowhere and cut through him like a knife. Such was the power of the See-All, with little information she could bring about a poetic point which offered more truth than most are able to offer themselves.

Nothing spoken could be considered offensive, no implication out of place, and no words brought about anything that could be considered new information. Still, there was something about being made fully aware of something James knew all along that startled him more than he would ever want to let show. To have such things brought up so suddenly and so mysteriously put was a shock, and James was beyond intrigued.

'I've never really had a taste for fish,' he replied eventually.

'I never said you were eating them,' Dahlia's smile grew wider, it was the kind of smile James recognised on people when they knew they had hit the right nerve.

'So I take the fish and guide them back to the river. Is that it?'

'You guide, suggest, influence,' Dahlia waved her hand in the air as though conjuring something, 'but you starve yourself in the process.'

'Nothing wrong with a hobby,' James said defensively. Dahlia set her glass back on the coffee table after taking a large sip, a quiet scoff escaping her as she did so.

'We'll begin with a schedule that I will e-mail to you later in the week,' she said.

'Thank you, Doctor Noore,' James said happily, suddenly unsure as to how to address her. He decided to stick to formality, as he had often found was the best idea, until corrected.

'This offer is not without condition, James,' Dahlia's smirk vanished as she lifted her glass back up off the table, leading James to wonder why she had set it down in the first place. 'You are to come to me every Monday evening for therapy both to talk about yourself and share your thoughts on your own patients.'

'What? Why?' James spluttered the words out, momentarily forgetting whose company he was in.

'It is not uncommon for therapists to have therapists,' she returned to making deliberate yet careful eye contact. 'When you're dealing with all the problems and dealings of others and are, by whatever means, forbidden to speak of them, then it can become difficult to worry about yourself.

'Particularly empathetic individuals will find it difficult to cope with the emotional weight placed upon them, not to mention the expectations of their role, be it profession or hobby. It's only natural that I offer to provide you with some respite to talk about yourself, and offer my own opinion on how you're dealing with your own patients.'

James couldn't think of a single argument against Dahlia's logic, though the idea made him uncomfortable enough to try.

'I'm fine,' he said curtly.

'This condition is non-negotiable.'

'Then fine,' James admitted defeat, not that he had fought very hard.

'It's settled, then,' Dahlia's smile returned as she stood up and walked over to her desk. She took out a piece of paper and began to hastily write something on it. James also stood, figuring it was time he got going, and took his empty glass over to the drinks stand.

'Thank you again,' he said as he walked to the door.

'James,' Dahlia said just as he placed his hand on the handle. He turned to look at her and found her sparkling blue eyes already looking in to his as though she knew exactly where to look in order to demand his full attention.

'Yes?' he said.

'Don't forget to indulge in life's pleasures while you manage their lows. If you starve yourself for too long out there then a helpless fish lost off the river may start to look like dinner. Deny yourself proper meals, and you just might find yourself swallowing something rotten.'

***

James chewed on Dahlia's words as he waited for his lift to take him to his floor. The See-All had certainly not lost her touch, not that he had been expecting her to.

Every word of every sentence was set in its proper place like a well built wall that no one could scale. Even the poetic monologues seemed physically heavier than mere words should ever be, but that was what James liked about his old mentor and why he had fought tooth and nail to get her as his supervisor when he was a student. Still, a weekly therapy session seemed like a hefty price to pay.

James received a text from Charlotte asking how the meeting went, a question he wasn't sure he knew he knew the answer to. He was yet to reply.

As the lift doors opened James once again felt the presence of another in his waiting room, a feeling that had come to be like a sixth sense to him. He rounded the corner to see a man around his own age if not slightly younger with short brown hair. He was wearing a thick jacket that seemed to suit him despite being a touch too big.

James had no idea who he was.

'Hi,' the man said with a sudden and nervous smile, as though the sound of the lift had not been enough to advertise James' presence.

'Hello,' James replied awkwardly.

'Sorry,' the man said quickly, pushing past James and entering the lift. 'I thought I'd stop by, but I have to go.'

James just watched, confused, as the doors closed and the lift began its descent, taking his unexpected guest with it.

Something sparked in James then, something different yet not wholly unfamiliar. A feeling that left him smiling to himself, a twinge of selfish happiness within the confusion that he neither understood nor questioned.

Once inside his flat, James took his usual seat in the rocking chair and opened his phone, replying to Charlotte with a simple sentence.

I've decided to take up fishing. x

3.

'Do you... do you think I'm worthless?' David was close to sobbing, but he held it back as he often did.

James always had the impression that his friend refused to cry in front of people in order to maintain some ridiculous sense of masculinity. Though he had observed over the years that such outdated attitudes were still very much prevalent in children of religious households.

'Of course I don't,' James said convincingly. 'If I did then you wouldn't be here right now. It's not like I have any real professional obligation.'

'Yeah,' David smiled meekly, 'I suppose that's true.'

'I need caffeine,' James said as he stood up, wanting a break from David's repetitive complaining more than anything else. 'Want anything?'

'Do you have any chai?' David perked up slightly.

'I think so,' James replied as he left. Of course he had chai, it was the only thing David ever drank. The fact that he needed to ask told James more about the state of their friendship than David likely realised, not that that was a problem.

The light on the kettle indicated that it had been switched on, the blue glow clashed with the dark red of the kettle's casing in a combination James never liked but had learned to live with. It was much less hassle to put up with a functioning appliance than replace it. As it boiled and James made the drinks he had time to reflect on his friendship with David, a friendship that was soon to fade.

David and James had been friends since they were twelve, first meeting in their assigned home room early in high school. Together, the two of them along with Lorraine had been good friends, practically inseparable. When David began to grow quiet during the brief period James and Lorraine were seeing each other it was generally assumed that he was simply uncomfortable as a third wheel.

A drunken night during a study break instead revealed that David had had feelings for Lorraine since they were children and she had rejected him just before James asked her out.

Those feelings had no bearing on David now, but James couldn't help but feel that they acted as a catalyst to the subsequent spiral into self-loathing that had plagued David for years. He had no shred of self worth or confidence, and James could relate to a degree, though not in a way that offered any real insight.

The click of the kettle informed him that the water had finished boiling and he mixed the drinks without another thought on matters of the past.

David had been, in many ways, James' first friend as well as his first patient.

'Worthless, huh?' James said as he carefully handed over the hot tea and returned to his chair, sitting carefully so the rocking didn't disturb the cup too much. 'What made you ask that, anyway?'

'I suppose,' David shifted in his spot on the sofa, 'I started trying to go out with guys, you know, like you do. I thought it would help me feel confident, but I... I couldn't make it work.'

James allowed for a short pause to allow David to continue if he had more to say. After long enough James grit is teeth and looked to David with a harsh glare.

'Idiot,' he barked.

'What?' David started, he looked hurt.

'What does it matter, exactly?' James found himself speaking in an angrier tone than he had expected, though just how mad David had made him was also something of a shock. 'If you don't like something then you can't force yourself to like it. Even acquired tastes are not universal, I thought you'd be smart enough to know that.

'Besides, what good does it do you to spend your life comparing yourself to others? If you chase after a taste of other people's happiness then of course you're never going to feel any of your own. No wonder you're such a mess.'

One of the reasons James had never attempted a career in psychiatry was his complete inability to tolerate idiocy. He knew he wasn't particularly intelligent, and he was far from infallible, but he had long since come to understand just how uncommon common sense was. He had no patience for people who avoided simple solutions and chased idiotic ones for the sake of clinging on to some vague sense of joy that they should have known from the beginning would never be theirs.

James encountered such irritation far too frequently to hide his impatience every time.

'So,' David sniffed, 'what do I do then?'

'Stop trying to act like other people,' James breathed deeply in an attempt to calm himself down. 'Find your own happiness, if you can't love yourself then don't try to love others, regardless of what's behind their zippers.' James looked out the window and surprised himself with what he said next. 'Only an idiot would take someone's happiness at face value, but it takes a special kind of moron to trust anyone who refuses to allow themselves to even pretend.'

David saw himself out once his tea was finished, and James once again found himself somewhat taken aback by the emptiness. As well as the normal sense of absence there was also the lingering smell of the chai tea and thickness of James' words that remained in the air as though they had been blown out as a dense smoke.

James knew the uneasiness with which most people lived, social media and online galleries showed smiling faces and fun, interesting times in people's lives. All too often were posts considered to be perfect examples of people's moods, peeks into the standards of their lives.

After all, it would be rude to let such sadness or weakness show so publically. Seeking help from friends was a too-rare occurrence because if someone knows just how much you're struggling then why would you be invited out? Who would want to go out or drink with such someone so open about how down they can sometimes feel?

Few people could tolerate such a person, much less like them, and the idea that someone would be so stupid as to think they could both tell the truth and be accepted was ridiculous.

Two hours passed and James found himself deep in an old psychology textbook when his phone rang. He expected a telemarketer as he took the phone out of his pocket to reveal Andy's name on the screen. He answered it happily without knowing why.

'Black Fox. Ten minutes,' was all Andy deigned to say.

'Wait, what are you doing on this end of to-'

'Just get here,' Andy hung up without another word. Despite how quickly and directly Andy spoke there was no real urgency in his voice. Still, such brashness was unusual and James had to admit that he had nothing better to do.

It didn't take long for James to put on his coat and head out the door. Andy didn't joke around when it came to drinking, even on a weekday. It was one of the things James liked about him.

'What took you?' Andy asked with a grin on his face as James approached the table. The weekday crowds were thin and they had managed to secure a booth.

'You gave me ten minutes when you know I live fifteen minutes away. For me this is early and you know it,' James took off his coat.

'No excuse,' Andy winked. 'It's your round.'

'Fine,' James knew better than to argue, 'What do you guys wa-' he stopped when he noticed who was sitting beside Andy.

Looking to James with a warm smile was the man who had been waiting outside his flat several nights previously.

'You're...' James began.

'Luke,' he held out his hand, reaching around Andy to do so.

'James,' he replied, Andy had to lean back to allow them to shake hands.

For whatever reason, it seemed obvious that Luke wanted to keep their previous encounter under wraps. James obliged.

The bartender promised to bring the drinks to the table and James thanked him happily. The reason he and Andy frequented that bar so much was because they were given table service if the staff weren't too busy, a too-rare treat for any regular drinker in the city. James had not been charged for the drinks, meaning Andy had set up a tab and was joking when he called for a round.

It was going to be a long night.

'So what was the rush?' James asked as he sat down.

'We haven't drank together in ages,' Andy beamed.

'It's been two weeks.'

'That's ages for us,' Andy seemed in an exceedingly good mood. James never really trusted such vague answers.

'How do you two know each other?' Luke asked once their drinks had arrived.

'We met in uni-'

'We used to date,' James cut Andy off without meaning to.

'I need to piss,' Andy got up, seeming a little annoyed. James knew it would be temporary, though he did still feel guilty.

'So, same question,' James turned to Luke, hoping to get rid of the slight tension he had created.

'Huh?' Luke looked up.

'How did you guys meet?'

'Oh, um,' he stammered, 'online.'

'Ah,' James understood. When a man admits to meeting another man online with such apparent hesitation it normally meant one thing.

James recalled something Charlotte had told him the week before.

'So,' James said, wondering if there was a way to phrase his words without sounding rude, 'you're the dating type and the hook up type. Must make a love life difficult.'

'Jesus,' Luke's eyes went wide though he couldn't fight a smile, 'you really don't hold back, do you?'

'Sorry,' James laughed, somewhat embarrassed, 'comes with the job.'

'Don't apologise,' Luke said sincerely, 'you do have a point.'

'Is that why you were-'

'Has he talked your ear off already?' Andy sat back down. He didn't take long in the restroom, leaving James to wonder if he had forgotten to wash his hands, something he only ever did when he was nervous.

As the evening went on James was happy to see Luke become talkative and involved. James knew not to mention either Andy or Luke's last visits to his flat, and instead allowed the conversation to become light, happy, a gathering amongst friends. He didn't need to be a psychiatrist for a while.

Though he still found it difficult to turn off the more worrying parts of his brain.

Luke was sarcastic, chatty, a little on the camp side and projected a naïveté that James believed was superficial. He was sweet but forward, and very much aware of his words.

Luke was not Andy's type at all.

With the tab paid and their coats half on, Andy offered James a cigarette while Luke excused himself to the restroom. James was more willing to accept the cigarette than he thought he'd be, only after a moment of hesitation did he remember Dahlia's words to him about enjoying life's pleasures.

Andy handed a lighter to James as the two stepped outside and James lit his cigarette with hands shivering from the sudden chill the evening had brought.

'What are you doing, Andy?' James asked coldly.

'Hm?' Andy was busy lighting his own cigarette.

'He seems sweet. If you're just messing around then you need to either knock it off or tell him.'

'What are you getting at?' Andy looked to James with anger in his eyes. James knew he was crossing a line, speaking out of turn, but he had seen and heard too much to trust his old friend's intentions.

'A rebound is fine, even expected,' he went on, knowing it was too late to retract his words, 'but if you're not serious about him then you need to let him know.'

'It's not just a-'

'He's been grinning like an idiot all night, man. He's infatuated. I don't want to see you fuck him around.'

James had no idea where his mind was going. He tried to blame the alcohol, convince himself that he was just misunderstanding both the situation and his place, but even that wouldn't explain his sudden wish to get involved outside of his own business in order to defend a stranger.

Something had come over him. Something he wasn't sure he liked.

'You know, James,' Andy's hands were shaking from something other than the cold, 'one of these days someone's going to break you down and play you just like you play everyone else,' he took a deep drag of his cigarette. 'This isn't one of our sessions, and it's none of your business. So butt out.'

'Everything okay?' Luke asked from behind them.

'Fine,' Andy said quietly, his upper lip trembling. 'Make sure he gets home safe,' he said to James before bidding them both an apathetic farewell and wandering in the direction of the taxi rank.

'You're not coming over?' Luke asked. James didn't detect much disappointment in his voice, he thought then that perhaps the two of them were a good fit after all. His accusations began to sour in his mind.

'I've got work tomorrow,' Andy said. The three of them knew it was a lie.

James had never known Andy to be the sensitive type, not to the opinions of others anyway. He could see that his words had hurt him, that he had been wrong. James knew then that he either should have phrased his thoughts better or kept his mouth shut.

'I hate cutting nights short,' Luke sighed, he was more relaxed than James thought he'd be, less willing to question Andy's sudden change in mood.

'Me too,' James replied, stomping out his cigarette and turning to Luke. 'Don't suppose you've got any beer?'

Luke looked to him with a smile that rang more of gleeful mischief than it did of happiness, it was an expression that was as familiar to James as it was welcome in new friends.

Luke's flat was on the first floor of a building just round the corner from James' own flat. It was a modest dwelling that was small enough to be comfortable without being confining. Small but cosy, it seemed perfect for one person to live alone though James found it difficult to imagine two people living there happily.

James made himself comfortable on the soft sofa of the living room while Luke brought two beers from the open plan kitchen and sat cross-legged on the floor, insisting that he found it more comfortable than any of his furniture.

'So, I gotta ask,' James began, realising that alcohol had once again begun to make him care about things his sober mind would have found unimportant. 'Why did you come to my flat that time? Wouldn't it have been easier to just introduce yourself?'

Luke forced a laugh that was meant to dispel any awkward air, it managed to do exactly the opposite.

'It's pretty embarrassing,' Luke rubbed the back of his neck, 'Andy never seems to shut up about you, though he doesn't say anything about you in relation to himself. We've been going out for a few weeks now and I guess I wanted to, well... I got concerned.'

'You came to see if I was a threat?' James laughed loudly at the notion.

'Something like that,' Luke blushed.

'Well?' James said with a wide grin, he leaned forward with a feigned sense of expectant intrigue.

'I was relieved,' Luke said calmly, 'I don't know him all that well, at least not as well as you do. But when I saw you I knew right away that you really aren't his type.'

James had not been expecting that. While it was true that he and Andy had turned out to be a less-than-perfect fit, to hear that observation coming from a stranger after an encounter so brief was enough to catch James off guard. It was a statement with both the potential for offence and hilarity.

In truth, James didn't care enough to be offended, but also couldn't bring himself to laugh. The time he and Andy had spent together was nice, after all, and he had believed their parting was mutually beneficial aside from some drama that's to be expected with any breakup.

'Is that right?' was all James could bring himself to say. He put on a smile but found himself fumbling with his can of beer, looking at it as though it were the most interesting thing in the world.

Andy wasn't the kind of person to be obsessive, he wasn't prone to overt enthusiasm or worship, even about his favourite things. The idea that Andy apparently wouldn't shut up about him was something James knew likely meant nothing, but it was something to keep in mind none the less.

A feeling came over him then, a familiar sense of random emotion that had come to him when he watched Luke disappear behind the lift doors. Something that was a mix of intoxication and perhaps spite left his skin shaking as though he were outside in the cold once more.

James set his beer on the floor and leaned forward off the sofa. His mind had gone entirely blank, his movements only partially conscious. For reasons he couldn't comprehend and explanations just beyond his reach, James was acting on something short of instinct and profound desire as he kissed Luke softly on the lips.

Fragments of James' mind returned the moment they touched and he expected resistance, he even began to form an apology in his head despite not knowing exactly what he was doing himself. Instead of the expected backlash James felt Luke's hand cup and then grasp the hair on the back of his head.

Luke leant backwards and pulled James with him until they were lying on the floor. With one hand holding himself up, James reached up with his free arm and took Luke's hand in his. Their fingers interlocked and the Luke's hold on the back of James' head tightened.

A noise James didn't recognise sounded down the hall, followed swiftly by a pressure on his chest as Luke pushed James away. Reclined on the sofa, his knuckle to his lips, James breathed heavily and stared at the ground as Luke apologised quietly. They sat opposite each other for a few seconds, the short distance between them in the small living room suddenly felt like an expanse as wide as any desert.

Luke stood up and went to leave the room, only then did James realise that the noise he heard had been Luke's doorbell. He already had one sleeve in his coat when he heard Andy's voice.

'You're still here?' Andy asked as James entered the hallway.

'Just leaving,' he replied, stopping at the door and thanking Luke for the drink. Luke smiled in response before bidding him an overly fond farewell.

'Not like you to want to cut a night short,' Andy said, an angry tone still lingered behind his almost accusatory words.

'I have some work to do,' James said, faking a yawn without knowing why.

'I'll be in touch,' Andy said coldly.

'I don't doubt it,' James said from the top of the stairs, taking care with his volume so as not to disturb Luke's neighbours. 'G'night guys.'

The cold of the streets outside again surprised James as he took his first step outside the front door. With a loud shiver he plunged his hands into his pockets, grinding his teeth as he did so in a physical attempt to make his mind shut up.

James was home in less than ten minutes and found his waiting room to be gratifyingly empty. He fumbled with his keys in his numb fingers before getting them into the lock and shutting the door quickly behind him. Had anyone been watching it would have seemed as though he was being chased by something. It wasn't entirely untrue.

The moment he was inside, James planted his back firmly against the door, allowing himself to catch his breath. His heart was pounding harder in his chest than it ought to and his ears rang from the cold. He grabbed his forehead and held on to it as though it might fall off his skull. He cursed under his breath, insulting himself with a few quick whispered syllables.

James had no idea what had come over him. He wanted to blame the alcohol but knew it wasn't entirely true. He had kissed Luke because he had wanted to kiss him, and he couldn't ignore how happy he had felt when his desire was reciprocated. Though now it only made him feel sick.

It wasn't just what he had done that was confusing him, it was why he had done it. While considering that Luke didn't seem like Andy's type, James also knew that the same was true for him. Luke was a stranger, a friend of a friend at most, and he wasn't comparable to anyone James had been attracted to in the past.

Even if it wasn't true, James never knew himself to be the sort of person to make a first move, especially not one so brash and thoughtless. He had betrayed both Andy and himself with little concurrent regard for the consequences of what he was doing.

All in all, James had scared himself. To act so impulsively wasn't an entirely new sensation, though he had been dwelling more on the fact that he had taken Luke's hand. If he was just horny then he would have allowed his hands to wonder to more intimate places, instead he had unconsciously made a gesture that could be construed as far more romantic than James would allow himself to be with someone like Luke. It meant nothing, and he knew it meant nothing, but it still bothered him.

He took a deep breath and silenced a deeper longing that he had learned to more or less ignore. With naught but a shake of his head James dispelled the overthinking with an arguable degree of success.

He felt like an idiot for getting so caught up in something so small, so meaningless. It didn't matter, it didn't mean anything. He was drunk and lonely, he'd wake up the next day hungover and embarrassed, he'd wait it out and that would be that.

James considered a whisky as he walked into his living room and threw his coat on the sofa, but the sight of the still unopened package on the coffee table made him realise that brushing his teeth and going to bed were preferable solutions. He made a mental note to throw the package out the next day and walked slowly to his room, a sudden fatigue had hit him hard.

It would be hours before James was able to nod off. Throughout the night he couldn't get the thought of Andy and Luke being together in that exact moment as he lay in bed, in his flat, alone as he always was. It was a thought that he found more humiliating than hurtful.

***

James spent his Sunday undisturbed and well caffeinated. He found himself in higher spirits than he had been in a while and was not looking to question why. The Monday came fast, though, and he was still in a good mood as he sat opposite Dahlia Noore for their first therapy session.

The downside of being in a good mood was that James found himself with very little to say.

Being an early afternoon session, Dahlia had prepared coffee in lieu of whisky, it was a cortado in a small and expensive looking cup. It was strong and effective without being overpowering, the perfect brew.

'So James,' Dahlia began after some comfortable preamble, 'let's start by discussing your life since graduation. Tell me, what's a normal day for you?'

This was the kind of question James found difficult to answer. Vague, half-hearted enquiries that a hundred boring answers. To begin with a question as open-ended as it was inoffensive was just what he had expected, though hadn't really prepared for.

'Not much to say,' he replied, 'I wake up early enough in the morning, get up not long after and spend the day either killing time, reading or doing what you're doing now.'

'Interesting that you don't consider reading to be killing time,' Dahlia picked up on the smallest detail immediately, James knew she would the moment the words came out of his mouth.

'Reading feels productive,' he had his answer ready, 'even some trashy nonsense or badly written horror, reading makes me feel like I'm doing something. It makes me think,' James set his cup down on the glass table before him, the noise of the porcelain hitting the class was louder than he anticipated and made him wince. Dahlia didn't seem to notice, though James was sure she did.

'Is horror your genre of choice, then?' Dahlia asked. She had a peculiar way of asking questions that made even the most mundane things seem to be of paramount importance.

'Not really,' James replied, 'I'm not very picky.'

'And what about when you're in my position?' Dahlia sipped her coffee, 'Are you picky about your patients?'

'Isn't that a bit of a stretch?' James smirked as he lifted his own cup back off the table, making a note to himself to not set it down again.

'It would be if I weren't sure of one thing,' Dahlia cocked her head slightly to the side. James braced himself. 'Do you know why I have so many seats in my office?'

James looked around the office, reminding himself of the layout. It only occurred to him then that the office he had been in many times had not changed at all, but he had never sat in the seat by the window until the week before. Every conversation he had had with Doctor Noore over the years had taken place at her desk or on the small grey sofa by the door.

James only thought to question then why an office occupied by one person would require so many places to sit. Between Dahlia's own chair and the two at her desk, the sofa and the chairs in which they sat then, there was enough space for eight people, maybe more.

'You've noticed it, haven't you?' Dahlia asked, 'I use these seats for patients, the desk for professional calls and the sofa for personal ones.

'I remember you telling me that you've always wanted to own a rocking chair, I can assume that you both have that chair and you use it for reading, social and not-so-social engagements, correct?'

'Correct,' James said, raising an eyebrow. He wasn't entirely sure what she was getting at.

'I make this distinction within my own space because I believe it's important to differentiate between what and where. If you use a space to regularly take on hardships, then how can you expect to be happy using that same space for recreation. I think it's correct to say that this negative association has made your pastimes have become less fulfilling in recent years, right?'

James couldn't argue, he saw her point clearly enough. One of the reasons he had disliked the idea of therapy was because he hated having important revelations pointed out as though they were the most obvious ideas in the world. James knew it was the point, but it didn't stop him from feeling like an idiot.

'I must say you look well rested,' Dahlia smiled warmly, 'you barely slept when you were my student. While I can't say I approve of how you've been using your time I must say that a more leisurely life seems to have somewhat become you.'

'I don't know what to say,' James blushed slightly.

'But of course your life wasn't exactly without leisure before, was it?' Dahlia smirked again. 'Before we go any further,' she said, lifting a briefcase from beside her chair and producing several papers. She handed the papers to James and sat back, an air of anticipation on her face as he looked over them.

'Wait,' James said, confused, 'bank details?'

'I've decided to offer you not an internship or shadowing position,' she finished her coffee and set the cup down on the table soundlessly, 'but a role as a paid assistant. I think you're more than qualified.'

'I didn't come looking for a job,' James tried not to sound ungrateful.

'Your father's money isn't going to last forever,' Dahlia's tone turned more serious, 'when I learned that you weren't going to continue your education I was disappointed, but more than that I was concerned that your hedonistic and promiscuous tendencies had won over your equally academic ones.'

'I need to start thinking about the future, huh?' James looked again to the forms.

'Exactly,' Dahlia said, her seriousness remained but behind it James could hear a caring tone. 'I don't need a response right away.'

'When would I start?' James asked, intrigued. He wasn't about to overlook how great of an opportunity this was, the kind of offer most undergrads would kill for.

'We'll have something of an introduction this Wednesday, then from next week you'll be working from me Tuesdays through Thursdays. Our Monday sessions would remain a condition, of course.'

James was ashamed to admit that he had never really put much thought into what he would do for work when the time came. He had been too busy of late enjoying something of a respite from responsibility to think about the future. Dahlia, of course, had made some excellent points, and he had been meaning to replace is old sofa.

'I have to admit,' Dahlia turned to look out the window, 'I was surprised when I saw you again. When you became quiet in your second year I began to worry that you had fallen too far, that. You were angry and focussed yet somehow apathetic, too.'

James had not wanted to talk about this so soon, he remained quiet knowing anything he said, even in defiance, would only give Dahlia more to work with.

'But seeing you here now,' she went on, 'you seem much happier. I'd like to ask, what happened to you?'

'Then or now?' James set his empty cup down, the noise didn't bother him.

'Either, I'm sure we'll get to both eventually,' Dahlia said confidently.

'The former is ancient history, the latter is something I don't want to question.'

'I suppose that's fair for now,' Dahlia leant back, sure in the knowledge that that she would get the answers she wanted in time. The See-All knew very well that first sessions were more often than not an assessment and re-adjustment of boundaries between patient and therapist. The meeting they were in was an ice breaker, and what was beneath that ice would show itself eventually in as much detail as she desired.

'Perhaps I am being too forward for an opening session,' she said, 'how about we table this for now and catch up?'

'Shouldn't we move to the sofa, then?' James joked.

'Not this time,' Dahlia replied quickly, she did not match his tone.

James found himself in no worse spirits as he left Dahlia's office. Even the sight of Andy's scowling face waiting for him outside wasn't enough to dampen his spirits.

'We need to talk,' Andy folded his arms.

'Well good afternoon to you too.'

'Charlotte told me you'd be here,' Andy ignored James' sarcasm.

'Okay...'

'You free or not?'

'That depends,' James made his way to the lift, Andy followed behind. 'What do we need to talk about?'

'I really don't appreciate what you said on Saturday, you know?' Andy stared into his coffee. James had gone for a lemonade as he still found himself buzzing from earlier.

'I know, man,' he replied, relieved that Luke had apparently chosen not to tell Andy what had happened. 'Look, I was insensitive, I was just concerned.'

'Is it so hard to believe that a guy like me can be with someone unless I'm using them?'

'That's not what I meant,' James said quickly. He knew he had no right to be upset, but he didn't care for Andy's tone.

'Then what did you mean?' Andy looked up. In that moment James saw in his eyes something that wasn't anger, he knew then that if Andy had been holding a grudge he would have said so sooner. He had been chewing on James' words, likely not believing them but still feeling as though they came from a place of truth. James needed to be careful.

'He just didn't seem like your type to me,' he spoke truthfully, 'though I should have gathered from what you said before that you're not the one playing around here.'

'What?' Andy's eyes went wide as though James had offended him.

'I mean, you're insecure enough and, let's face it, not long out of what was a promising relationship. That can make someone vulnerable, I'm still trying to look out for you I guess.'

'Appreciated,' Andy said half-heartedly. 'He wants to see you, by the way.'

'Me? Why?'

'For sessions I guess, maybe just to talk. Don't ask me why.'

James didn't like that, though he had to accept the expectations placed on his role, albeit with some discomfort.

'I've gotta ask,' Andy lifted his coffee to his lips, 'Did something happen between you two?'

There it was, James was faced with the terrible yet familiar problem of choosing between a potentially painful truth and an arguably white lie. He was not so righteous that he thought his actions didn't have consequences, but he also wasn't so naïve to think that all truths would be uncovered in time.

'No,' he answered.

'Okay. I'm sorry to ask, but I'm really trying to make this work.'

James nodded, acknowledging once again the expectations that came with a man of his reputation. He did not need to think about why Andy had seen fit to ask, the question wouldn't have been without reason even if nothing had happened.

'I gave him your number,' Andy said emotionlessly, 'hope that's okay?'

'Of course,' James said, not sure if he meant it. 'Hey Andy, I just want to let you know that our past is just that. We're friends, yeah? I care about you.'

James spoke these words with a genuine sincerity. Andy was his friend, and while he could be cold sometimes, James knew that he wouldn't have said what he said if he didn't mean it. By the time the two of them parted ways for the day James still didn't know which stung him more, the words Andy had said in response, or the frank uncaring tone with which he said them.

'Sure thing.'

4.

James sipped at a weak, milky coffee as he pored over the contract and attached forms that Dahlia had given him earlier that day. A Bluetooth speaker filled the room with a calming playlist that had gone unchanged from the day James put it together.

Sure enough, the See-All had included mandatory therapy sessions every Monday as a clause, meaning that there was absolutely no way of wriggling out of it. The salary offered was modest but not insulting and the hours of his three work days looked manageable. James had no doubt that Dahlia had put the contract together with James in mind rather than using a standard employee form.

Having completed reading, James found himself surprised by his own hesitation. The offer for work as a paid assistant to one of the most renowned psychologists in the country was a dream his student self would have found too perfect to trust. Yet there he was, three years since graduation, wondering if it was what he really wanted.

The request to shadow Doctor Noore had been on a whim born of a half-drunk conversation, and James wondered if he had really spoiled himself so much that a dream job was something he was trying to find a reason to get out of, something he considered rejecting.

Whenever faced with a decision that he had been wrestling with, James often found that the answer came to him in a moment of unconscious cancellation of thought. He referred to these as 'fuck-it moments', the exact instant where the body decides for the mind and a path is chosen.

With the mental equivalent of a slap in the face, James grabbed a pen and signed the contract without another second's thought. He would enter the rest of the details later, for now his signature was the only thing he needed to solidify the decision in his mind. Besides, the relaxing music echoing off his walls put him far from the mood to begin rifling through files and documents that he knew weren't even remotely organised to look for details and insurance numbers.

Instead, James took out his phone and began browsing through online furniture outlets for sofas and chairs that caught his fancy. He had plenty of room for more furniture and was more than happy to use the good doctor's advice as the kick he needed to finally get something done about it.

After a few purchases based more on impulse than taste, James fished a cigarette out of his pocket and lit it. He had little problem with smoking indoors. His ceilings were high enough and James smoked infrequently enough so the smell of tobacco rarely lingered for too long.

The cigarette he enjoyed then was the first he had had since the one Andy had given him, which itself was the first in months. James felt a change coming to his life that wasn't just to do with the contract he just signed. Things had been looming, invisible things that made him feel more anxious and vulnerable than he had in a while. He smoked to return to a simpler, albeit less sure, time in his life. He still knew to keep an eye on how much he smoked, that slope was far slipperier than even the legally mandated package warnings seemed to advertise.

Aside from the convenience, James found smoking indoors to be a pleasant reminder of the fact that it was his flat and he was free to live in it as he saw fit. He had been living alone before and after Andy lived there and had found sharing the flat to be something of a nuisance, though he had since found his own company to be just as tiring as the company of others.

A crystal ash tray sat on the windowsill beside him, it had been a gift from his father some time ago, a silent message that his habit was no longer a secret but he wasn't going to be reprimanded for it. James flicked his cigarette over the tray and watched the grey specks scatter on impact, sullying the clear dish.

Several loud knocks sounded at the door, distracting him from a deep thought he knew he wouldn't remember. He checked his phone and saw that it was nearly eight in the evening, too late for a delivery or solicitor. Normally James would greet guests at the door, but good moods often made him lazy.

'It's open,' he called out, unsure if the door actually was open. He put out his cigarette and stood up when he heard the heavy door creak, knowing he'd likely have to offer his guest something from the kitchen.

'Hello?' A voice sounded, almost singing, just before James got to the hallway. It was a familiar voice, though not a voice that had ever been heard within those walls.

He stepped into the hall to see Luke's smiling face, he had a plastic shopping bag in each hand and wore the same coat he had been wearing the first time the two of them met, if one could indeed call that a meeting.

Andy had mentioned that Luke wanted to see him, but James had not expected him to call over so abruptly, much less so soon.

'Luke,' James greeted, 'this is a pleasant surprise.'

'Sorry,' Luke made his own way into the kitchen and set his bags on the counter, 'I wasn't sure whether or not to call first. What's the etiquette here?'

'There sort of isn't one,' James laughed awkwardly.

'I think I know it well enough, though,' Luke said, reaching in to the shopping bag and producing two bottles of red wine and several expensive looking beers.

'That'll pretty much do it,' James smiled, going to the cabinet to fetch two glasses. 'On a school night, though?'

'What's the harm in one or two?' Luke beamed.

'So why so abrupt?' James asked once they had sat down. He had gone for a beer in a pint glass, Luke for wine. The decision was not entirely based on taste as James owned only one wine glass that he didn't remember buying. 'Didn't Andy give you my number?

'Oh, you've been talking to him?' Luke flinched.

'Earlier today,' James spoke reassuringly, 'he wasn't too happy about something I said on Saturday.'

'Said, huh? Is that why he was in such a mood?'

'Seems so,' James sipped his beer, it tasted hoppy and strong. Luke either had tastes similar to Charlotte's, or he had asked for advice. Either way, Luke's decision to call didn't ring of a simple matter of being in the neighbourhood.

'He was in a foul mood that night, but wouldn't talk about why. I figured it was something to do with you,' Luke said with some hesitation. 'I was actually hoping you could fill me in. I don't like the idea of him just randomly switching moods without letting me know what's up.'

'I told him to be honest if he was just messing around with you,' James answered, seeing no reason to hide his words, 'you seemed pretty happy with him, and I didn't want to see you hurt.'

'You accused him of that for my sake?' Luke stopped just before taking a sip of his wine.

'I didn't want him hurting someone else over some bitter feelings,' James explained. It was a half-truth, as James himself wasn't sure why he had spoken so harshly to defend Luke that night.

'I appreciate it,' Luke said, 'and I appreciate you telling me. But I can take care of myself.'

'I didn't mean-'

'I'm a big boy,' Luke said with a forced smile, 'I know what I'm doing.'

'Andy mentioned you wanted to speak to me, was it about this?' James found himself hoping that the answer wasn't yes, though he wasn't wanting to discuss any dark or troublesome matters while his spirits were still so high, especially when the origin of his good mood still eluded him.

'I suppose not,' Luke said after some thought, 'but it's nothing that can't wait,' he smiled a wide smile, a warmth in his eyes gave James an odd feeling of comfort, as though the mere act of seeing someone be happy rubbed off on him more than it should have. Mirror neurons, he figured, or something of the like.

James knew what the feeling was deep down, if Luke had wanted to talk only about what Andy was upset about then he could have done it over text, if he wanted to talk about more serious matters then he could have done. But the fact was that Luke was there on a social call, and James' happiness at that also bore a sadness in realising just how rare that circumstance was.

'What exactly do you make of Andy?' Luke asked, 'I mean, really make of him?'

'Hmm?' James was mid-swig.

'We both seem to disagree about what his type is, so we must see him differently, right?'

The question was thought out, well reasoned and oddly timed. James didn't really know what to make of it, much less why he hadn't figured the same thing himself.

'He's... interesting,' James said without much thought. Luke burst out laughing.

'That bad, huh?'

'Um...' James couldn't help but snicker himself, 'I mean, like, he's got a lot going on. One minute he's happy as ever, next he's quiet and solemn. I don't think he's ever really been sure of himself.'

'Is anyone?' Luke asked once he got control of his laughter.

'I suppose not, though people who try too hard to be certain of everything normally end up being the most disappointed with themselves.'

'Deep.'

'Sorry,' James rubbed the back of his neck which had suddenly become stiff, 'I've been with a friend all afternoon who speaks very profoundly, guess she rubbed off on me.'

'The See-All, right?' Luke asked.

'Charlotte?' James faked a glare.

'Yup. She's a talker,' Luke grinned. A bad feeling came over James then, though it was small enough to ignore.

James wanted to bring up, or at least apologise for, kissing Luke that night. But as the intent to do so travelled from his brain to his tongue he found himself hesitating, as though the words themselves were caught in his mouth, held back by a subconscious judgement that was for neither better nor worse. Regardless of how much he forced his body to act, James couldn't bring himself to say anything out loud.

'It's hard,' Luke said, swishing the wine in his glass, 'to put stock in something like a relationship without really knowing the person you're with. It adds to the intrigue, but it doesn't make it any more secure.'

'You're a man who needs to be sure, then?' James wasn't sure what Luke was getting at.

'Not exactly, but consistency is nice,' he said plainly, 'though it can get, I dunno, boring?'

'You were testing the waters,' James said, unable to stop an impressed smile from appearing on his face, 'I said the right thing to the wrong person, didn't I?'

'Maybe,' Luke said, 'Andy is interesting, as you said, but maybe not boyfriend material,' the words could have been construed as cruel were it not for the sadness in his voice.

James had seen this more times than he could count, more often than not relationships tended to end because one person was more willing than the other, more caring. So often the reason a relationship failed was the result of a one-way street that the other wasn't aware of.

That was the difference between an attachment and a bond. Andy wanted to make it work, Luke wasn't sure it could. James had been on both ends of this far too many times. It was impossible to make someone care about you as much as you care about them, and the realisation of that, depending on how it became apparent, was the most painful thing in the world.

Luke's visit was turning out not to be as social as Luke had led James to believe.

'Don't tell him,' Luke said, 'I don't want to give up just yet. And maybe don't tell him about that night, if you haven't already.'

'I haven't,' James said, remembering Andy's words from earlier, 'but I will tell you what I told him. If you're playing around then you need to tell him, otherwise it's not fair.'

'I know that, I've been on the wrong end of players far too often,' Luke stared into his wine, to James it seemed as though he was looking at his reflection in the shimmering red liquid.

'Are you looking to avoid them,' James cocked his head, 'or become one yourself?'

Luke chuckled but said nothing in response.

'Mind if I get another?' James asked once his beer was finished.

'Of course,' Luke said, holding his glass out, 'only if you don't mind topping me up?'

'Sure thing, though I'd rather not get too drunk if that's alright,' James said as he took the glass from Luke, 'I've got a session tomorrow that it's not good to be hungover for.'

'Works for me,' Luke replied, 'I've got work anyway.'

James grabbed a beer from the fridge and took more time to examine the bottle, he remembered seeing it in the supermarket not so long before, and noted that it looked much more expensive than it was. The same went for the wine that Luke was drinking, a simple sketch on the label made it seem like an expensive batch to a layman like James, but he had no doubt that it, too, was cheaper than one might think upon seeing it.

He filled the wine glass to the same level that Luke seemed to have filled it earlier and decided to drink the beer from the bottle over the glass that he had accidentally left in the living room.

As he handed the glass back to Luke, who immediately rested it on the sofa's arm, James was stopped from returning to his chair by a sudden grip on his wrist as Luke pulled him down to the sofa and kissed him hard. James managed to set his beer on the floor without spilling it.

James didn't wrestle against the kiss, he had no better judgement to fight against. Instead he took the back of Luke's head in his hand and pulled him closer, lifting Luke to him in an embrace. As Luke wrapped his arms around James' back he pulled away from the kiss only to lower his mouth to Luke's neck, making him shiver slightly. James didn't stop as he undid a button from Luke's shirt.

Luke's breathing grew heavier as he held his hand on James' head and pushed him further into his neck, using just the right amount of force. James knew to resist the urge to give a love bite, though it took a lot of willpower to do so.

A snap of realisation came to James then, whether it was out of conscience or judgement he couldn't tell. He stood up suddenly, Luke didn't try to cling on and instead sat back on the sofa, his partially opened shirt slipping off one of his shoulders, a smile gracing his visage.

'Maybe,' James noticed only then how out of breath he felt, he felt as though something had suddenly scared him. He had no end to that sentence and he abandoned it, replacing the words in his mouth with a cigarette as he lifted his beer and sat back down. He lit up without any regard for his guest and inhaled deeply.

'Testing the waters again?' James said with once the air and humour returned to his mind.

'Something like that,' Luke lifted his wineglass without buttoning his shirt. 'I have to say I wasn't expecting you to hesitate. These aren't new waters for you, are they?'

'What do you mean?' James flicked his cigarette over the ashtray.

'You had a reputation in university, one I have to say you're not exactly living up to.'

'How do you-'

'Charlotte.'

'Ah.'

'But,' Luke went on, 'it's not like I'm disappointed.'

'What are you doing, Luke?' James asked after a short silence. 'Why are you doing this?'

'I...' Luke seemed to have an answer ready, but second guessed himself after one word escaped him, 'I don't know.'

James watched as Luke looked again into his wine, twirling the glass slowly in his hand. Directionless, acting on desire, knowing what one wants without knowing what one needs. James knew the feeling all too well.

'Thanks,' Luke said, a weak smile returning to his face, 'I'm glad I came.'

James thought on returning the sentiment, telling Luke he was also happy to see him that evening, but without fully knowing why he couldn't bring himself to say anything. Instead he simply took another drag of his cigarette and tried to make the grin on his face less obvious.

'Hope this doesn't bother you,' James said.

'Not at all, I used to live in halls that reeked of weed,' Luke said, wincing at the thought, 'so regular smoke is no big deal.'

'Cool.'

'So who's this person you've got tomorrow?'

'A friend,' James replied, making it clear that he wasn't willing to share details.

'Fair enough,' Luke looked to the high ceiling.

'Why aren't you seeing Andy tonight?' James asked plainly. 'He did mention he was free.'

'I told him I wasn't,' Luke turned to James, his mischief returning to his face. James couldn't help but chuckle slightly.

'I'll ask again,' James said, more confidant he'd get an answer this time, 'what are you doing, Luke?'

'I think I'm trying to figure out what I want,' Luke said after a few careful sips, 'and I think I'm using Andy to do it.'

'You know why that's not fair,' James said, crossing his legs.

'I know,' Luke sighed heavily, 'I know it's dumb and I know it's selfish, I wanted to give some new friends a try and wanted to latch on to his. But as for a relationship with him, I just don't know.'

'Sounds like you two have some things to talk about,' James said, putting out his cigarette. 'Andy isn't the kind to become attached so quickly, so if he is trying to make it work with you then the sooner you let him know the better.'

'You mean,' Luke stopped swirling his glass, 'you're not going to tell him?'

'Of course not,' James remembered his promise from earlier, 'I didn't get the reputation I have by being a loudmouth.'

'Thanks,' Luke smiled warmly. 'Can I ask you for a favour?'

'Sure,' James shrugged.

'If Andy and I do break up, can I keep talking to you? You seem like a good friend.'

'Of course,' James said, hiding the skipping of his heart behind a sip of the beer that he presumed was stronger than it tasted.

'Thanks,' Luke returned his attention to the wine, 'I feel better than I have in a while.'

James needed only a moment to think then on what it was that made him feel protective of Luke, why he had said those words to Andy that night. He wondered about his reaction to seeing Luke for the first time and his profound delight at seeing him happy. A less experienced man may conflict these feelings as romantic attachment, but James knew it was something different, something he couldn't put his finger on.

He was not in love with Luke, not by a long shot, but there was something Luke's smile offered him that gave James a joy he hadn't felt in some time, but hadn't realised he had been without.

Still, James knew that you didn't need love to want to see someone happy. The deeper reasons could wait until later, or so he told himself as a fuck-it moment came over him once again.

He got up walked over to Luke, whose smile widened with each step James took. Leaning down to get to the same level, James moved forward and picked up where they had left off just a few minutes before. Something was different about it that time, something good.

This time James knew he wouldn't stop.

***

Given that James had given up on drinking after two beers, the following morning brought no hangover, though it did bring a headache that James had not been prepared to deal with. Once conscious, James sat up in bed and rubbed his forehead, wondering if he had any cause to reach for the painkillers or if he just needed some hydration.

Beside him, sleeping soundly, was Luke.

James was familiar with the art of getting out of bed without someone noticing, even in his own flat, and had no trouble getting showered and dressed without disturbing his guest.

With a coffee made and messages checked, James sat back in his rocking chair and relaxed. In the old days he would have lit up a smoke with his morning coffee, but he had found that habit easier to quit than he had been told.

It was ten in the morning, and the sun still shone strong into his living room, warming it well with a soothing light that had made James want to buy the flat in the first place.

Charlotte wouldn't be arriving until two in the afternoon, giving James plenty of time to sort through his documents, the only problem being that they were all in cabinets he kept in his bedroom. Instead, he turned on his television and loaded up a show he knew he could zone out too.

As the voices droned in the plot of a show that had taken his fancy at one time or another, James found himself less buried in his thoughts than he believed he would be. He wasn't mad at himself, nor was he in a state of regret that normally followed morally questionable yet ultimately innocent acts. He didn't even ask why he had allowed the previous night to happen.

Perhaps it was the effect Luke seemed to have on him, the fact that he had all but announced intentions to break it off with Andy, or just because James was bored, horny and overthinking it. These were the answers to a question James wasn't asking, mostly because he didn't care.

Such was the beauty of afterglow, or so he told himself.

It wasn't long before there was movement from down the hall and Luke wandered in to the living room, James noticed that he was wearing a pair of sweats and a long white t-shirt that he seemed to have taken from James' own wardrobe.

'Morning,' he greeted. 'Coffee?'

'Yeah, if that's okay?' Luke smiled, James was relieved to see that he also wasn't regretful. To help out with someone else's problem was one thing, to know you were the source of the problem was a much heavier issue.

'Of course,' James got up. 'How do you take it?'

Luke thanked James for the coffee and let out a loud, satisfied sigh after taking his first sip.

'Sleep well?' James asked, hitting pause on the show and taking his usual seat.

'Yeah, really well,' Luke beamed, 'that's one hell of a bed. Memory foam?'

'Yu-huh,' James sipped his own coffee, it was stronger than he meant it to be, 'best thing I ever bought.'

'Set you back much?'

'I don't remember, couple of hundred I think.'

'Will have to look into one myself,' Luke raised his head and looked out the window from his seat, 'I wouldn't mind sleeping on one of those regularly.'

James enjoyed the insinuation, whether it was deliberate or not eluded him. It hadn't occurred to him whether or not he wanted it to happen again.

'I want last night to happen again,' Luke said bluntly, James paused mid-sip, he didn't like the thought of people being in his head. 'I had fun, and I wanna be around you more,' Luke blushed as he spoke.

With a smile James himself didn't trust, he got off his chair and kissed Luke softly on the lips.

***

Luke was long gone by the time James heard a knock on his door, he thought to himself that he should consider installing a doorbell. He opened the door without checking the peephole.

'Hey Charlotte,' he smiled, 'how're things?'

'Okay,' she marched through the door without wiping her feet, 'I mean awful. No, fuck it, yeah, I mean awful.'

'Yikes,' James said without thinking, he made it sound lighter than he meant to. Charlotte didn't notice, she was already in the living room by the time he had spoken.

'Got any booze?' Charlotte asked, knowing full well that James had booze.

'It's two o'clock,' James said from the living room door.

'And?'

'Let's just start with a coffee, huh?'

'Only if it's Irish,' she said. James pretended to think she was joking.

Charlotte didn't complain when she was handed her non-alcoholic beverage, though James could see that she wanted to.

'So what's been happening?' James said, taking a seat.

'Ugh,' Charlotte grunted, 'I've been dealing with Andy for the last four days. He's freaking out about the new guy and I don't know what to tell him, he's not acting like himself at all and it's stressing me the fuck out.'

'Andy has been acting out of character,' James nodded, 'but I didn't ask about him.'

'My course supervisor's been getting to me, he says he doesn't think I can finish my thesis in time.'

'Why not ask for an extension?'

'I've had too many as it is,' Charlotte looked away.

'That reminds me,' James had been sitting on a question for a while, 'what exactly happened with that? You used to get your work done early.'

'Things,' Charlotte sighed, 'just things.'

'I thought you were here to talk,' James said, 'that's why you come here isn't it?'

'Sometimes I come to see you,' Charlotte sniffed. 'So, anyone I know?'

'What?'

'I smell aftershave I know isn't yours,' Charlotte winked, the sudden and forced return to her usual joviality worried James.

'I have guests, you know,' James smiled, 'you've really gotta work on that one track mind.'

'You're relaxed,' Charlotte said confidently, 'you haven't stopped smirking since I got here and you haven't done that weird knee crossing thing. Admit it, you hooked up.'

'Charlotte,' James glared, 'I don't want to talk about this.'

'I see,' Charlotte bit her lip, 'so it is someone I know. I'll get it out of you,' she smiled.

'Careful,' James adjusted in his chair, 'this is bar talk.'

'You're right,' Charlotte sighed, remembering their deal, 'still, kudos.'

James felt uncomfortable then, he hadn't seen Charlotte act so erratically since she had wanted to drop out of her course.

'What have you been up to lately?' James tried to sound professional, something he'd never really get used to.

He understood then that he had tried to dive in to whatever it was Charlotte had wanted to talk about that day, as though he could take her problems head-on. He normally started with vague, inoffensive questions before digging slowly into the root of whatever was bothering people.

This sudden bout of confidence in his own skill was something he'd look into later, for the time being he needed to focus on his friend.

By the time Charlotte was getting ready to leave James had no more answers than before. Small, petty problems that wouldn't have bothered her before suddenly seemed to weigh on her mind. It had been their first session in months, and James had been bracing himself for something earth shattering, but what he got was worse.

Charlotte was deeply bothered by something and was hiding it poorly. She had not referred to Luke by name despite the fact that she seemed to have been in regular touch with him, though James speculated that was because she wasn't aware that they had met yet. Charlotte danced around questions of her own escapades and spent too much time asking James about his.

'Drinks tonight?' James asked as Charlotte put on her scarf.

'Nah thanks,' Charlotte said with a yawn, she changed her mind about booze rather quickly, which was unlike her. 'I've got way too much coursework. I think a bunch of us are doing something on Friday, though. I'll let you know.'

'Sure,' James was trying to cheer her up.

'See ya,' Charlotte said quietly as she made her own way out. The front door had closed behind her by the time James got to the hallway.

He looked down the hall for a moment, it seemed darker than he remembered. James had always considered one of the few good things about himself to be the trust people seemed to place in him, trust he was willing to accept and turn into a helping hand.

People had always looked to him for advice, for an ear, a place to vent. He had accepted that role gladly as he saw little use for himself otherwise.

His goals in doing so were not selfless, however. If he could see a smile on someone's face or know that someone he cared about was happy then he could sleep well at night. But if he knew that he had something to do with that happiness then he could relax and think, just for a little while, that maybe he wasn't such a bad person after all.

It was what he did for his friends that made him happy, made him go on. He didn't put a lot of stock in himself, but he put his stock in his friends, friends he was grateful for. And to watch Charlotte walk away knowing he couldn't help her, knowing she wouldn't talk to him for reasons he didn't know, stung him more than he felt it ought to.

James felt helpless.

As he entered the air of absence in his living room once again, he noticed a scent that hadn't been obvious to him before. Charlotte had been right, the faint smell of an aftershave or cologne still lingered in the flat, it wasn't a fragrance James used. He didn't know how he didn't notice it before, but it must have meant that Luke had brought it with him, meaning there was a chance that he had been intending to spend the night long before he had shown up.

James was perturbed by how happy that thought made him, but decided to focus on that happiness instead of the doubt. He flicked the television back on to the programme he'd been watching earlier before remembering the forms he was still yet to fill out. Leaving the television on, he made his way to the bedroom where his various details could be found.

***

James entered the psychology building the following afternoon, well aware of the fact that he wasn't expected. Next to Doctor Noore's room was the office of the department secretary, shared with her assistant. The room was a shoebox in comparison to Noore's, and James wondered if it was even legal to make two people work in such a cramped space.

'Good afternoon,' the friendly middle aged woman said from behind her desk, the size of her office didn't seem to bother her, at least not anymore.

'Hi,' James said, 'I have some forms for Doctor Noore?'

'Ah, Angela deals with the Doctor's affairs,' the woman took off her glasses, 'she's stepped out for a moment, but you're free to wait in the lounge if you like. I believe she wanted to speak to you.'

The woman read out the code to the lounge that James recognised as unchanged since he learned it in his second year. The lounge had two comfortable sofas, two computers, a water cooler and a printer. James wondered if his old university password still worked before realising that he had long since forgotten it.

Unintentionally, James sat in the same place on the sofa where he had sat as a student and brought the forms out of his satchel, wondering why he had been asked to stick around when he only needed to hand in some forms. Surely he could have just left them on this Angela's desk?

The water cooler bubbled as James poured out a cup, he wasn't thirsty and was killing time more than anything else. He waited for twenty minutes, wondering how he had ever spent hours on end, with the odd smoke break, in that room doing coursework.

He had a flat back then, of course, that he shared with his friends, or more accurately, people a computer had matched him with. Getting along was easier than living uncomfortably, so they had taken to calling each other friends whether it was accurate or not.

He wondered then why he had chosen to work in that lounge, on campus, away from his own home.

He looked outside the glass wall and saw the seminar room opposite, he remembered immediately why he had worked for so long in that space that suddenly felt a lot more cramped than he remembered. He hadn't worked there for ease or comfort, he had worked there because of that seminar room, because of who had seminars in that room.

'Mister Steele?' James jumped at the sound of a voice, he hadn't heard the door open.

'Y-yes,' James looked up to see a woman around his age with long chestnut hair tied in a ponytail. Her glasses were small and a pen was tucked behind her ear to compliment the clipboard she carried.

'I'm Angela. Doctor Noore is out today,' she said, adjusting her glasses and looking at the clipboard, 'but she told me to speak to you in her stead. We can go to her office if you like?'

'Sure,' James stood up.

The two of them made their way down the long hallway and arrived at Dahlia's office. Angela fished a key out of her pocket and opened the door, as James walked in behind her he realised that he had absolutely no idea where to sit.

He looked to the desk and thought about how rude it would be to use it without Dahlia's permission, he then looked to the sofa and thought about how awkward such closeness could seem between strangers. As he did his best to make up his mind he saw that Angela had already taken a seat over at the chairs that Dahlia reserved for patients, the chair James normally sat in.

'What's this about?' James said, thinly hiding his discomfort as he took Dahlia's seat. The chairs were identical, but something about the placement felt far too wrong.

'Doctor Noore asked me to give you your interview if you showed up without her around,' Angela said, flipping a page on her clipboard.

'Interview?'

'Yes. You have your forms, right?'

'Oh yeah,' James handed them over. Angela didn't examine them before setting them on the coffee table between them.

'The questions were prepared by the doctor herself, I'm sure you know what to expect,' Angela said with a slight laugh in her voice. James wondered how long she had been working with the See-All.

'I'm sure I don't,' he joked.

'First off, what is your dream for the future?'

'What? I...' James stammered, he hadn't been given much time to collect his thoughts.

He wasn't expecting an interview at all, but he knew that this was likely one of Dahlia's games. His answers wouldn't determine whether or not he got the job, he had already signed the contract after all, this was another therapy session. But why then and why Angela had been instructed to conduct it James had no idea.

He didn't doubt that Angela had been told exactly where to sit as well.

'Take your time,' Angela said, writing something down.

'To be happy,' James said concisely.

'Is that all?'

'Of course not,' he felt a rush of confidence, 'but it's the culmination of what I want. I want to be happy, that's the simplest answer I've got.'

'Interesting,' Angela furrowed her brow. 'Where do you see yourself in five years?'

'Exactly where I am now,' he decided he would play into the See-All's hands a little. Without her around she would be easier to mess with, though perhaps that was her intent. 'I don't want anything to change.'

'If you don't want anything to change then why take this job?' Angela asked.

'Is that on the list?'

'Actually, yes.' Angela smirked. James felt slightly annoyed.

'Damn See-All,' he mumbled, realising that was the first time he had said the nickname out loud in that office. 'Because I'm curious,' he went on, 'because I want to see what happens.'

'Okay,' Angela wrote a few more things down. James toyed with the idea that she wasn't actually writing anything, but dismissed it as nonsense. 'How long do you plan on sleeping with everyone who crosses your path?'

'Excuse me?' James feared his eyes would pop out of his head, 'I'm sorry but what do you-'

'Please just answer the question,' Angela said quickly.

'I'm afraid I don't,' James began to stammer, 'I don't know what you mean.'

'Maybe we should just move to the next question,' she scribbled something down quickly.

'Please,' James said sharply, he was starting to feel angry.

'Why did you do your coursework in the psychology lounge instead of at home?'

James leant back, suddenly he wanted desperately to leave but found his body relaxing as his mind raced faster and faster. The confidence he felt was gone, the game had turned into something worse. He was to answer these questions in front of a stranger, as honestly as he could. It would all come out eventually, but he hoped it would happen in more privacy than this.

'I wanted to see someone,' he sighed, knowing it would be better to get it out of the way, 'or, I wanted someone to see me.'

'And this someone is?'

'Someone who doesn't matter anymore,' James glared.

'Good enough,' Angela made a tick, as though the possible answers were written out as multiple choice. The See-All had really outdone herself if that was the case.

'What's next? What brand of condom I use?' James said with a snide tone.

'Nothing that personal,' Angela said. James restrained himself from saying it was far too late for that. 'Would you say your brand of therapy works?'

'I would,' he hesitated. 'If it didn't then why would people come to me?' James trailed off as he spoke as he realised he didn't quite believe the words himself.

Would they come to him just because they didn't know any better? Because he didn't charge? Because he was there and had the time?

'Next,' Angela seemed oblivious to James' discomfort, 'why do you think people come to you?'

'I... I don't know,' James said quietly. 'Can we take a break?'

'Just one last question,' Angela smiled at him, trying a little too hard to look reassuring. 'How many of your patients do you consider to be your friends?'

'All of the-' James stopped, thinking harder on that. He could count on one hand, two at a stretch, about how many people he had seen who he really considered to be friends, people he himself could trust. 'A few,' he breathed more than spoke the words, 'I think.'

'Excellent,' Angela stood up, still smiling, and gathered the forms from the coffee table. 'That'll be all, James. Please see yourself out when you're ready.'

James stayed put for a moment after Angela left, staring at the empty chair across from him. He was a lot of things, but out of all the emotions that had flurried inside of him in such a short space of time and under such bizarre circumstances, he felt one come out on top.

James was more pissed off than he had been in a long time.

He got up with the intention of leaving immediately, but instead he paced back and forth, muttering panicked and angry curses under his breath. He considered pouring himself a drink, thinking it would be rude before coming to the conclusion that Dahlia owed it to him.

He approached the drinks stand and paused as he reached for the whisky upon seeing a note that was stuck to the bottle.

Help yourself.

While he couldn't help but let out a snort of laughter, the note only fed his anger more. Dahlia wanted James to know he was being messed with, that the job offer was part of a game that he was losing. He knew not to mess with the See-All, but he never expected her to be the type to mess with him.

He shakily poured a generous snifter and sipped at it while he continued his pacing.

How had Dahlia known about the lounge? Had she set it up so when he arrived he would have to wait there to be reminded of it? How had she known that he would show up with the forms that day? Did she even know? The See-All did not bank on lucky guesses, if she ever had to guess anything in her life. There was something James wasn't seeing, something that made him nervous.

He had a choice to make, then. He could turn down the job and forget it ever happened, but the moment that thought entered his head he knew he wouldn't do it. He wouldn't give up, back down or quit after one weird day before he had even started.

He calmed down more and more with each sip as his pacing slowed. He understood that it was all perhaps a joke, albeit one in poor taste. It would certainly fit into Dahlia's sense of humour, at least as far as James knew, and he had no real right to be mad about any of it.

He believed then that if he had just taken to the therapy sessions with more gusto, feigned or not, then perhaps he would have been spared the events of that afternoon. And the only way to make sure it didn't happen again would be to answer Dahlia's future questions in earnest without looking to avoid them.

It was a joke, a game, it was punishment for obfuscation. All of these thing culminating to a display of power. It was Dahlia's way of telling him that for as long as he was in her domain, she would get the answers she needed from him, and the only way to make it easy was to play by her rules and answer her questions.

James knew when he was beaten.

With a heavy gulp that he had to brace himself for, he drank the rest of the whisky and set the empty glass back on the drink stand. He knew it wouldn't be his last drink of the day headed out the door with his head held high to see Doctor Noore waiting for him in the hallway outside, Angela's clipboard in her hand.

'Four minutes,' she said, looking at her watch, 'I expected longer.'

'I take it that was supposed to be funny?' James said, unsure as to where his acceptance of loss had vanished to.

'An expected side effect, yes,' Dahlia smiled, 'but more interesting than funny. Why don't you head back in my office?'

'It's not Monday,' James stood aside to make room as she passed him and entered the room. He felt his phone vibrate briefly in his pocket.

'This will be a friendly chat,' Dahlia said, leaving the door open, 'a sofa conversation.'

James reluctantly followed her inside and took a seat where he had been told.

'Another?' Dahlia asked as she poured herself a drink.

'No thanks,' James replied quietly, 'I've had enough for now I think.'

'Fair enough,' she said, walking over and taking a seat beside James. She sat too close, James' body tensed. 'I used to see you, back then, in that lounge. You spent more time in there than anyone.'

'I was doing coursework,' James said defensively.

'You were, but I knew that wasn't why you were there. It was just before you left, wasn't it? Even for a little while after. When you came back you were a different person. You were quieter, more withdrawn, but somehow more outgoing.'

James knew what she meant by all of those. He stared at his hands and said nothing.

'It still bothers you, doesn't it?'

'Only when I think about it,' James spoke honestly, 'which isn't all that often anymore. You could have just asked, you know?'

'I did, and you put your guard up.'

'So you decided to catch me off guard,' James realised what had been going on. 'Doctor Noore,' he went on, 'why exactly do you care? The past is in the past.'

'Call it professional curiosity,' she said before sipping her whisky, 'or call it concern from a friend.'

'I want to know one thing,' James sat up straight, 'you told me to take advantage of life's pleasures, so why did you bring up my sex life so blatantly?'

'I don't know what you mean,' Dahlia looked to him, the confusion in her eyes seemed genuine.

'About how long I plan to sleep with basically everyone I meet?'

Dahlia stood up and walked over to her window. James remained seated, watching her as she folded her arms and sighed.

'I think we should continue our conversation on Monday, James. Until then,' she turned to him with a wide grin, 'go and have some fun.'

James looked at his phone the moment he was outside, he had one message from Andy asking if he could come over. James replied with his ETA for The Regal and shoved the phone inside his pocket. It was nearing four in the afternoon, and James couldn't wait to get a pint in him.

Dahlia watched James walk away with purpose in his stride and sighed heavily. Her door slowly opened, an action known only to Dahlia by the sound of the door brushing gently against the carpet.

'You wanted to see me, Doctor?' Angela said as she closed the door behind her.

'I did,' Dahlia turned around and looked to her secretary with a glare in his eyes that would send weaker subordinates into nervous breakdowns.

'Angela,' she spoke calmly and quietly, though her tone was as cutting as a knife, 'if you ever feel like messing with one of my patients again, then I suggest you channel that energy into finding yourself another job.'

***

It was almost six by the time Andy was at the bar. Having arrived first, James had forsaken Charlotte's usual seat and instead gone with a pair of armchairs by a wall decorated with vague abstract art and a wooden cuckoo clock that somehow didn't look out of place amidst a myriad of clashing colours.

'You're late,' James said, he was already towards the end of his second pint, 'and you've got some catching up to do.'

'Damn,' Andy said, trying to force a laugh. 'Got a tab?'

'Nah, may as well open one, though.'

Andy nodded and went to the bar, returning with two pints, a stronger one for himself.

'So what's wrong?' James asked, hoping he didn't already know the answer.

'What makes you think something's wrong?' Andy took his first sip and winced slightly at the acidity.

'Since when do you ask permission to come to my flat?' James' glare was complimented by a small smirk.

'Fair enough,' Andy chuckled nervously, 'Luke's been acting really distant.' He wasted no time in getting to the point, meaning James had successfully projected that he wasn't in the mood for preamble.

'So break up,' James said plainly, surprised at his own lack of tact. He waited for Andy to respond but got nothing. 'You're stressing so much and you haven't been dating that long. If you feel strung along or uncomfortable then get out. Simple as that.'

'Jesus,' Andy shivered at James' words as though they really were as cold as they sounded.

'Sorry, but I mean, it makes sense, right?'

'Yeah, but,' Andy paused, 'you're normally less blunt.'

'I'm in the mood for candour,' James said, somehow already feeling much better.

'Maybe you're right, but first off what the hell's gotten into you today?'

'Doctor Noore,' James sighed, 'she really messed with me today.'

'The See-All? That doesn't sound like something she'd do.'

'Yes it does. Maybe it's her assistant or secretary or whatever,' James yawned despite not being tired, 'either way I needed this,' he held up his glass.

'Well that makes two of us,' Andy smiled wearily.

'So,' James said after a hearty swig, 'what's your deal today, then?'

'My deal?'

'Come on, man,' James flashed a knowing look.

'Okay, fine,' Andy admitted, 'Luke's not been replying to me much, we haven't met up in a week. I get that he's probably busy with work but I dunno.'

'This isn't at all like you,' James said worriedly, 'since when do you get so hung up like this?'

'Since you,' Andy said quickly. His body relaxed immediately and he slumped back in the chair as though the words had been a hefty burden to him.

'Since me?'

'I thought we were going somewhere, you were my first real relationship. I understand that we didn't work out, but I want that again.'

'I see,' James felt guilty. He wanted to apologise, but didn't know for what.

Relationships didn't always work out, sometimes it's no one's fault. But to think that the time the two of them had spent together had affected Andy so much was hard for James to take in. But what really stuck in his head was the fact that he didn't share Andy's feelings on the matter, he appreciated the time they had spent as a couple but hadn't attributed such meaning to something he saw as an experiment, a trial that proved to be error.

'It's not your fault,' Andy said, he recognised the look on James' face, 'it was just an awakening for me. I don't want to just mess around anymore, or be messed with.'

'I understand,' James said. He saw then that Andy had really grown up more than he had been given credit for. He wasn't messing around, he wasn't rebounding, he was dating. He was looking for someone to share himself with.

'But hey,' he said with a smile that looked real, 'they can't all work out, right?'

'I guess not,' James suddenly felt a lot more drunk than he felt he should. 'I don't even know what I'm looking for these days.'

'Since when do you look for anything?' Andy chuckled.

'True enough,' James decided to take it as a compliment.

James' phone vibrated then, a message from Luke saying he was out with Charlotte and if James wanted to join. He decided to reply to it later.

'What's up?' Andy asked when he saw that James put his phone away after little more than a glance.

'Nothing important,' James said convincingly, 'you got plans tomorrow?'

'Not anymore,' Andy looked away.

'Good, because I'm not even close to done drinking.' James smirked.

'Think Charlotte would wanna join us?' Andy asked.

'You kidding? I'm surprised she doesn't just move in upstairs.'

The two of them laughed together, neither of them wanting to point out how long it had been since they had really felt like friends.

'Why don't we invite her?' Andy said, bringing out his phone.

Reflecting on the knowledge that Luke was with her, James was about to reject Andy's idea before realising that he would be out of the way of any kind of blame. It would be good for them to all be together, even if not immediately. Besides, it had been a long time since James had been given the opportunity to rock the boat without any direct consequences falling on him.

That, and he really wanted to see Luke.

'Why don't we?' James said happily.

'Luke?' Andy almost stood to attention, 'I thought you had plans tonight?'

'Well yeah,' Luke pointed to Charlotte.

'That was kind of a dumb question,' James snickered.

'We should find a bigger table,' Charlotte said as Luke went to the bar, she didn't even glance around.

'Let me guess,' James sighed as he stood up, he had already admitted defeat. Together he and Andy went to Charlotte's favourite table while Charlotte stayed behind to help Luke carry the round.

'You okay?' James asked once they were sat, noticing Andy had gone pale.

'I am,' Andy said unconvincingly, 'I just had it in my head that we'd break up the next time we met.'

'Nothing wrong with enjoying the time anyway, right?' James was in a much better mood than before, Andy seemed worse.

'I think it's really nice,' Charlotte's voice could be heard as she approached the bar with two pints in hand.

'Thanks,' Luke said happily, 'I took kind of a chance on it but it's grown on me.'

'Well it's grown on me too,' Charlotte took a seat next to Andy while Luke sat by James on the other side of the table.

'What are you talking about?' James asked.

'Oh,' Charlotte smiled a wide smile, 'I was just telling Luke how much I absolutely love his new aftershave,' she flashed James a knowing look.

'I hadn't noticed,' James said.

'Why would you?' Charlotte cocked her head to the side. James was starting to get annoyed. Neither Luke nor Andy seem to notice.

'Thanks for the drink,' Andy said happily.

'No worries, Charlotte's been buying every round so far so I figured it was about time.'

'You never buy me that many drinks,' James said playfully.

'You never have anything interesting to say, and you're rich,' Charlotte joked. Her words stung a little. 'So how's the good doctor treating you?'

'Like a plaything,' James said, 'but I kind of expected that.'

'What do you mean?' Andy asked.

'It's not important,' James sighed, 'but her secretary might have it in for me.'

'Secretary?' Charlotte thought out loud.

'Yeah, Angela. You know her?'

'Not really,' Charlotte's trailed off.

'Anyway,' Luke stretched out the word for a few syllables, 'what's new with you two?'

'Work's a drag,' Andy began, 'we got a new guy in who's some kind of pharmaceutical prodigy. I think he's the See-All's nephew or something.'

'Can't escape the Noore family, huh?' James smirked.

'Apparently not. He's a dreamer, though. Got a shit tonne of ideas and it's pissing everyone else off.'

'Isn't it an oversight to let a kid like that in a lab?' Charlotte said, 'I mean, prodigy or not surely there are rules for this kind of thing.'

'He says he wants to cure the world or some nonsense,' Andy said, 'the bosses have taken to him and I think they're looking the other way.'

'You can't fight that family,' James said into his glass, 'better to go along with it.'

'Ugh,' Andy snorted and took a heavy swig of his beer.

'He doesn't really like to play by others' rules,' Luke laughed.

'Apparently none of us do,' Charlotte chimed in, no amount of warning looks from James seemed enough to make her stop.

***

Charlotte and Andy shared a cab despite Charlotte's insistence that James had beer and they should all hang out at his. James did, in fact, have beer in his fridge but found Charlotte's enthusiasm to stick around a touch unnerving given in was a weekday. She conceded eventually when Andy reminded her about her upcoming deadlines.

'Next time!' Charlotte called out before closing the cab door. She seemed far more drunk than the rest of them and James sent a text to Andy asking him to get her home safe the moment the cab left.

'Looks like rain,' Luke said as James put his phone back in his pocket. 'Your place or mine?'

'Huh?' James wasn't sure why the question caught him off guard, but he was too drunk to think of any reason to answer in the negative. 'Mine,' he said, 'I could use a smoke.'

***

James' eyes blinked open to the harsh light of noon, a strong headache thudding in his skull woke him up more than the light did. Beside him, once again, was Luke, who was sleeping peacefully.

A happiness came over James then, the same sort of calm, baseless joy that he felt whenever Luke was around, but with it came a lingering feeling of something that James attributed to most of his hangovers.

James knew that for the next eight hours or so he would occasionally feel like he just wanted to not exist for a while, like he could erase the entire previous night despite none of it being regrettable or embarrassing. He felt ashamed, but not for anything in particular, not even the obvious reasons.

James thought on the questions he had been asked in Dahlia's office. He wondered if he was really making a difference in anyone's lives. Did people really just come to him out of habit shared by word of mouth? James shook his head and immediately regretted doing so as the pain sloshed around his brain like a bucket of water.

He prepared his hangover smoothie, using more painkillers than perhaps he ought to, and settled on to the sofa for fear of the rocking chair knocking more pain loose in his aching noggin. A sense of déjà vu came over him as he set the television to a show he could drown out. It didn't take as long for Luke to wake up this time.

'Morning,' James turned his head to see Luke, wearing his clothes from the night before, the bags under his eyes and groan in his voice betrayed both how hungover he was and how little rest his sleep had given him.

'Hey,' he croaked out while staring at the floor.

'Y'alright?' James asked, suddenly concerned.

'Yeah,' Luke responded unconvincingly, he lifted his head only slightly to look into the middle distance. 'Look, I gotta go.'

'Sure,' James muted the show and stood up, 'but can I get you a-'

'No,' Luke held up his hand, still refusing to look at James. 'Hey, you haven't told Andy about any of this, have you?'

'No, I didn't think it was my place,' James replied. It was a half-truth, James had also simply wanted to avoid an awkward conversation as much as possible.

'Anyone else?' Luke sounded almost mad.

'I think Charlotte's figured it out on her own,' James said, remembering her odd behaviour the night before.

'Okay,' Luke said after taking a deep, shaky breath. 'I'll message you later.'

James didn't move as Luke made his way out the door and let himself out of the flat.

Something in Luke's tone showed more than just hangover or fatigue. He seemed angry, regretful. While it was true that an odd air had been hanging over James as well, he had just assumed it was the alcohol. Even with the negativity hanging around his hurting head, the happiness James felt was still winning out in the long run. Luke seemed down, almost angry, at the idea that they had been found out. Or worse, at the idea that they had slept together at all.

Something was amiss, but James wasn't even remotely capable of figuring things out that day. He plugged his phone into the wall socket in his bedroom and decided to leave it alone for the day. He would ignore any callers, grab a blanket and not leave his sofa for any reason that wasn't urgent, focussing only on silencing his idiotic, probably still drunk thoughts.

Over the course of the day two messages would go to James' phone, messages he wouldn't see until going to bed to get a less restful sleep than he'd like.

One was a text from Charlotte apologising for how she had acted the night before, the other was a message from Luke that James would read over and over in an attempt to find some deeper meaning behind the words, knowing he should have been happy to read them instead of giving in to a deep pit of something that wasn't quite despair.

I'm going to try to make it work with Andy.

5.

'I feel I owe you an apology,' Dahlia said once the her and James had sat down.

'You're damn right you do,' James said plainly. He wasn't still mad about the interview, but he wasn't feeling great about it either.

'While I am sorry for the way you were treated, I can't help but feel as though it will do us both well to keep such things in the foreground of our conversations.'

'Why?' James leant back with a sigh, Dahlia's apology did not sound like an apology, but he was willing to take it nonetheless.

'Because that's what these sessions are.'

'Heartbreak happens to everyone one day or another,' James said, 'I just got caught off guard and reacted badly. It's all in the past, I told you.'

'Then why don't you want to talk about it?'

'Because it's embarrassing,' James barked, 'can you honestly tell me you have no teenage regrets that you'd rather not think or talk about?'

Dahlia chuckled softly to herself. 'You have a point,' she said, though James knew she wouldn't drop it so easily, 'so let's talk instead about why you're in such a sour mood.'

'I haven't been sleeping well,' James admitted, 'and I haven't had many sessions myself lately.'

'Surely that's a good thing,' Dahlia began to make notes, 'it means your patients are getting better, doesn't it?'

'Yeah, I get that,' James said before hesitating. He never found it easy to give words to stewing thoughts.

Almost a week had gone by since James had last spoken to anyone in person. Ever since Luke left his flat that morning James had become sequestered, listening for a knock on his door or the buzz of his phone. He had heard nothing, not even from David, and he had grown to realise just how lonely he really was.

He had time to think about a lot of things, though no matter what he tried to focus on his mind always wandered back to Luke.

James had always found a comfort in seeing his friends happy, even moreso when their happiness was in some way because of him. But something about seeing Luke smile, hearing him laugh was special. He knew that what he had been feeling was something he had regained after being unaware that he had lost it.

James had been a lot more confident in himself since Luke entered his life. He hadn't considered a relationship with Luke at all, but he had found a comfort in the reciprocation of care that he had believed he had been shown.

Before long James understood that the only reciprocation had been sexual, and Luke hadn't shown anything to prove that he had any real fondness or love for James at all, as a friend or otherwise.

That got James thinking about the others.

He was invited out for drinks, but often as a last resort or for last minute advice, social calls and invitations that didn't imply sex were rarer in recent years, and people he had considered long time friends were beginning to fall off his radar. The only person who he could really convince himself to consider a friend was Charlotte.

He felt petty for thinking these were real problems, and refused to believe that they were anything worth speaking about to anyone. He was embarrassed, but he couldn't get the thoughts out of his head, they simply ended up swimming around his bored brain with no sign of drowning.

He felt used, he felt alone, and he felt like he needed to buck the hell up and get over himself.

'I've found myself in an interesting situation,' James said, calming down, 'y'see, I know a couple, a couple I'm not sure fit together. I know enough about them both to ensure a breakup, and if they stay together then I'm worried I'm going to lose them to each other.'

'I see,' Dahlia said quizzically, 'what is it about them being together that makes you think you'll lose them?'

'Because I might be in love with one of them,' James said, knowing it wasn't exactly true but unable to really say anything else without sounding like the randy scumbag he was starting to believe he was.

'So it would be a purely selfish action, then,' Dahlia stated.

'It would, but aren't humans inherently selfish creatures?' James looked out the window, 'is it so wrong to feel jealousy or want something my way?'

'Something, no. Someone, yes. But James,' Dahlia took a moment to consider her words, a rare action for her, 'are you sure what you're feeling isn't envy?'

'What do you mean?'

'Jealousy is being scared that someone will take what you have, envy is simply wanting something someone else has. The differences are not so subtle in definition, but they can be in practice.'

'I'm not entirely sure,' James thought out loud.

'You'll be starting work here tomorrow,' Dahlia was quick to change the subject, 'maybe we should focus on that for now.'

'Yeah,' James realised he had absolutely no idea what he was going to do in that office, but he couldn't shake the feeling like he was being toyed with. 'I'm looking forward to it.'

They both knew it was a lie.

James heard someone call his name from across the university plaza. He stopped and looked around, thinking it was meant for someone else before he saw Charlotte waving him down from the library entrance.

'Hey,' he said as he approached, a wide smile on his face. He was happier to see her than he thought he'd be.

'What's up?' Charlotte hoisted her satchel over her shoulder, 'I'm just done with studying, you free? Fancy a drink?'

'You know I do,' James' smile grew wider, 'you sure it's a good idea, though?'

'Eh, I'm all out of study brain,' Charlotte said, acting more tired than she was, 'besides, I think I've earned it.'

The Lothian University campus had three bars across a quarter mile stretch, frequented by students and faculty alike. James had come to miss his old haunts and had often wanted to return but always figured he'd feel too creeped out by himself to do so.

The campus bars were where his happiest memories from university were, and upon entering with Charlotte he recalled fondly the times he had spent getting far too drunk for his own good.

'Been a while for us,' James said as he sat down with their drinks, 'what've you been up to?'

'Sorry,' Charlotte smiled, 'was studying all week and then had a wild night on Friday, took ages to recover.'

'I shudder to think what you call a wild night,' James chuckled.

'Okay, it wasn't *wild* wild, but it was up there. Loads of us were out at the clubs. Everyone was there.'

'Everyone?' James' smile started to feel heavy.

'Yeah!' Charlotte beamed, oblivious, 'but man, I needed like two days to recover. We even got Gregg out, if you can believe it. Poor guy did not take well to Luke.'

'Jealous, huh?'

'Definitely,' Charlotte emphasised the word.

'Charlotte,' James dropped his smile, 'I know you know about me and Luke. I gotta ask, is this going to be a problem.'

'No,' she was very quick to answer.

'Good,' James let out a sigh of relief and looked to his drink, he couldn't help but chuckle a little. 'I guess I haven't changed that much, huh?'

'None of us have,' Charlotte said, an exhausted tone in her voice as though this was a conversation they had had a hundred times before. 'But I don't think that's a bad thing.'

'No?'

'Well, we're all the same, sure. But most of the baggage is gone, right? Like, we can enjoy being young without being as naïve as we were back then.'

'Oddly profound for you,' James said flippantly.

'I can have deep thoughts too, y'know?' Charlotte snorted.

'How's the studying going?' James decided to move on to more light hearted conversation.

'It's going, all right,' Charlotte sighed, 'mind if we don't talk about it, though? I'm so sick of my course. You had the right idea man, shoulda got out when I had the chance.'

'Doctor Noore would disagree,' James held his chin in his hands.

'I know she would, hell it was her that got me to stay.'

'It was?'

'Yeah, she was my therapist for a while when you, y'know...' Charlotte trailed off.

'Disappeared,' James concluded. 'Charlotte, look,' he went on.

'Relax,' she smiled as she held up a hand to stop him talking, 'you don't owe me an explanation, not after all these years.'

'Thanks,' James smiled warmly. There was something different about the way Charlotte spoke, her usual energy seemed to have vanished and he was left with a calmer, more restrained and thoughtful version of his friend. James wasn't sure he liked the change, but chalked it up to fatigue from studying.

It was a lazy assumption, but it worked.

'You spoken to Luke, then?' Charlotte asked once they decided that yes, they did want another round.

'Not since that morning,' James sighed, 'but you know how it goes with me. If I don't hear from someone-'

'He's okay,' Charlotte cut him off, she didn't want to hear James' excuses any more. James understood. His smile started to feel a little lighter.

'That's good,' he said earnestly, 'I was beginning to think heartbreak was on the way.'

'For who, I wonder?' Charlotte said quietly, James pretended not to hear.

'So how's Gregg?'

'Why did you sleep with Luke?' Charlotte completely ignored James' question, knowing full well that he didn't really want to know the answer.

'What?'

'Why him? He's not even remotely your type and I've never known you to take part in infidelity, not deliberately anyway.'

'It just kind of happened, Charlotte,' James answered with a tinge of anger, he felt he didn't owe her an explanation. 'It's not like we were courting.'

'*Courting*,' Charlotte snorted.

'You know what I mean,' James rolled his eyes.

'It's just kind of weird,' Charlotte began to swirl her glass in her hand, a few drops spilling over the side. 'Andy doesn't know, probably never will, and you're both just happy to keep the secret, huh?'

'Are you telling me you'd wanna know if you were Andy?'

'Are you telling me what he doesn't know can't hurt 'im?'

'Yes,' James answered frankly. It was a rule he knew was childish, but one he couldn't find an argument against. Ignorance was bliss, and the truth often hurt more than it should.

'Am I naïve for thinking otherwise?' Charlotte took a swig.

'No,' James mused, 'more idealistic.'

'Some might say that's a good thing.'

'You know it's not,' James sipped at his beer.

'You'd know better than me,' Charlotte raised her eyebrows.

The two sat in a less-than-comfortable silence for a little while, neither of them sure where to go in the conversation or how to proceed without hurting any feelings or bringing up bad memories.

Charlotte was the one to break the silence, as James had anticipated. She had a look on her face that he recognised in someone with something to say but was lost on the words necessary to convey it.

'You should drop him,' she said, her shoulders becoming stiff, 'Luke, I mean.'

'Huh? Why?'

'He's,' she stopped again to gather her thoughts, 'well, I've known him for a month or so now and, he's not a bad person or anything, but he's just,' she stopped again.

'Where's this coming from?' James set down his drink.

'He's a pretty shitty friend, James,' she spoke quickly, 'he comes out with these things, like little snide things, or will just up and leave when a conversation or night isn't going his way. He probably doesn't even know whose bed he's gonna wake up in half the time.'

'Sounds like you should be telling Andy this,' James acted like he wasn't that interested.

'Andy knows and, well, he's pretty submissive about it,'

'What?'

'Like, I've seen Luke drunk and angry over nothing, saying and doing really shitty things. Then the next day Andy tells me he's off to apologise to him.'

'What's the hesitation? Since when are you slow to call out someone's bullshit?'

James' concern was getting harder to hide. Andy was never one to apologise first, much less when he wasn't in the right. He believed Charlotte, but only because he didn't know her to lie. If anyone else was telling them this he would have dismissed it as hyperbole, and he knew that meant that he really was protective of Luke.

Even on hearing Charlotte's warning, James found himself scrambling for excuses as to his apparent behaviour.

'That's the thing,' Charlotte furrowed her brow, 'I did. He has this way of flipping things. He can be a real asshole, but somehow manages to make you feel bad for pointing it out.'

'Why are you telling me this, Charlotte?'

'Because I don't want to see you hurt again.'

'I don't know what you-'

'Cut the shit,' she took a heavy swig, 'I know you're feeling something for him. I don't know what it is but every time you get involved it fucks you up.'

'I think you're being unfair,' James forced his body to appear relaxed.

'That's what he tends to say,' Charlotte shook her head, 'I think he's bad news, James. And I think if you treat him as anything other than a patient then you're gonna have a lot more to talk about in therapy.'

'This isn't like you, Charlotte,' James wanted to change the subject, 'what's going on?'

'I don't think he's playing around, and I don't think he means it,' Charlotte ignored James' question again, 'but there's something the See-All once told me, something that's been in my head lately,' she looked to her beer and began swirling it around again, James already knew what she was going to say.

'Sometimes,' James finished her thought for her, 'the world's worst monsters are those who don't know just how much they hurt others.'

It was a warning that Dahlia had given Charlotte whenever she spoke about James. They both knew it well.

He wondered then if Charlotte was really talking about Luke, or if she was hiding behind her thoughts on him to get to the root of what James was fearing to be true, that he really hadn't changed much after all.

Eventually they finished their beers and made plans for the weekend, effectively putting their chat on hold for the time being.

***

James lay in his bed that night feeling lightheaded. Daytime drinking always felt different to him, it always seemed to hit him harder and last longer than night drinking. James found himself with less tact and more focus, but at the cost of some equilibrium and clarity of thought. Even hours later he felt as though the two pints he had drank with Charlotte still lingered in his stomach, brain and liver.

'Jealousy or envy, huh?' he said out loud, turning to the empty side of his bed. In the three years he had been living in that flat he had shared that bed with only three people.

Out of all of them, James found himself wishing Luke was there, sleeping peacefully as he often seemed to, even with a hangover brewing in his head. It was ridiculous to him, the idea that he would miss someone he had only known for a fortnight and met four times.

If Luke really was the kind of person Charlotte made him out to be, then James just had to wait for evidence. Until then, it changed nothing. But if it did happen, and he really did get hurt, James had no idea how or if we would react at all.

He had no idea if he was jealous or envious. Jealousy would mean that he wanted Luke more than Andy did, which didn't sit right in his head. Envy would mean that he simply wanted whatever it was they had, and since sex was the only real thing he and Luke had shared, it just came down to libido.

Neither answer was satisfactory, and both were embarrassing. James rolled over to face away from the rest of the bed and cursed himself under his breath. He had no idea what was going to happen the next day, and decided to focus on possible circumstances of his first day working for Doctor Noore and planning his reactions to those things. Sleep found him before long, a deep sleep with heavy and painful dreams that he wouldn't remember upon waking.

***

The air was brisk and chilling as the morning sun shone down on the university plaza where the students shuffled silently towards their early morning lectures. It was the first morning that really felt like winter.

James couldn't tell how much smoke was from his breath and how much was from his cigarette as he stood outside the psychology building, wondering if he had shown up at a good enough time. He had looked over his copy of the contract again before leaving but didn't find any real details that give him any clue as to what to expect, only vague statements regarding assistance to Doctor Noore's work, errands and whatever else she may need.

In truth, James felt happy to have a reason to get up again, he had expected some resistance from his body clock but instead seemed to have energy to spare as he made himself a coffee that morning, energy that seemed to come with a sense of purpose that he allowed himself to revel in.

Still, he couldn't help but feel nervous about entering the building that he had been in a hundred times before. He felt like a fresher again, a first year who had no idea what the looming, imposing buildings and new responsibilities had in store for him or his future.

He took a deep drag of his cigarette, wondering what he would say to his first year self if he got the chance, if indeed he would say anything at all. It was a nice feeling to consider changing nothing if given the opportunity, it made James feel as though he really was okay with the way his life turned out.

As he put out his cigarette in a nearby bin and entered the building as an employee for the first time, James had his head held high in a sense of pride he hadn't felt in years.

'Ah, good morning James,' Dahlia greeted him from the hallway. She was talking with a faculty member James didn't recognise, a tall man with messy stubble and an odd grin that made him look somehow younger than he likely was.

'Good morning,' James returned the greeting, he suddenly felt as though his morning coffee was wearing off.

'Is this the new guy?' the man asked.

'Yes, he'll be starting here today,' Dahlia handed him an envelope that she had tucked under his arm. 'I take it this will cover another month?'

'Absolutely,' the man grinned wider before taking his leave, he briefly rested his hand on James' shoulder as he walked past and an icy shiver ran down his spine, something he hadn't felt from human contact since he was younger.

It was all James could do to not turn his head and stare wide-eyed at the man who could change his entire disposition with nothing more than a few words and a brief touch.

'Who was that?' James asked once he was sure the man was far enough away.

'One of my family's benefactors,' Dahlia folded her arms and looked past James down the hallway. 'He's supporting my nephew's work in one of our pharmaceutical labs. I believe your friend Andy works there, too.'

'I remember him saying something about it,' James said, his voice shaking slightly. Dahlia smirked her half-mouthed smirk.

'Imposing, isn't he?' she said.

'Yeah,' James nodded quickly.

'Never mind that now, I'll show you to your work station,' Dahlia turned round and motioned for James to follow her. Together they walked past her office and further down the corridor to the psychology lounge where a desk had been set up in place of one of the computer stands.

'This is my office?' James couldn't hide his disdain at the idea, though he was relieved that Dahlia hadn't tried to cram a third desk into Angela's space.

'I thought it would be fitting,' Dahlia entered the code to the lounge and opened the door.

'What exactly is my job, then?' James said, taking a seat on the desk chair that was far more comfortable than he thought it would be. It felt new, though he somehow doubted it was.

'I'll be forwarding e-mails to you that I feel could use your advice rather than mine, patient requests, enquiries and the like. Other than that you're to offer your help to any student that uses this room to do their coursework like you used to.'

'Mentoring, huh?' James fiddled with the chair's settings.

'More advising,' Dahlia said, 'I'll be screening the e-mails you send, of course. And I also want to be kept in the loop of any student you talk to.'

'And that's it?' James said, unsure why he was using an accusatory tone.

'That's it,' Dahlia leaned against the doorway, 'I have an appointment now,' she checked her watch without needing to. 'Have fun, James.'

James switched on his computer and logged on, he was immediately urged to change his password before continuing and took nearly ten minutes to decide on what to enter.

The desktop was standard, brand new with little more than an internet browser and e-mail shortcut on the dash. He wondered just how much he would be allowed to customise his computer, and remembered at least being able to change the wallpaper for his login when he was student.

With a smirk to himself, James went online and found the cartoon fox wallpaper he had used as a student. It was a kind-of joke to himself, though seeing it filled him with a pleasant nostalgia that he couldn't help but warm to. The sound of the door opening made James look up.

'Mister Steele?' Angela walked in, a file under her arm.

'Oh, James, please,' he felt uncomfortable at the correction, but not as uncomfortable as he felt about unnecessary formality.

'Okay,' Angela fixed her glasses, 'I came to give you your forms.'

'Oh, I already filled those out,' he said.

'These are your report forms,' Angela set the file on the table, 'you're to fill them out at the end of each day, one for every student you speak to in person.'

'Ah, thanks,' James said, he was made more uncomfortable by Angela's decision to hover awkwardly around his desk.

'James, I want to apologise for the last time we spoke,' she said. James suddenly realised that the report papers were likely supposed to be on his desk to begin with, but Angela wanted a decent excuse to bring up what had happened. 'It was over the line, I shouldn't have done that and I'm sorry.'

'Don't worry about it,' James smiled to her, 'it woke me up if nothing else,' he laughed. The bitterness was gone, though Angela had unknowingly given James confirmation that at least some of the questions she had asked were by her own design. All he didn't know was why.

'Thanks,' she said, unhappiness in her voice. 'James,' she continued, 'you don't remember me, do you?'

Her phone began to ring in her pocket as James scrambled for an answer that he didn't have. As far as he was consciously aware he had never met this woman in his life before she sat him down in Dahlia's office.

'Hello?' she answered her phone and stood to attention, regaining her professional composure despite her and James still being the only ones in the room. 'Yes, of course. I'll have them on your desk by noon,' she said as she left the room. James toyed with the idea that it was a fake phone call to get her out of an awkward conversation that she started. He knew that wasn't the case, but found the idea funny anyway.

He decided to shelve the conversation in his mind and think on it later. He had met a lot of people in passing as a student and shared his course with hundreds more who he had spoken to or worked with briefly in group presentations or lab projects. He didn't see any real reason to worry, so he didn't. He wished then that the rest of his petty concerns could flitter away so easily.

Not a single student entered the psychology lounge in the hours James spent there, though many did gawk in through the glass walls as they passed by to see why the layout was different and whisper amongst themselves about who the new guy behind the desk was.

It didn't make James as uncomfortable as he thought he would be, though he did occasionally find himself glancing up at the seminar room outside, somehow feeling as though he would catch a glimpse of him. He knew it was nonsense, but that didn't stop him from looking and, for reasons that utterly escaped him, hoping.

He chuckled to himself more than once. Dahlia had really outdone herself this time.

***

Dahlia had left the office by the time James packed up to go. All in all he found the day to be more boring than he had anticipated. Other than his pseudo-conversation with. Angela he had nothing really of note for the day, his only forwarded emails were vague questions about mental health, coursework assignments and a few asking for directions. James realised quickly that his job amounted to little more than dealing with messages that were below Dahlia's pay grade, though he didn't know why he didn't expect that.

The weird feeling he got from the man he encountered with Dahlia was a distant memory as he lit up his cigarette outside the building. At five o'clock, the sky was already mostly dark and the outdoor lights around the campus were in full effect, making the plaza seem more like a Christmas market or street fair than a university.

'Hey,' Angela came out behind James, 'how was your first day?'

'Dull,' James said as he turned around, trying to make it sound more like a joke than a complaint, Angela's smile made it seem as though he had succeeded.

She was wearing a long grey coat and a chequered scarf. Seeing her made James realise how cold he actually felt, he made a mental note to bundle up better.

'Don't get used to that,' she chuckled, 'when end of term comes up every student and their mother wants a piece of us, sometimes literally.'

'I look forward to it,' James took a drag of his cigarette. 'So, sorry, but how exactly do we know each other?' he surprised himself, something in his brain had decided to go for a fuck-it moment and the words came out from curiosity rather than anything else.

'Oh, it's not important,' Angela blushed, 'but if you want we can go for a drink sometime this weekend, to celebrate the new job? I'll buy.'

'Seems like drinking's all I do lately,' James half-joked.

'Don't make a habit of it on weekdays,' Angela warned, 'Doctor Noore doesn't take kindly to hungover staff.'

'Somehow that doesn't surprise me,' James put his cigarette out.

'Anyway, I have a bus to catch,' Angela began walking, 'I'll see you tomorrow James,' she waved.

'Yeah,' was all James could say, his brain still scrambling to remember how he knew her. Something about the way she bid her farewell rang a bell in the back of his mind, he had known her before, but not in passing. He remembered then about how Charlotte had reacted when he brought her up. As though on a timer, he brought his phone out quickly and sent a text to Charlotte.

Tell me about Angela. Do I know her? x

He put the phone in his pocket and made his way to the tram stop, wondering above all else what thoughts were going to keep him awake that night, all the while distracting himself from the desire to text Luke the instant he had brought out his phone to send the message to Charlotte.

'A bad person, huh?' he thought out loud, his determination to not tempt fate faded faster than he had assumed, and once he was on the tram he messaged Luke to see how he was, a vague text from what could be called a friend wouldn't seem to out of the blue. James felt flush after sending it, ashamed of himself without knowing why. It was a feeling he was beginning to get used to.

Lying to partners, ditching friends for casual sex, hedonism and deception hidden behind a somewhat charming façade, and the ability to make others apologise when they were wronged. James saw enough of his old self in what Charlotte had said about Luke, and where there should have been a cautious and defensive instinct there was instead an intrigue that James couldn't shake, the potential for a dangerous game that James had played before.

James wouldn't admit it, but part of him wanted to lose.

Neither Charlotte nor Luke had replied by the time James got home. His waiting room was once again empty and his zeal for playful thoughts had vanished along with his energy.

It was seven o'clock, but it looked like night time. Winter had certainly begun, and James didn't care for it. He had stopped for beer on the way home, but upon entering his well-heated flat he realised that a cold one may not sit right.

He put the beers in the fridge and prepared a whisky without ice, something he had acquired a taste for since he sat down with Dahlia what seemed like a long time ago. He jumped a little as he felt his phone vibrated.

She was your patient. x

James looked at his whisky and realised that he simply wasn't ready to call it a night, but he also knew that showing up the next day hungover was a bad idea. He downed the rest of his drink in one, knowing it was all he needed, and turned his attention back to his phone.

***

Angela arrived early at the office. She had bought a bottle of wine on her way home the evening before and wanted to leave it on James' desk as a show of good faith. Upon her arrival to the psychology lounge entrance she was surprised to find James already at his work station.

He didn't seem to notice her as he mindlessly looked half-awake at his monitor. Angela hesitated, clutching her satchel with the wine. She froze and turned to walk away, embarrassed.

'Angie?' she heard someone behind her. She knew who it was before she turned around, only two people had ever called her by that name in her life.

'Hey, long time,' Angela turned to see Charlotte standing behind her in the corridor. It was the first time the two had spoken since Charlotte cancelled her therapy.

'Yeah,' Charlotte looked happy, Angela was glad to see it, 'what have you been up to?'

'Just work,' Angela said, fixing her glasses unnecessarily, 'was just gonna drop by a little welcome to the office present for the new guy.'

'"The new guy", huh?' Charlotte looked into the lounge. She recognised the look on James' face and knew he hadn't gotten much sleep. 'He really doesn't remember you, does he?'

'It was a while ago,' Angela had forgotten how cutting Charlotte's honesty could be, 'it's not his fault.'

'He was a different person, then,' Charlotte rested her hand on Angela's shoulder, 'don't beat yourself up, okay?' she smiled warmly.

'I know,' Angela said, 'still...' she trailed off, Charlotte recognised the look on her face all too well. 'What are you doing here, anyway?'

'Oh, I have an appointment with Doctor Noore.'

'Oh, are you back in therapy?' Angela asked without thinking.

'No, no, just a consultation of sorts,' Charlotte deflected awkwardly. 'speaking of, I should get going,' she fixed the bag on her shoulder and began to make her way down the hall.

'Sure,' Angela said, 'we should catch up sometime soon.'

'I'd like that,' Charlotte said, stopping just by Angela and lowering her voice to make sure James couldn't hear them. 'I'd let it go if I were you,' she said, her voice serious, 'he's not the kind of person fragile people should get involved with.'

'What?' Angela wasn't sure what to make of Charlotte's words.

'The person he was is still in there, and I'd hate to see you get hurt again.'

With that, Charlotte continued down the hallway towards Dahlia's office, humming a happy tune while Angela stayed put, staring at nothing in particular as she thought on the words that had come out of nowhere. The lounge door opened beside her, making her jump, she hadn't seen James move.

'Mornin',' he yawned.

'Good morning, James,' Angela replied, unable to match his low energy. 'Not had your coffee yet, huh?'

'I had one at home,' James stood up straight and cracked his back with a groan that was louder than it should have been, 'but I'm gonna get another now. You fancy one?'

'Sure,' Angela nodded happily. She didn't need a coffee, but company was nice.

'Long night?' Angela asked as James put a pod in the coffee machine, 'I did warn you about hangovers.'

'I'm not hungover,' James said, 'I'm just tired.'

'Not sleeping well?'

'Oh he slept,' Dahlia said as she walked into the room, 'eventually.'

'Doctor Noore,' Angela stood to attention, 'good morning.'

'Morning Angela,' she smiled, 'James.'

'Mornin',' he replied without looking, taking his coffee from the stand the moment it was finished.

'Back to your old habits, are we?' Dahlia asked, her smirk made it seem like a joke, though they both knew it wasn't.

'I'll perk up after this,' he sipped the bitter espresso and sighed heavily, he didn't bother adding milk.

'Be sure that you do,' Dahlia said.

'Oh, Doctor Noore,' Angela said quickly, 'your nine o'clock is here.'

'Earlier than I thought,' Dahlia mused, 'thank you, Angela,' she took her leave. James wondered why she had come into the kitchen to begin with.

'She's scary, huh?' Angela said quietly.

'Dahlia? Sure. You're not used to it?'

'Not really,' Angela hugged herself, 'I guess you're used to being around scary people,' she said, her mind returning to her run in with Charlotte.

'Huh?' James couldn't quite focus.

'Nothing,' Angela said with a smile. She decided to hold off on giving James the wine, wondering if it was a good idea at all.

'Anyway,' James said, scratching the back of his head, 'I guess we should get to work.'

***

'It's like you said,' Charlotte said, looking out the window, 'he doesn't seem willing to believe me about Luke.'

'Assuming you are telling the truth,' Dahlia began, pouring a coffee from her personal machine in the corner of the room. She handed one to Charlotte, who thanked her quietly.

'You think I'm not?' Charlotte said before taking a sip.

'I wouldn't know,' Dahlia sat down, 'despite my reputation and unfortunate nickname, I can't actually see everything, and James hasn't been bringing Luke up in our sessions.'

'They're too alike,' Charlotte said, 'superficially they're night and day, but Luke's just like he was when he was younger. Maybe even now.'

'Are you worried about Luke turning James back to that life?'

'Not exactly,' Charlotte took a seat, 'because I think the old him is still very much in there.'

'Yes, I looked in on him like you said,' Dahlia crossed her legs, 'he isn't hungover, there's no smell of alcohol. He was out late, but not drinking.'

'What do you think it means?' Charlotte's voice began to shake.

'I think it means his wounds are opening,' Dahlia sipped her coffee, 'and I think it means he's acquiring a taste for rotten fish.'

6.

'I'm just, I'm so scared,' James sobbed, he couldn't remember the last time he cried so much. It felt good, it felt necessary, it felt awful.

He grabbed onto whatever clothing he could, barely able to speak over the rushing emotions. 'I don't want you to not care about me.'

He felt a hand take his wrist, and for a moment he thought everything would be okay. He felt something of a smile return to his face before a harsh force threw him from the bed and sent him crashing to the floor, his head hitting the brick wall hard enough to blur his vision.

'Pathetic.'

James woke up suddenly, drenched in a layer of sweat that made his pyjama top stick to him in a cold bind. He got out of bed and threw the shirt into the corner of the room. He breathed heavily and ran a hand through his damp hair.

'Fuck,' he said out loud, gripping his chest. It had been a while since he'd had such a nightmare, or at least since he'd remembered one, and he didn't care for it at all.

He was angry, but at no one in particular, he cursed his brain more than anything else, as though his unconscious self had deliberately betrayed him. In a way it was true.

Nightmares and uncomfortable dreams were par for the course, and normally nothing that James couldn't handle. But a resurfaced memory was a different animal, something that would shake him for hours if he didn't get a firm grip on himself.

With a fresh pyjama shirt on, James lay down on the other side of the bed, the wrong side.

Luke's side.

He checked his phone, it was nearly five in the morning, though dawn would still be a few hours away. He grit his teeth and remembered just how much he hated the winter.

He assumed he wouldn't sleep again, but in what seemed like a blink his dark and musty room transformed into a sunlit haven, he didn't know if it was the light that woke him or the incoming message on his phone. James' heart leapt in a manner his newly woken body was barely able to handle when he saw Luke's name on his screen.

You don't work Fridays, right? Wanna hang out?

Above the words was the message that James had sent two days earlier asking how he was. He ignored the sinking feeling in his stomach and replied saying he'd let him know later. It was coming up to eight o'clock, and James turned his alarm off before its shrill screeching disturbed what was already a terrible morning mood.

The nightmare was still in his head by the time he lit his cigarette to go with his first coffee of the day. He leant against the window and saw his eyes reflected back at him, a transparent version of himself that looked in to the empty flat instead of out over the grizzly morning. Thick grey clouds moved in his eyes and he knew that snowfall wasn't far off.

James turned to put his back against the glass and sipped at his coffee, his cigarette burned quietly in his hand as he thought about the near future. His new furniture would be arriving the next day, he'd find a place for his old sofa somewhere in the large dwelling, there was plenty of room for it.

He'd be constructing all day and wondered if he knew anyone who'd be willing to help in exchange for a beer or two. He had put Tuesday night behind him, though his thoughts lingered on Angela for a while, he just couldn't figure out where he knew her from or how bad to feel for not remembering her at all.

His phone vibrated in his pocket, he set his coffee down by the unopened package on the table and flicked his cigarette over the ashtray on the windowsill. He switched on the screen to read the message without opening it.

Can't wait.

***

By the time he arrived at his office, James felt like a new man. His mood was elevated as he took his chair and booted up his computer, entering the password that, in his more mentally sharpened state, seemed like an unfortunate decision.

He already had an email waiting for him despite the fact that he was yet to see anyone in the office. It was labelled *SAD*, seasonal affective disorder, one of the topics of James' dissertation. The email wasn't forwarded like all the others, but was addressed directly from Dahlia.

Good morning, James.

The department heads have asked me to give a presentation on SAD in Manchester in one week's time, and I would like to request your attendance to assist and talk alongside me as part of your dissertation will be used as source material.

The conference will last the weekend and your accommodation and expenses will be provided. I trust you will keep your schedule open.

Regards,
Dr. See-All

James smirked at the signoff, he knew she disliked the nickname and he appreciated the joke. His mood lightened further and, while the idea of public speaking didn't sit well with him, nor did the idea of going to Manchester, he found himself appreciating the invitation, thankful for an opportunity he would have scoffed at just a month before.

With no one else around and no more emails to get through, James went online and sent messages out to everyone he knew asking them if they'd help him build furniture the next day.

As he sent out his final request, James pondered on the chore with happiness in his heart, the idea of having a few friends over to drink some beer and complain about how shitty flat pack furniture was to put together was the kind of thing good memories were made of. His most fond recollections were beginning to age poorly, and he needed to replace them.

In setting out to make those memories, James had promised himself to try harder to make life something more than just a series of time killers and difficult conversations.

The lounge door opened and James looked up to see Dahlia, cortado coffee in hand, smiling at him from the threshold.

'Good morning,' he smiled.

'Morning, James,' she smiled back, 'you're looking much better today. Did you sleep well?'

'Not really, but I feel pretty good.'

'I'm glad to hear it. Did you get my invitation?'

'I did, I'll be free,' James said, unsure whether or not it would be appropriate to thank his boss for effectively giving him a work-related task. Though he realised then that he hadn't actually replied to the email.

'Excellent, I'll send you more details later,' she said before taking an immediate leave.

As the door closed behind her, James found himself feeling oddly empty. The brief social contact he had being replaced once again with solitude rang oddly to him. His body felt hollow as all the energy and good will of the past hour seemed to leave him for no obvious reason.

He stood up, fighting any nonsense thoughts that entered his mind, and decided to make himself a coffee.

It was around lunch time when three young students came into the lounge, their lively conversation stopping the moment the door was open. James looked up with a friendly smile to acknowledge their presence, but was met with hesitant looks as they sat down and got their laptops out. One of them began listening to music while the other two engaged in hushed and intermittent conversation.

James hadn't felt so awkward in years, and by the time the three of them left he let out a heavy sigh as he realised he had been tense the entire time the students were there.

It didn't seem right, he had no way of starting a conversation despite the fact that it was part of his job. For some reason he had expected the students to come to him, and wondered if it would help to set up a sign or memorandum to let the student body know that he wasn't just some creepy post grad who had set up shop in a communal space.

Instead of attempting to enforce either of these ideas, James opened his internet browser again and sent a message to Luke saying that he was definitely up for drinks that evening.

***

James felt sullen as he stepped out into the freezing eve. He had remembered to grab his thickest winter coat and a scarf, but hadn't yet donned his gloves as he still wanted to light up a smoke before heading for the tram.

It took him a few seconds to see Angela standing outside, holding onto her satchel with both hands. She wore a pair of fingerless gloves, James wondered why he didn't own a pair himself.

'Hey,' he said after taking his first drag, 'sorry, I didn't see you there.'

'It is getting darker,' she chuckled, 'just wanted to know if you're still up for some drinks tomorrow?'

'Oh, of course,' James smiled, hoping he was able to hide the fact that he had completely forgotten about their vague plans.

'Cool,' she said, the word somehow didn't suit her. 'I hope you don't mind I got your number from Doctor Noore. I'll text you tomorrow, yeah?'

'Not at all,' James said happily. 'Sounds good.'

'Okay, see you then. Enjoy your day off!' she waved before heading on her way.

James' smile dropped as she walked away, he felt foolish for feeling so glum. Charlotte and David had given him a maybe for the following day and Luke and Andy both claimed to have plans. There was no word at all from Lorraine or Gregg.

His opportunity for a fun day was seeming out of reach, but he knew he needed to stop dwelling on it. He was meeting Luke in an hour and couldn't face a friend in a sad state, he wouldn't allow himself to be rude enough to let his low mood show in front of someone.

That wasn't what good friends did, after all, and he didn't want Luke to think of him as a downer.

***

'Glad you could make it,' Luke greeted him from the comfortable armchairs in the corner of The Regal.

'Happy for the invite,' James hung his coat on the back of the chair, relieved to see a drink already awaiting him, though it looked like it had been there for a while. 'Sorry I'm late.'

'No worries, I've taken it as a given that you will be.'

'Charlotte always gives me grief,' James chuckled.

'Yeah, she seems like the type.'

James' body tensed at Luke's tone. He had expected something venomous, but he hadn't been expecting it anywhere near that quickly. He sighed quietly, knowing he should have known better than to think Luke had simply wanted to see him for the pleasure of his company.

'Eh, she's under a lot of pressure.'

'She hates me,' Luke said, he sounded more angry than upset, 'you know that, don't you?'

'She doesn't hate you, Luke,' James said awkwardly, taking a seat and wanting more than anything to just have a relaxing drink with his friend.

'She does, but I don't care,' he said defensively, 'I'm just being me. Fuck her for thinking otherwise.'

'Jesus, calm down,' James felt uncomfortable.

'Don't tell me to calm down,' Luke snapped. The two sat in an awkward silence, James didn't know why he was surprised, though he did wish that just once he wouldn't have to be an ear for everyone's problems. He wanted to help, but he needed a break.

He hadn't even had a sip of beer yet.

'I just-'

'I'm sorry,' Luke said, 'I just don't like being judged like that.'

James didn't really know what to say to any of it. If Luke really was cheating on Andy with strangers and making others aware of it, then he felt like it was his responsibility to speak up.

He could either let Andy know or call Luke out then and there, but from knowing Andy and listening to Charlotte, James knew that either action would result in a backlash.

And if James really was going to go to Andy, then he'd have to let him know that he and Luke had been sleeping together too, and that was fault he would have no choice but to accept, at least partially.

He was stuck between a rock and a hard place, and he was already starting to lose faith in those he had so far been referring to as friends. James had to put on a happy face.

'Hey, it's okay, I get it,' James said, opting temporarily to take the third option of total ignorance.

Though he took care to remain cautious around Luke, if he really was as two-faced as Charlotte had warned, and if he really was unaware or unapologetic of the harm he was causing, then James needed to be discreetly defensive.

It was still a game, and James' current move was looking for evidence to back up Charlotte's words. Though calling it a game suddenly didn't seem right, not as he sat opposite the other player.

'So how was your day, anyway?' Luke asked half-heartedly. James couldn't help but frown a little at the idea that he was likely only asking to be polite.

'Same old same old,' he said, knowing that Luke had no idea what that meant.

'Sounds bad.'

'What about yours?'

'Can't complain,' Luke said, 'I've got the day off tomorrow, don't know what I'm gonna do with it th-' he stopped himself, remembering as James did the message he had sent him not three hours ago saying he was too busy to help build furniture.

'Must be nice,' James smiled heartily, pretending not to notice, 'what's a day off to you, then?'

'Might clean the flat, might hang out with Andy, though I think he said he had plans.' Luke visibly tensed, he hadn't meant to shine a light back on his lie. James was losing his patience, but hardened himself to it.

'Productive,' he mused, 'My days off normally amount to playing videogames.'

'I haven't had the time for videogames in ages,' Luke sighed.

Finally, James found an opening for more relaxed conversation.

'What do you play?'

The two spent the evening drinking and chatting, the chatting and banter becoming lighter as the evening went on. Despite James' insistence that he didn't want to get too drunk, he found himself two sheets to the wind while grabbing beers from his fridge while Luke sat himself down on the living room sofa as opposed to the floor, where ne normally chose to stay.

Upon entering the living room, James saw Luke sitting on the sofa and realised he would likely be the last person to sit in that exact spot. He had no idea what he was going to do with the creaky old thing, but thinking about it made his head already start to hurt as though his future hangover was coming back in time to taunt him.

He sat in his rocking chair after handing a beer to Luke and began to sway back and forth comfortably. He could feel the walls he had so deliberately built start to become eroded by alcohol and did his best to keep himself to himself. That evening wasn't about him, he couldn't make it about him, though his blurry vision and uneasy stomach made worse by the rocking weakened his resolve.

'So what exactly has Charlotte said about me?' Luke asked after taking a swig. He seemed down, tense, as though the sofa itself was taking comfort from him rather than providing it.

It was a sudden change.

'That's not a conversation either of us wants to have,' James replied, 'and you should be talking to her and not me, anyway.'

'Sounds about right,' Luke scoffed, 'you like to help people, but when the chips are down you're just a coward, huh?'

'Excuse me?'

'Nothing.'

'Look, man,' James sighed, ignoring Luke's words as the accidental projections of a drunk, 'it's not like I'm not here for you, but I'm also not going to spread gossip or he said she said nonsense because it's just not my place, okay?'

'This is why we don't invite you, you know?' Luke's upper lip trembled with rage, his teeth were bared, though his voice remained calm. 'You want to be everyone's friend, but you know you're just a therapist.'

'Luke, I don't think you know what you're-'

'I didn't come here to drink a beer on your ratty old sofa, you know,' Luke turned his attention to the ceiling, 'I should have gone home with that guy at the bar. Christ you can be a downer.'

'What the hell is going on with you?' James slammed his fist on the arm chair, balancing himself with his feet as it rocked forward. He was angry, and had lost his will to listen.

'You know what?' Luke stood up and quickly put his jacket on, quickly making tracks. He was already dialling on his phone by the time James had followed him to the hallway.

'Luke, wai-'

'I'm not here for this,' Luke barked, his phone to his ear, 'these aren't my problems and you can go fuck yourself if you think you can put them on me,' he pushed James away with his free hand and opened the front door, stopping it with his foot as he turned to look back into the flat.

'Let me know when you're gonna stop acting weird,' Luke said exhaustedly before making his way towards the lift. 'Hello?' he said into his phone, James could hear him from where he stood, frozen in the middle of his hallway. 'Yeah, it's me. Night was a dud, I can still make it over to yours after all.'

The lift doors closed and James was left in silence, he stared at the door he could only kind of see in the dark corridor. He felt as though he was about to sneeze, but knew it was something else when he felt a warm tear run down his face.

He didn't sob, nor did he break down, he simply stared at the closed door and listened to his breath grow faster and faster as a deep sorrow mixed with an even deeper rage.

'What the fuck?' he said through his teeth.

***

It wasn't even an hour since the furniture arrived when the Allen wrench had already begun to dig uncomfortably into James' palm. He had a new red sofa with two matching armchairs to put together, and he was beginning to wish he had found someone to hire to put them together for him.

He had a new rocking chair for his bedroom, too. He managed to put it together with ease as it was the same model as the one he already had and it was a fifteen minute job at most even if he hadn't done it before. The armchairs and the sofa were more of a pain.

With each turn of the wrench James got angrier and angrier. Small increments of rage that he channelled into ignoring the pain in his hands. Every squeak of a screw turning into place brought with it something Luke had said, and with each recollection came the energy and will to turn the wrench one more time.

'I'm not here for this,' he growled to himself, 'these aren't my problems, night was a dud, go fuck yourself,' he paused on the last one and chuckled slightly. 'Go fuck yourself.'

He knew he looked crazy, but he didn't care. Talking to yourself was odd, sure, but he found something oddly cathartic in repeating Luke's words to himself. And the fact that it made his work easier was a welcome side effect as well.

He leant back on his floor and wiped his brow, he wasn't actually sweating but he felt like it was something people did when taking a break from building things.

He was angry with Luke, of course, but he was also angry with himself. He had failed in his role as a helper, he had lost his temper. People said hurtful things to him all the time, and he knew better of himself than to try to let his own insecurities come up with people he had wanted to keep as friends.

James couldn't shake a feeling that had been gnawing at him from the moment he woke up, and thanked whatever deities there were that his head was free from pain, the decision to go straight to bed with a glass of water after Luke had stormed out clearly being a good one.

But a deep, painful question had been eating away at his mind and heart, a question born of a drunken outrage that had seemingly come out of nowhere.

Was Luke the only one who thought that way?

It all hurt, sure, but James had recently been questioning how effective he had really been in helping people. He wasn't a real psychiatrist, but he always assumed he had meant something to those people.

He thought about Lorraine, about David, and all the others who had left his flat one day and never spoke to him again. They didn't care about him, he was just a pair of ears and occasionally a dick for people to use.

He awoke that morning, remembering the furniture he had to build and how he would have to do it on his own, and he felt a crushing loneliness that he knew he had been fighting for years.

If Luke really was just the only one with the balls to say what everyone was really thinking, if his problems and hardships really did mean nothing to anyone but himself, then he had been living his life in an alcoholic fantasy land where he had been pretending that people cared about his wellbeing.

He considered testing this thought out, but couldn't figure out how to without just pushing more of himself on others. It had been a long time since he had felt so idiotically over-reactive.

Why was it so important to him what Luke thought? What did a guy who had only ever given him something of a confidence boost hold over his life on the whole?

It was then that it hit him. It was the confidence, sure, but it was something else. What kept James going, what made him want to see Luke smile, was a genuine feeling of caring that he knew then was much rarer than it should have been.

David, Lorraine, even Andy and Charlotte, he had responded to their problems and offered up advice with a gusto that he normally had to force. He wasn't proud of it, though he did allow himself to believe that his willingness to try made up for what could arguably be called apathy.

But he had, for reasons he still couldn't grasp, really grown to care for Luke in a profound way that made him as happy as it did uncomfortable. If Luke really didn't care about him, hell, if no one cared about him, then he was in no position to argue at all. He had no right to feel down, and the idea that he had allowed himself to wallow in hurt disgusted him.

He lay reclined on the floor with a heavy heart and a buzzing mind for a few minutes before he decided that he needed a coffee if he was going to keep up the work at any reasonable pace.

James stood up with a loud groan that made him feel like an old man and turned on his speaker to set up his calm playlist. He wasn't really in the mood for music, but he knew that silence was not going to be his friend that day.

As the ugly kettle boiled, a knock came on James' door.

'It's open!' he called out. The door opened quickly and light footsteps made their way into the kitchen.

'Yo!' Charlotte greeted happily as she walked in. James was relieved to see that it was her.

'Hey,' he greeted in return, 'what are you doing here?'

'You sent a message yesterday,' she replied, setting her satchel down on the kitchen floor. 'I came over after my morning seminars, you haven't finished already have you?'

'Not even close,' James sighed.

'Isn't Luke helping you?'

'Huh? No. Why?'

'You guys were out last night, right? He messaged me saying how hungover he was. Said his memories got fuzzy around the time you left the bar so I assumed he spent the night here.'

'Um...' James hesitated.

'Don't worry,' Charlotte said, 'I know that when Luke 'blacks out', it normally means he did something shitty that he doesn't want to remember,' she said with an awkward smirk, 'tell me about it over some tools, and get that kettle off! I'm not working without a beer.'

James laughed and went to the fridge. He knew he could always count on Charlotte to alleviate a bad mood.

'He said what?' Charlotte nearly spat out her beer.

The two had finished one of the armchairs and were halfway through the second when they decided to take a break and lay on the floor with a couple of drinks. Indulging Charlotte's curiosity, James lit a cigarette and recounted the events of the night before.

'Yeah, kind of came out of nowhere. Then he got mad because I got mad and I have no idea,' James sighed, flicking his cigarette above the ashtray that was overdue for a cleaning. 'It all feels like some bullshit high school stuff.'

'You got that right,' Charlotte said, rolling a screw between her fingers with surprising dexterity, 'I don't know what's going on any more, and Andy's just eating it up.'

'It's sad,' James said, 'I didn't realise Andy was that lonely.'

'I don't think it's that,' Charlotte mused, 'I think he's wanting to see where it goes. More boredom than loneliness. Haven't you said anything in your sessions?'

'Haven't had a session in a while. What was Luke doing messaging you, anyway, I thought you guys didn't get along.'

'When he's sober we're fine,' Charlotte stopped playing with the screw, 'but when he's drunk he fucks up, we fall out and then he's magically forgotten all about it the next day.'

'He thinks you hate him.'

'I kinda do,' Charlotte said hesitantly, 'I get it if people are assholes sometimes, but it's when they're unapologetic about it that I can't stand it at all. I don't wanna be a bitch, but I promise you the next time you hear from Luke he'll act like the two of you are best buds.'

'And calling him out just makes things worse, right?' James suddenly felt like a gossip, like what was supposed to be him venting was turning into them just talking behind Luke's back.

'That's my beer done,' he said, wanting to change the subject, 'shall we get back to work?'

'Aye aye,' Charlotte set her own empty beer bottle down and picked herself up.

'What are your plans for tonight, anyway?' Charlotte asked, handing James a part that she could see he was looking for.

'Angela wants to take me out for a drink, celebrate the first week of the new job.'

'That sounds fun,' Charlotte said, a hint of something playful in her voice that James ignored.

'It will be, but it feels kind of awkward,' he said, stressing the last word as he put all his strength into screwing in the final piece of one of the arms. 'I still don't remember how I know her and I don't want to hurt her feelings.'

'I'm sure it'll be a good time,' Charlotte flipped the chair over and prepared the next arm, James handed her the wrench she'd need. 'Wrong one,' she said before finding the larger one on the floor beside her.

'Maybe, at least I won't have to be on guard like last night,' he held the chair steady while Charlotte worked in the screws. 'The last thing I need is to let the dam burst again.'

'Don't,' Charlotte pointed the Allen wrench like a gun in James' direction, a glare on her face that he knew wasn't a joke. 'Don't you dare apologise for how some asshole treated you. Whatever about last night is your fault is your fault, but don't for a second think he doesn't owe you an apology, too.'

'Okay,' James held up on of his hands in jest and used the other one to mark an X on his chest with his index finger. 'Cross my heart.'

'You remember?'

'Of course I do,' he beamed, 'it was our favourite song.'

'It's still mine,' Charlotte got back to work, 'speaking of, why are you using your calm playlist? Doesn't seem like physical labour music.'

'First thing I thought of,' James admitted, returning to his job of keeping the chair steady while Charlotte put in the final screws.

'And done.'

The two of them lifted the chair and set it on its legs. It felt good to be productive on something practical on a day off, it felt even better to do it with a friend. Though the two of them still grimaced at the idea that they were yet to even start on the sofa.

James reflected on just how much his mood had turned, how happy Charlotte's company had made him. He didn't say so out loud, however, both because he knew his friend was already well aware, and also because of just how fragile he feared this upturn was.

***

'You sure you don't want to stick around?' James said as he locked the door behind him, 'I'm sure Angela wouldn't mind you coming along.'

'Nah,' Charlotte replied, taking a deep breath, 'I've got a lot of studying to do and am on an empty stomach. Any more booze and I'll be way too far ahead of you guys to have fun.'

'Sounds like you should just blow off the studying,' James pressed the button for the lift.

'No can do, but thanks for the invite.'

'Thanks for the help, the living room looks great now.'

'It always did, but to be honest I may not want to sit on that sofa for a while, I know the evil that lies within it.'

'It will be a difficult association to shake,' James laughed, 'but it'll come in time.'

'Yeah, well, time is definitely what I need,' Charlotte said with a yawn, 'I gotta stop letting you be such a bad influence on me.'

'Role reversal much?'

'Up yours!' Charlotte giggled.

The two parted ways once they were out of the block, Angela wanted to meet at one of the campus bars while Charlotte lived in the opposite direction. They bid their farewells and James made his way to the tram stop, wondering why Angela wanted to meet on campus on a Friday night. While he did see the merit in the campus being quieter than most bars in town, it still seemed like an odd decision.

His wonderings aside, James checked his phone twenty times in the forty minute journey without really knowing why.

***

'Hey!' James called out from across the plaza when he saw Angela waiting outside. It was just before five and he hadn't expected her to be waiting for him yet.

'Hey,' she waited to greet him until he was close enough for her to avoid yelling.

'Sorry, am I late?'

'Not at all, Dahlia knew I had plans so she let me leave early,'

'Nice of her,' James didn't bring up the fact that that was the first time Angela had referred to Doctor Noore by her first name. 'So where are we going?'

'The Omega,' Angela started walking, 'you remember it?'

'Yeah!' James sounded more enthused than he meant to, 'I haven't been there in ages.'

'I thought it would be a good call,' Angela smiled warmly.

The Omega was one of the more popular places on campus. It was a large, old fashioned pub that was most commonly visited by post-grads and faculty than the younger members of the student body.

'So why campus?' James asked after he returned with two drinks, a beer for himself and a large red wine for Angela. He had insisted on getting the first round.

'I actually live here,' she answered after thanking him for the drink, 'I'm doing my doctorate under Doctor Noore.'

'Ah cool, what on?'

'SAD mostly,' she said, 'various forms of depression and whatnot. I've actually read your dissertation, it's fascinating stuff.'

'Nice, are you coming to the conference next weekend?'

'Yeah, our area of the department is effectively closing for it. I'm so nervous about getting up to speak, though.'

'Me too, I haven't given a presentation in front of a crowd since my undergrad,' James shivered at the thought. 'We'll be okay, though. You know me and some classmates used to do tequila shots right here in this bar before we had to give big talks.'

'Really?' Angela laughed. 'Did it work?'

'Nah, but we did it anyway.'

'Sounds like fun.'

'It was,' James recalled fondly, 'so how do you deal with it?'

'Grit my teeth and wait for it to be over,' Angela said humourlessly.

'So, hey,' James began awkwardly, 'how do we actually know each other, then?' he wanted to say how much he'd been wracking his brain trying to recall, but didn't want to risk insulting her.

'We lived next to each other in first year,' she said after a short pause and a sip of her wine, 'you used to talk to me when I was having a hard time. I almost quit because I didn't fit in with anyone, but you talked me out of it. You used to joke that I'd be a traitor if I left.'

'Oh, uh, sorry,' James was beginning to remember how tactless he could be.

'Don't be,' she smiled, 'it actually helped. You always knew what to say to make people feel better.'

'I don't get it, though,' James felt sombre, 'I feel like I should remember that.'

'Your mind was always somewhere else, even when we were talking,' she said, she matched his tone but maintained a happy visage. 'You were going out with the guy next door I think, he seemed to consume you. I wasn't surprised that you didn't remember me, don't worry.'

'I still feel bad but,' James took a deep breath, 'yeah, he really did consume my thoughts back then, huh?'

'Wanna talk about it?'

'No,' he answered quickly, he realised he had almost barked the answer, 'it's ancient history,' he smiled a wide smile that he hoped would be convincing. Between his nightmare a few days before and Luke's anger, James couldn't think of anything worse than spending any length of time talking about himself.

'Okay,' she didn't seem convinced by James' demeanour, but she was at least unwilling to push, which was enough to allow him to relax.

'So you and Charlotte, are you close?'

'We were, she didn't tell you? We took the same criminology minor as freshers but I dropped out at the end of the year and we lost touch.'

'Huh, I thought you and her might be tight. She calls you Angie.'

'You used to call me that too.'

'I did? Huh,' he blushed, 'sorry if you didn't like it.'

'You still apologise too much,' she giggled. Something in her laugh made James almost remember spending time with her back then, though no solid memories came to mind. Still, he felt happy to be with her.

'Y'know,' she said, looking into his eyes, 'you really don't seem like you've changed that much.'

'Huh?'

'You still look at your drink when you're not sure what to say, and you apologise when you think you've dug yourself into a corner. You still look out for others.'

'I think I've changed a little,' James smirked playfully.

'Not to me.'

***

James awoke with an aching back and stiff arms, his head was pounding and his mouth was dry as a bone. His bed felt smaller and the sun shining through his window had a blue hue from curtains he immediately knew weren't his.

He sat up slowly, careful not to move too quickly, and noticed that he was in a single bed. He looked to his left and saw Angela sleeping soundly beside him. He looked around and recognised the brick walls, the sink by the door and the desk at the window. He even recognised the view from the window through a crack in the curtain. It was the same building where they had lived in their first year, it was probably the same room.

James didn't need to check to know that he was naked.

Gritting his teeth silently, James held his aching head in one hand.

'Fuck,' he whispered.

7.

'There's something about coffee with you that feels weird,' Charlotte said, stirring in her third pack of sugar.

'You mean because we're always getting smashed when we're together?' James added milk.

'Exactly.'

The Sunday afternoon brought a chill with it that seemed colder to James than the previous days, though the weather reports showed it to be a few degrees warmer. Were it any other season, James would have wanted to sit outside and drink his coffee with a cigarette, but not even the simple pleasure of a smoke with a coffee was a comfortable possibility for the next few months.

Instead they sat in the crowded café that felt far too warm with a person in every seat and the heating cranked up to its limits.

'God I hate winter,' James sighed.

'You always did,' Charlotte sipped her coffee, 'I'm not surprised, you never remember to bundle up.'

'I do, I just don't deal well with cold,'

'All your coats are ten years old at least, I don't think they have any lining left. Half of your pockets have holes, too.'

'I rock the scruffy look,' James shrugged.

'Cocky shit.'

'Always.'

'So how was Friday night? Angie doing well?'

'Yeah, y'know she was actually pretty nice about me not remembering her. She filled in a lot of blanks.'

'So you've talked about the night you slept together, then?'

'What?' James nearly spilled his drink, 'How did you know about that?'

'You kidding? Everybody knew, even made you-know-who jealous.'

'We slept together back then?' James realised as he finished asking just what he'd given away, he hoped Charlotte hadn't noticed.

'Well, yeah,' she looked confused, 'you didn't talk about it? Wait. You didn't.'

'I-'

'You fucking idiot,' she growled, 'you better call her right the fuck now.'

'What? Why?'

'Oh my God,' Charlotte shook her head and let out a heavy sigh, 'you really are a fucking idiot.'

'I don't know what you're-'

'You and Angie slept together in first year,' Charlotte spoke as though she was giving a movie synopsis in bullet points, 'and then you just up and vanished without a word, remember?'

'The night before...' James struggled to remember.

'Look,' Charlotte took a deep breath to calm herself, it didn't seem to work, 'when you go in tomorrow just call in on her, okay? She freaked the fuck out last time so just,' she paused, 'don't be a dick, okay?'

'I won't,' James felt offended, but didn't want to point it out. 'I've really earned this kind of reputation, haven't I?'

'I really thought you'd changed, James.'

'I have, haven't I?'

'Not enough,' Charlotte didn't look him in the eye, her tone became sullen as she gripped her coffee cup right with both hands before letting it go completely and standing up, putting her coat on.

'Charlotte?'

'Coffee's paid for, man,' she tied her scarf, 'I think I'm awake enough.'

James watched her walk away without trying to stop her, he had no words to say nor the will to defend himself. As she opened the door to leave, everyone who sat near the entrance tensed and shivered as the cold air blew in momentarily. The chill didn't hit James, but he shivered nonetheless.

He looked to his coffee and saw his own tired eyes staring back at him. He had spent the previous day organising his new furniture, opting to put his grey sofa against his otherwise bare back wall with the coffee table in front of it. Sitting there he had smoked five cigarettes in a row while staring at the package on the table and wondering how Angela really felt about what they had done.

He had gotten it out of his head, and had planned on calling in on Angela on Monday anyway. But there he sat, disgraced and alone, with absolutely no memory of what had happened the day before he abandoned everything.

Luke hated him, Andy hadn't been in touch and he hadn't held a session in weeks. Now Charlotte, the one person he felt he could still call a friend without any doubt, had walked away from him.

He had spent the better part of four years trying to have as little to do with his former self as possible, but he seemed to have been losing his way. His new and somewhat happy life was in freefall.

He lifted his coffee mug and closed his eyes while he took a bitter sip, knowing that he had no one to blame for himself, though the catalyst for his own change wasn't hard to spot.

Everything had changed from the moment he met Luke.

***

'You've got to be kidding me,' James said as he stepped out of the lift to see Luke, magazine in hand, sitting in his waiting room.

'Well good afternoon to you too,' Luke smiled in greeting.

'What are you doing here?'

'I came to see you,' he stood up, setting the magazine on his chair, 'I wanted to see how you were.'

'You've got to be kidding me,' James repeated, suddenly not in the mood for any kind of social interaction, much less whatever game Luke was playing this time.

'No?' Luke seemed offended, James ignored the guilt he felt at causing the offence and made his way to the door.

'What even happened on Thursday?' Luke chuckled nervously, 'I woke up in some rando's bed.'

'Rando, huh?' James recalled Luke calling someone before he left.

'Yeah, totally crazy,' Luke walked in behind James, who hadn't held the door for him. 'Did I ditch you?'

'Sure,' James went to the kitchen and filled the kettle, the coffee in the café had been far too weak for his liking.

'I do that,' he said, chuckling.

'And you're okay with that?' James didn't hide his impatience.

'What do you mean? Everyone knows the score. I'm just having fun,' he opened the fridge and lifted out a beer, 'may I?'

'No.'

'What's going on with you, man?'

'You really aren't joking, are you? Do you really not remember?'

'Hey, did I say something? Are you mad at me?'

'Of course I am,' James kept his voice calm, but refused to hide his anger.

'Talk to me, man.'

'You're so confusing,' James said mostly to himself before turning his attention back to Luke. 'You told me you didn't want to deal with my problems, you told me to go fuck myself for thinking I could, and you told me you had no interest in being here for any reason other than sex.'

'So?' Luke said bluntly before shaking his head quickly, James was too taken aback to get another word in before Luke spoke up again. 'I mean, like, yeah, the sex is great, but it's just that you can't take drunk talk seriously.'

'Drunk talk isn't telling someone the night's a dud when they try speaking to you,' James got the instant coffee from the cupboard and poured it, without a spoon, into his mug. 'Drunk talk isn't telling someone that they have no friends.'

'Jesus, I mean, you know I didn't mean it, right?'

James did not know that, what he did know was that he was pissed off.

He poured the boiled water into his mug and stirred it with a spoon he lifted from the counter without checking its cleanliness.

Luke was standing in front of the fridge, James settled on having his coffee black. He picked up his drink and started making his way to the living room. Luke grabbed onto his jacket as he moved past, hot coffee spilled onto James' hand, making him wince. Luke didn't seem to notice.

'Talk to me, man,' Luke repeated, 'we're friends, right?'

'We're not friends, Luke,' James said, a calm running through his body, washing away everything but a dull rage that became the driving force for his words. 'I'm just your psychiatrist, remember?'

'We slept together.'

'Well I never promised professionalism, did I?' he took the coffee in his other hand and shook his arm free with more force than he meant to. 'Get out, Luke. Sessions are cancelled for the day.'

He went into the living room, hoping he wouldn't be followed.

'Okay,' he heard Luke say solemnly from the kitchen. James wasn't in the mood to find out if what followed was a sniff from oncoming tears or the beginnings of a cold. At that moment, he simply didn't care.

Luke was just as Charlotte had said, unapologetic.

Even if Luke really didn't remember, James felt like he couldn't have been more clear about how upset he was. Even so, all Luke seemed to do was hide behind alcohol and blackouts. And James got angrier and angrier with every excuse.

To demand an apology seemed childish, but to need to have an apology demanded of you was even worse. No one was the good guy, but James wouldn't let himself think he was in the wrong.

The moment he heard the front door close, James felt as though he had made a terrible mistake, though his sudden and intense feeling of pride would never let him act on it right away.

***

Confidant

James sat on the bottom of the stairs, turning a penny between his fingers with little luck. His hands were too small to do the trick he had seen his father do since he could remember.

The yelling from the kitchen would be a lot harder to hear from his room, but he was told to sit where he was and breaking a rule was a one way ticket to a smack. James rubbed his face at the thought, as though he could feel the sting from the last time he had spilled his juice on the breakfast bar

The kitchen door flew open, making James jump and almost drop his penny. His mother stormed out, a look of anger on her face that made him curl himself into a ball.

'Get out of my sight,' she spoke to her son through clenched teeth, 'selfish piece of shit.'

With that, she made her way down the corridor and out the front door. James was almost relieved to see her go, like he had eluded a great monster from one of his videogames.

'Don't do it, son,' a voice spoke from the kitchen doorway. James looked up to see a tear in his father's eye and a red mark across his face. 'Never fall in love with a whore.'

James opened his eyes to find himself alone and in his own bed, two facts he felt the need to double check.

He looked to the ceiling and sighed. His dreams lately had been long buried memories that he hadn't thought about in years, and the distinction between the conscious and unconscious was starting to blur too much already.

James had no idea what anyone really thought of him, and his lot in life that he had relied on so heavily was starting to feel insecure and fragile. Even his dreams were betraying him as he seemed to betray himself, he couldn't even count on sleep to get himself away from whatever the hell was going on.

He had hoped that any lingering regret about the way he had treated Luke would escape him by the next morning, but he awoke with a pit in his stomach and a heavy heart as he shook a headache that had nothing to do with a hangover.

He had failed himself in every facet. He had let his emotions get the better of him. He felt wronged, he felt insulted, but it wasn't his place to call anyone out on it and he knew it.

'Who the hell do you think you are?' he said to himself as he clutched his hair in his hands and curled himself into a ball on his bed, he considered screaming into his pillow before getting a hold of himself and jumping out of bed so fast he gave himself a head rush and stumbled back for a moment.

James realised then that he had been sleeping on the wrong side of his bed, something he couldn't remember ever doing before, at least not accidentally. His flat was freezing and he was wearing only his pyjama bottoms and a thin t-shirt, the covers on his bed were bunched up in a thick cocoon. James knew then that his first priority was turning the heating on.

'Better to be one,' he held his rushing head in his hand, 'than to fall in love with one.'

The boiler groaned as James turned it on and the radiators started to crackle in a way that always made him nervous. He had to leave for his session in half an hour, but would keep the heating on all day to make sure he returned to a warm home, and damn the expense.

Still in his pyjamas, James was preparing a coffee when several loud knocks sounded at his door.

'What now?' he said to himself, leaving the kettle on the boil and answering the door. Andy scowled at him from the other side of the doorway, he had already made his way past James and inside by the time James could attempt a greeting.

'What did you say to Luke?' Andy barked, taking his coat off and hanging it on the crackling radiator.

'What? Dude, it's eight in the morning.'

'He called me last night in tears,' Andy marched into the kitchen and started helping himself to the instant coffee, using one of James' rubber takeaway cups to do so. 'I had to go to his place. Don't you think Charlotte's giving him enough shit as it is?'

'You don't live here anymore,' James said, a quietly seething rage boiling in his only half-awake body.

'You were gonna offer anyway, and it's your fault I've barely slept.'

'Couldn't this wait until later?' James rubbed the back of his head. Andy filled James' cup before his own while James grabbed the milk from the fridge.

'I want to talk about it now,' he barked, grabbing the sugar from the cabinet.

'You know he's been cheating on you, right?' James leant against the wall and sipped his coffee.

'It's called an open relationship, asshole' Andy said, setting the lid on his cup, 'a concept I assumed you'd have a grasp on.'

'That's not your bag and you know it.'

'Would you fuck off with that!?' Andy slammed his palm on the countertop, 'I'm not here for your invasive advice, I'm here for a damn apology!'

'Well you're wasting your time,' James went into the living room and grabbed his cigarettes from the coffee table, he offered one to Andy in the hopes that it would calm him down.

'You can't treat people like that,' Andy took the cigarette without thanking him, 'you need to start taking responsibility.'

'You're joking, right?' James lit his cigarette. He wanted to sit in his rocking chair and relax, but figured doing so might make him seem more aloof than he was. Though he also acknowledged that it was probably a bit late to worry about that.

'No, James,' Andy said after a drag, 'I'm not. Whatever you think he said to you, and however right you think you were yesterday, it's not cool. He doesn't remember and he's just being himself. It's not like you have any right to complain, anyway!'

'What are you-'

'Don't play innocent here, don't give me that 'ancient history' bullshit! You think you don't owe us an apology, too?'

'I've been trying to make up for what I did,' James felt his offence was losing his edge as he struggled to find the words to defend himself.

'Yeah, with this helping others nonsense, right? I bet it feels real good to give advice and lend an ear to people you clearly don't give a shit about.'

'Hey, man, that's out of line. You know I care.'

'No, I don't,' Andy took another drag, the ash from his cigarette fell on the floor, he either didn't notice or didn't care. 'You think you have any right to faun over my boyfriend and then feel betrayed when he doesn't spend the night?'

'That's not what-'

'You think you can sit in that chair and look down on all of us and then wonder why we don't invite you out anymore?'

'Andy-'

'You think you're really so betrayed here when you're the one playing some stupid game with our fucking *lives*!?'

The two stood in silence for a moment, their cigarettes burning slowly in their hands while their coffees cooled too quickly. Andy was breathing heavily from the outburst and some movement from below them told James that he had likely woken his neighbours.

'And as for your advice,' Andy went on, quieter but still enraged, 'Lorraine and Travis are getting a divorce.'

'What?'

'Luke and I are stronger than ever because we stuck at it despite what you said and David's dating Gregg. And guess what? They're happy together. So it's not just your friendship that isn't worth spit these days.'

'I didn't know any of that,' James looked to the floor.

'Because it's none of your business,' Andy opened a window and threw his still burning cigarette to the street below.

'I didn't know,' James said, 'I thought things had been different since I met Luke but-'

'Don't you *dare* blame Luke for your shit,' Andy barked, 'you've started to change from the moment that package arrived,' he pointed to the brown box on the coffee table. 'What? You thought I hadn't noticed? I was here when it arrived, remember? I know that address and I know it's been changing you back. But, y'know what? I'm done caring about any of that.

'Whatever happened to you back then,' Andy turned and walked towards the hallway, James followed to see him setting his coffee on the floor and putting his jacket back on, '*if* anything even happened to you at all, you probably fuckin' deserved it. And I'm not the only one who thinks so.'

James held his coffee in both hands, his fingers still numb from the cold despite the flat's rapidly increasing temperature.

'The new you really was working, James,' Andy said with a sigh as he opened the front door with his free hand, 'but if you can't hold on to it, then for everyone's sake you need to get and stay the hell out of our lives.'

***

'I feel like I'm not really me,' James said emotionlessly as he stared out Dahlia's window. She sipped at her coffee without sound, he had politely refused to take one for himself. 'It's like I'm a stranger in my own body, like I don't know who I am.'

'The things Andy said to you,' Dahlia breathed deeply, 'why are they bothering you so much?'

'It's not just him, it's everything. Luke and Charlotte are mad and I don't know what Angela must think. I thought Luke was just being a dick, and I was willing to overlook it all even if it did hurt, but he's not the only one. You can't deny the common denominator is me. I can't have that many people feel wronged by me and still think it's not my fault, can I?'

'You're the only one who can ever truly explain your own actions, James. No one can read your thoughts.'

'But when I say what's on my mind people just get mad,' James bit his lip, 'it was always a one way street for that reason. I was there to listen, not to talk. I thought as long as I was helping other people everything would kind of work out.'

'You felt as though they owed you something?'

'What?'

'You help them, and they repay you with friendship. It was a give and take from the beginning. An equal exchange. When you added your own problems into the conversation it upset the equation and the scales became unbalanced, you were taking more than you were giving.'

'Sounds depressing when you put it that way,' James wondered if he really should have turned down that coffee.

'People normally repay friendship with friendship, kindness with kindness,' Dahlia finished her coffee and got up, bringing her cup to the machine and turning it on again. Unlike the one in the staff kitchen, hers was almost completely silent.

'What you've been doing,' she turned her back to the machine and looked at James, 'is offering up your own psychiatric services for friendship, something everyone seemed to go along with. But now you've thrown your own friendship into the mix and people don't know what to think.'

'They're my friends,' James said solemnly, 'but I can't be theirs?'

'Not without giving something more,' Dahlia took the small cup from the machine once it had finished and brought it over to James, offering it to him with a smile. He thanked her and took a sip.

'What more can I give?' James asked, finally ready to fully blame himself for what was going on. He wasn't mad at anyone anymore, not even himself, he was just beginning to see everyone's points.

Luke wanted nothing to do with James' own issues, Andy wanted James to stop trying and Charlotte was building a wall to protect herself from whatever she thought he was becoming.

The only thing he felt he could do was bottle up his problems, become a fair-weather friend who was all smiles and sunshine. It would be superficial, but that didn't matter, the only thing that mattered was what other people saw.

'I'm afraid that's something else only you can know,' Dahlia said, taking a seat, 'perhaps try being a friend before being a therapist.'

'It seems a little late for that,' James sighed.

'You can't live a life without friends, James. You need to trust that they won't stay angry at you forever. One day you'll have them back, and then you can try being what they are to you.'

James nodded, it was all good advice, not a word of it was arguable to him. Though he realised then that, despite the fact that he knew how important everyone was to him, he had absolutely no idea why. And that thought made him feel like the monster Andy had made him out to be, the selfish scumbag Luke had made him feel like, and the terrible person Charlotte seemed to be afraid of.

James sipped his coffee and smiled warmly at Dahlia, it was all he could do to not break down and cry right there and then.

He left the office that morning feeling like a hollow man, ready to be filled to the brim with the next passing emotion his erratic brain would feed him. He was numb, but not entirely unfeeling. He felt like a glass precariously balanced on the edge of a table ready to be either carefully set back into place or smashed on the floor depending on what fate and circumstance would allow.

'James?' Angela greeted him as he rounded a corner.

'Oh, hey Angela,' he put on his smile.

'I hope Doctor Noore took it easy on you today,' she said, reaching into her satchel. 'I was hoping to run into you, though, I forgot to give you this on Friday,' she took a bottle of wine out of her bag and handed it to him.

'Thanks, what's the occasion?' he said, pretending to check the label as though he knew anything about wine.

'The new job, of course,' she chuckled. 'Looking forward to the weekend?'

'Yeah,' he said, though he hadn't really thought about the conference, 'a break would be nice.'

'Too right,' Angela sighed, James only noticed then the large bags under her eyes, 'we're having a meeting about it tomorrow, so bring a notepad or something, okay?'

'Will do,' James managed to fit enough of the wine bottle in his jacket pocket. 'Hey, are you sleeping okay? You wanna grab a coffee at lunch?'

'Oh, no thanks, I've just been a bit busy. Speaking of, I need to run,' she fixed her glasses and rested a hand on the handle of Dahlia's office door. 'See you tomorrow!'

'See ya,' James replied, though she was already in the office and no longer listening.

He felt a small pang of happiness take him then, Angela seemed in good spirits despite Charlotte's concerns. Selfishly, James was also happy to see a life that he hadn't inadvertently made worse in recent days, he recalled Angela's gratitude that night, how she had thanked him for talking to her all those years ago.

The glass had shifted closer to the table's centre, and he felt a calm optimism that he hadn't expected to feel that day. He took his pack of cigarettes out of his pocket and had on in his mouth before he was even in the lift.

He would have a smoke, think again about how cold it was getting, and then call Charlotte and do his best not to sound smug when he told her Angela was fine.

The cold didn't bother him so much when he walked outside, a warm feeling within him seemed to keep his body from tensing up as the chilly air hit his exposed skin. With fingerless gloves he lit his cigarette, with a clear mind he smoked it, smiling to himself in a way he felt he didn't deserve to.

Things weren't looking up, but he had come to realise the truth behind an old adage about closed doors and opened windows. An ugly grin graced his face and he felt like a villain for daring to think that maybe total abandonment might not be so bad. If he really did deserve to have all those backs turned on him, then he would take a sick pride in any chance he could get to prove those same people wrong.

It was a feeling that would last only as long as the cigarette, but James made sure to enjoy it while it lasted.

'So she's fine, then?' Charlotte sounded bemused, 'at least you remembered to check.'

'Well yeah,' James had not been expecting her tone, 'I'm not a monster, Charlotte. She's fine, so we're all good.'

'You just don't get it, do you?' she sighed. Even over the phone James could imagine her rubbing her temples as she spoke. 'It's not about making sure people are okay after doing something, it's about not doing it in the first place.'

'What's gotten into you?' James felt down, 'it's not like you've never had a regretful hook up.'

'That's not the point.'

'Then what is the point?' James became painfully aware of the fact that the tram was packed and he was essentially having an argument in public.

'The point is that you can't act like Luke's breaking your heart, fuck someone else and then feel attacked.'

'Charlotte I don't know what you're-'

'I'm busy, James. I'll call in later in the week.'

'Okay,' James said solemnly, 'but if you need anything then-'

'See you,' she hung up.

James looked at his phone for a few seconds before putting it away. He was still ten minutes away from his stop, and he would spend that time avoiding any kind of inward thinking if he could.

He took his phone back out and sent a message to Lorraine, telling her he was sorry to hear about the divorce before deleting her number from his phone along with David's. He didn't really know why he was doing it, but in the deepest recesses of his mind he was beginning to form a decision for how to move forward.

He spent the rest of the journey scratching at his left wrist and wondering when it would start getting warmer again.

8.

The dark clouds that could be seen from the empty living room windows still threatened a snowstorm that James had expected days ago. He didn't care for snow, but he enjoyed watching it fall from a warm place, a place where he could be safe.

We swished the wine Angela had bought him in his only wine glass. He had never really had a taste for anything other than beer, but he felt it would be a nice way to enjoy the gift from the last person he expected to smile at him for some time.

It was a sad and petty thought, but Dahlia's advice had stopped him from feeling too sorry for himself. She was right, of course, about needing to offer more if he expected to be treated as a friend. Arguments and falling outs would happen, and as much as James was hurt by Andy's words that morning, he knew it wasn't the first time they had said such awful things to each other.

James knew that he had been repressing, or at least ignoring, his feelings for Luke. He had come to terms with the fact that it was both jealousy and envy he had been feeling, and while that didn't explain his actions of late, it at least explained some of the fuel for the fire that had been burning inside him.

He sat on his new red sofa, realising it was the first time he had done so, and found it softer than he had expected, far more comfortable than the grey mess he and his guests had tolerated for so long.

He had taken the chairs out from the front of his flat and piled them up in the hallway. He had no need for a waiting room anymore, the joke and gesture had both been played out and were long since stale.

He had received a message from a recently unknown number that simply thanked him for his condolences, and he deleted the thread without replying. He had three missed calls from Andy and one from Charlotte, though neither of them had sent any messages or left voicemails, meaning whatever they had to say wasn't important enough to rush.

The lights in the hallway were off and the music was at a low enough volume so it wouldn't be heard from outside, anyone who wanted to call on him would have to take the hint that the doctor was out for the day.

James considered ways to pass the time, but found that simply sitting with a glass of wine and appreciating the solitude he had begun to grow weary of was a pleasure that he had denied himself for too long. The future of his happiness was in the air, but still somewhat within his control, and he had to convince himself that he wasn't the terrible person everyone seemed to think he was, a task that was easier said than done.

He cleared his mind as much as he could and hummed along to the music, even taking the time to enjoy the songs that he would normally skip over. Some he hadn't listened to in a long time, some he would probably never listen to again.

If there was a knock on his door he would ignore it, if his phone vibrated he would put it in another room. If he really was going to figure himself out, then he needed some time to listen to his own thoughts instead of just reacting to them.

***

'Still no answer?' Luke asked as he handed a beer to Andy before taking his place on the floor.

'No,' Andy set his phone to the side, 'and I know he's not gonna listen to a voicemail.'

'Why don't you text him?' Luke held the bottle to his lips.

'If he's not answering the phone then he won't read a text,' Andy sighed.

'You feel bad, huh?'

'Yeah, I said some pretty terrible things.'

'So did he,' Luke put his hand on Andy's knee and rubbed it with his thumb, 'friendships aren't always gonna be brill. I'm sure he just needs time.'

'You're right,' Andy took Luke's hand in his, 'thanks for being here.'

'Hey,' Luke smiled, 'I'm always gonna be here.'

Andy excused himself to the bathroom and Luke was left alone on his floor for a moment, he looked at his phone and saw not one message or call from James. He was reluctant to apologise after the things James had said to him, he had gone to his flat the day before to try to see if he could sweep everything under the rug, bury whatever hatchet there was.

Sometimes people were assholes, and he knew that he was no exception, but life was easier to deal with when people were willing to just forget what had happened.

To apologise for what he had said would be admitting that he remembered saying it, to leave it hanging would only make James worse. Luke knew then that he needed to make a decision, a decision that would ultimately be based on just how much he wanted to keep James in his life.

Calling or texting so soon was out of the question, he'd wait for the weekend. A few drinks and some friendly conversation and it would all be forgotten, he was sure of it, then he could spend his time wondering if he wanted to keep James around or not. For the time being, Luke would focus those same thoughts on Andy.

'You okay?' Andy asked as he came back into the room, 'You look worried.'

'Not at all,' Luke put on his best smile, 'just wondering when I need to take the rubbish out.'

***

James sat at his computer in the psychology lounge, wondering when Angela's promise of more exciting work was going to come to pass. Every email was just more directions and timetable inquiries from students who should have known better after being in the university for over three months.

No students entered the lounge, and James began to wonder if that was normal or if his presence in the room really did make the undergrads uncomfortable.

Along with the mundane emails, which James considered might have been forged by Dahlia just to give him something to do, were notes and directions on travel to and from the conference in Manchester, as well as what to expect while there.

Dahlia had forwarded notes to both James and Angela regarding what to say while at the podium. They were given a page each that they were to read over and memorise to the best of their abilities to minimise tripping over the words on the day. It all seemed pretty straight forward, though James still couldn't help feeling nervous about the whole thing.

The dress code was strictly formal, meaning James would have to get his suit dry cleaned, which felt like more of a hassle than it was.

He hadn't told anyone that he was going to be away that weekend, not out of any attempt at secrecy, but more that he had simply neglected to pass on the information before letting himself fall out of touch for a while.

His pseudo-meditative state from the evening before had done little to make him arrive at any real conclusions about what to do, but had allowed him to carry himself that Tuesday with a certain clarity of thought that left his mind and movements unobstructed by hesitations born of ghosts from the recent past.

He didn't question his mental state, as no mood was better than a bad mood and less fragile than a good one. Even Dahlia seemed to notice a somewhat pleasant change in his demeanour even if he didn't notice it himself.

To seem more happy without feeling happy or trying too hard was enough for James to consider a win, and it would be that feeling that carried him through the week with little stress and dreamless nights.

Andy had stopped calling by Wednesday, and James was starting to feel bad about leaving him hanging. Either he was calling to chew him out more, or he was calling to apologise. James wasn't in the mood for either.

People stopped coming to him for sessions, even David, and the chai tea in James' kitchen cabinet was going unused. He considered throwing it away before trying a mug of the stuff for himself and changing his mind.

He needed little more than a rucksack to pack for the weekend and, while the trip was only a three hour train journey, James absent-mindedly packed his passport as well.

Friday evening came faster than he expected, though he was happy for the ease with which the week had passed. His plan was to use the weekend to get refreshed. It had been a long time since he had taken a holiday for any length of time, and the opportunity to use a less than familiar location and a hotel room to hit the reset button was far too good to pass up.

He had still not told anyone about the trip, if he was going to come back feeling as good and relaxed as he wanted then he would want absolute solitude. Better for someone to call on his flat or have a message ignored to assume he was busy with other plans rather than on a break and ignoring them.

That was the half logic that James was going with, though he knew the truth was that he didn't expect anyone to care where he was.

The only people he had left a good last impression on were Dahlia and Angela. He had no more reason to tell anyone else where he was going than a cashier or barista. He told himself that he was making the right call in keeping his whereabouts a secret, and that was good enough for him.

At ten o'clock on Thursday evening, twelve hours before his train was due to leave, a knock on James' door almost made him spill his mug of chai tea.

He checked the peephole to see Charlotte leaning against the wall in the outer corridor. With a haste he couldn't explain, he unlocked and opened the door.

'You got ridda the waitin' room,' Charlotte slurred before James could say a word.

'Yeah, I figured it was time for a change,' he said, 'are you drunk?'

'Yeah. Can I come in?' she didn't look at him as she talked.

'Sure,' James stepped to the side to let her in, he couldn't remember the last time someone had asked permission to enter his flat.

James handed Charlotte a glass of water as she sat on the sofa, a confused look on her face as she examined it, it seemed as though she had forgotten that they had built it together.

'Not got any beer?' she asked after half-heartedly thanking him for the water.

'You look like you needed this more,' James sat beside her on the sofa.

'Wow, thanks.'

'You okay? What happened?'

'You,' Charlotte said quietly, as though she didn't really want James to hear.

'What?'

'You, asshole,' she barked.

'Charlotte, I don't-'

'I thought,' she suddenly seemed out of breath, 'I thought you didn't, we didn't, because you weren't into girls anymore.'

'Ah, well, that's-'

'But one drunken night with Angela and suddenly you're Romeo again.'

'Look, it's not like I'm-'

'Why?' Charlotte began to sob, 'why not me?'

'Charlotte you know it's just-' James was interrupted one final time by Charlotte grabbing him by the shoulders and forcing him down to onto the sofa, her glass hit the floor without smashing and a pool of water spread rapidly on his hardwood.

Charlotte leaned in to kiss James, but he turned his head away.

'Charlotte,' he said calmly, 'please get off me so we can talk about this.'

'I'm don't wanna talk,' Charlotte attempted to sound seductive, her words were slurred and awkward and her breath reeked of vodka and beer. James tried not to visibly wince, he didn't want to hurt her feelings.

'Charlotte, please,' he pleaded. Her grip got harder for a moment before she released one of his wrists and slapped him in the face as hard as she could.

The room would have been in total silence were it not for the ringing in James' right ear. He didn't get mad, nor did he react until Charlotte climbed off him and sat back on the sofa, hiding her face behind her hands.

'I'm sorry,' she sobbed, 'I don't, I just don't-'

'It's okay,' James sat up, he tasted blood but didn't check to see if he was bleeding. 'I didn't know you felt that way, Charlotte.'

'I should go,' she went to stand up but was stopped when James took hold of her arm.

'Charlotte,' he began, 'I'm not in to women anymore, that night fucked me up a lot,' he wasn't sure just how much truth there was in his own words. 'But even if I wanted something to happen tonight, that doesn't change the fact that you're drunk and I'm not. There's just no way I'm going to become that kind of person.'

'That's fair,' Charlotte sniffed and sat back down, regaining some composure, 'I feel like an idiot.'

'Don't,' James placed a hand on her shoulder, 'if we were the kind of people to fall out over drunken mistakes then we wouldn't have made it a month as friends.'

'True,' she forced a laugh, 'thanks.'

'You should take the spare room,' James said, standing up and avoiding the pool of water on his floor, 'I'm gonna get something to clean this up.'

He placed a dishtowel over his shoulder and refilled the unbroken glass with water before grabbing a roll of paper towels from the counter. In the short amount of time he was alone, James reflected on what he had done.

It was just as Dahlia said, sometimes the world's worst monsters are those who don't know just how much they hurt others.

James had no idea that he had been hurting Charlotte the entire time. He spoke to her about the people he slept with, asked for relationship advice and even bragged about the odd one night stand. All the while she sat, smiled, drank and laughed along with him. Just how much had he hurt her over the years? How many times had he shared things and joked that only caused her more and more pain?

For the first time, James truly believed himself to be a monster.

'Hey,' Charlotte said with a sigh as he came back in.

'Hey,' he handed her the water and began to dab at the puddle with the paper towels.

'I know sex doesn't mean anything to you,' Charlotte began, her words were pointed but she wasn't entirely wrong. 'But did it mean anything with me? Or, Luke? Or, you know I don't even know what I'm asking.'

'It's okay,' James sat back down after soaking up enough to cover the remaining damp with the dish towel, 'honestly I don't know, I try not to think about it really. Sex is sex, y'know?'

'I know.'

'You gonna be okay?'

'I will be,' she took a sip of water, 'I think I'm gonna go lie down.'

'Sure,' he said, 'I have somewhere to be tomorrow morning, but I'll leave you a set of keys. You can stay here as long as you want.'

'Thanks man,' she looked to him with a smile he knew wasn't real, 'you're a good friend.'

Charlotte got up and insisted she could get to the room on her own. Like James she didn't often lose her balance while drunk, the fact that she was slurring her words was enough of a hint as to how much she had drank that night.

James' tea had long since cooled down, he considered microwaving it before realising that he would rather not be alone with his thoughts anymore. He went to bed and found sleep much easier than he thought he would, though far less restful than he would have liked.

***

James left his spare keys on the coffee table before hoisting his rucksack on his back and putting the train tickets Dahlia gave him in his wallet, double checking the time to make sure he didn't miss the departure.

Even though he hadn't been expecting Charlotte to be up, it was still a relief to him that she was still asleep as he prepared to leave. He didn't want to explain his rucksack or why he was turning the thermostat down and throwing out the perishables from the fridge.

As he crossed the threshold into his former waiting room, James paused. Something felt wrong to him, like he was saying goodbye to a life he had worked so hard to keep. It wasn't the case, he knew it wasn't, but something about walking out that door gave him a ominous feeling that jumped at him from out of a thick fog of uncertainty.

He left quickly, moving without thinking, and locked the door behind him before summoning the lift.

Once outside he stopped as a wet drop fell down his face, for a moment he thought he was crying before he looked up and saw the light snow that fell from the sky. Not a patch of blue was visible through the light grey clouds, though the morning's light seemed unobstructed.

James paused for a moment and held out his gloved hand, watching as the tiny white specs landed on the black fabric and vanished instantly to leave nothing but a small, shiny dot. He didn't feel a thing from it, but a cold air seemed to creep down the back of his neck.

James continued walking, keeping his head down so his face wasn't buffeted by any sudden winds. There was no breeze, but he was taking no chances, and the chill of the snowflakes was already making his skin feel uncomfortable.

He had been anticipating snow for weeks, yet only when he was about to leave did it finally begin to fall. James didn't know why, but the thought made him smirk.

He turned onto the main road and waited at a stop for the bus that would take him straight to the station. James struggled to remember the last time he had to take a bus, though he had read up on the new fare prices and made sure he had exact change before he left.

From his solitary spot under the plastic shelter, James could really stop and admire the beginnings of a white winter. The flakes danced and twirled as they fell to the ground to leave barely a trace on the tarmac. As he watched, James felt a melancholy sweep over him, a deep sadness and hesitation that still lingered from when he first set foot outside his flat.

'James?' he heard someone speak. He looked up to see Luke a few steps from him, a shirt and tie poking out from the coat that still seemed too big for him.

'Hey,' James hadn't been expecting to run into anyone, though he had forgotten that Luke lived on that street. He hated how good it felt to see him.

'You're out early, I thought you didn't work on Fridays.'

'I don't,' James had to use every ounce of willpower he had not to look at Luke while he spoke. 'Emergency faculty meeting.'

'Sounds rough,' Luke checked his watch, James stole a glance. He stood up and went to the road, he saw his bus turn in to the bottom of the street.

'It's fine, we had warning,' he tried to sound emotionless.

'Hey, so,' Luke sounded sad, 'a few of us are heading out tonight if you want to join.'

Something inside James broke. He didn't want to turn his back on Luke, he didn't want to walk away. He wanted with all his heart to take the invitation, or thank him for it at the very least.

'I don't think so,' he said, going against himself.

'It's just tha-'

'If I wanted to be yelled at for nothing and treated like an afterthought, I'd go visit my sister,' he turned and stared straight into Luke's eyes.

James told himself not to lose face, his heart was pounding wildly and every ounce of sense he had was telling him to stop talking.

'If I want to be told I'm worthless, I'll visit my mother.'

No.

'If I want to be ditched in the middle of the night, I'll hook up.'

Stop.

'If I wanted to have someone I loved tell me I don't mean anything, I'll give Andy a call.'

He didn't want this.

'And if I ever wanted to see you again,' the bus pulled up and opened its doors, James stepped on without looking, refusing to break eye contact, 'I'd have to be fucking insane.'

9.

'James? James, are you listening?' Dahlia's words snapped him back into reality.

James, Dahlia and Angela were sitting in first class, which was a surprise to no one. The Noore family had likely not ridden coach in generations, if they ever had to at all.

'Yeah, sorry,' James shuffled through his notes and reorganised his thoughts along with them.

'Where's your head today?' Angela asked, chewing on her pen.

'Not where it should be,' was the only answer James could say.

'Well get it here,' Dahlia said, flicking through pages on her lap. 'Now, the conference starts today, but our part isn't until tomorrow. So feel free to mingle all you like. Just be sure not to be drunk tonight or hungover tomorrow evening, at least not until after our segment.'

'Understood,' James said, his mind back in order.

'This isn't a school trip,' Dahlia smiled, 'I'm not your chaperone. This is a professional matter, so I expect you both to act like professionals, understand?'

Both of them simply nodded in response, though James couldn't help but feel as though the words were meant solely for him.

Phones normally only had weak, intermittent signal on train journeys, and James used this as an excuse to leave his in the rucksack which was crammed under his seat.

***

Luke sat at his desk, his tie feeling tight around his neck. He had expected James to still be standoffish, but he hadn't foreseen him still being that angry.

Either James was very good at holding on to grudges or something else had happened.

Luke was mad, he didn't think what he had said was all that bad, at least not from what he could remember, and it was one incident out of many. Were it anyone else he would have purged James from his life without a second thought, that kind of negativity was toxic in a person's life and Luke didn't need or want any of it.

But something made him keep going, he didn't want to lose hope in James being a good person, someone he could keep around. But if he was going to say such awful things without the excuse of alcohol and after being given plenty of time, then Luke knew he needed to be prepared to lose him.

The thought of losing James was more difficult than Luke felt it ought to be. Sometimes friendships just needed to be nipped in the bud, but there was a hesitation to do so this time that Luke really didn't care for.

'Luke?' Darren's head appeared over the cubicle wall.

'Yeah?' he said, successfully making it look as though he wasn't lost in thought.

'You got those returns for me? I need them by the afternoon.'

'Sure,' he said, opening the relevant tab on his desktop, 'I'll have it within the hour.'

James could wait, work would serve as a pleasant distraction until Luke had the time to deal with what had happened at the bus shelter that morning.

***

James, Angela and Dahlia stepped into the lobby of the Hawkside Hotel, taking down their umbrellas and shivering against the cold that could no longer reach them in the well-heated foyer.

Dahlia had booked them individual rooms, whether as an expense to the university or out of her own pocket, neither of them wanted to ask.

'It's huge,' Angela marvelled as Dahlia made her way to the reception desk.

'No kidding,' James looked at the high ceiling and felt himself grow dizzy, 'it's been a while since I've stayed in a hotel.'

'Same,' Angela spoke quietly as her and James both realised that the echoing room had the air of a library and should likely be treated with the same respect

'This is an annual conference, right?' James walked closer to her so he could keep his voice down. 'Have you never been to one before?'

'No, I've only been working there for a few months. I'm really getting nervous, apparently half the Noore family and their friends are here.'

'You're kidding.'

'Nope. Intimidating, huh? Your tequila idea may come in handy.'

James stifled laughter, he didn't know why he was surprised she remembered, but it was unexpected enough to make him chuckle.

'James,' Angela looked behind him and pointed at his rucksack, 'your phone's ringing.'

James hadn't noticed before Angela pointed it out, but there was a muffled vibrating noise coming from his bag.

'It's probably nothing,' he smiled, 'besides I'd feel weird answering it here. I'll let it ring out.'

'Yeah, I get that.'

Dahlia thanked the woman at the front desk and approached the two of them.

'Introductory drinks start in the ballroom at seven,' she said as she handed the envelopes with their key cards over, 'be early. I have some meetings beforehand. Don't wander off too far.'

James looked outside the glass doors at the cascade of rain that had been falling from the moment they stepped off the train.

'I don't think that's gonna be a problem.'

It was only three o'clock when James got to his hotel room and set his bag on an armchair in the corner.

It was a nice room with a double bed and an en suite shower and bath. Standard, clean feeling and normal, it was exactly what James had been expecting and he was happy to find nothing out of the ordinary.

He set the envelope and key card on the desk and began to unpack his things.

He got out his suit and patted it down on the bed along with the three white shirts he had packed. The room was equipped with an iron and trouser press, which came as a relief, and James got to work on making his shirts look as immaculate as possible.

He hadn't put so much work into ironing a shirt since his old boss threatened to fire him if he showed up with a single crease in his uniform. He always felt it was a little uppity for someone working as a waiter on a zero-hour contract, but back then he needed the money and wasn't in a position to argue.

The suit itself was a different case, he had bought it for his graduation formal and had only worn it twice since he left the tailor shop. The last time he had taken the pinstripe jacket and matching trousers from his wardrobe was on the morning of his father's funeral.

He had been wearing it when he was handed the envelope by his family's lawyer containing a cheque that he had to read twenty times over the course of a few minutes just to make sure he had read the numbers right.

The suit had gone unworn since, hidden away in his bedroom until he got it dry cleaned earlier in the week. He couldn't remember whether or not he got the suit cleaned after the last time he wore it, but it was a chance he wasn't willing to take if he was to make a good impression.

He realised then that he had been focussing on his work a lot more in the last two weeks. With his friendships in not-so-steady decline and his temperament changing unpredictably, his entry level pseudo-job seemed to be the only thing that was making sense to him both in his head and out.

A part of him really wanted to make a good impression at the conference, make a small mark in the world of professional psychology. He simply wanted to have something go his way, and the idea of getting something of a fresh start in a new community felt like exactly what he needed. That and maybe a whisky.

He still had over three hours to kill by the time he gingerly placed his perfectly prepared suit back onto the bed. He had chosen his black tie with small white dots over the shiny blue one, a decision based on nothing more than a gut feeling that the less ostentatious he dressed, the better, even if only by a small margin.

James took his phone from his bag, he had two missed calls from Charlotte and one from Luke, he ignored Luke's and opened the message from Charlotte thanking him for the night before and apologising for her behaviour. He replied saying not to worry about it and apologised for his silence that day, claiming that faculty meetings at the university were running long.

He still didn't really know why he had told no one about where he was, and he was starting to feel stupid about hiding it. Though it was too late to fess up, so he instead set his phone on the desk by his room key and sat in the small seating area in the corner. He looked out the window at the crashing rain that pelted his window while people walked quickly from shelter to shelter in the streets below.

The rain didn't seem like it was going to let up any time soon, though the outside temperature made James sure of the fact that it was going to turn to snow any minute.

A soft knock sounded at the door, accompanied by a voice before James could respond.

'James?' Angela said quietly, 'can I come in?'

James was about to tell her out of habit that she could come in before remembering that that wasn't how hotel rooms worked. He got up and went to the door.

'Nice suit,' Angela sounded surprised as she noticed it.

'Thanks, I got it years ago. I'm honestly surprised it still fits,' he chuckled.

'I was hoping to go over some of the stuff with you,' she took a seat in the chair where James had just been, 'is that okay?'

'O'course,' James said casually as he went to the dresser, 'coffee?'

'Please,' she smiled, fixing her glasses and crossing her legs the same way Dahlia had unknowingly influenced James to do when he spoke to patients.

***

Charlotte locked James' door behind her and posted the keys back through it. She had wanted to talk more to him but he hadn't been answering his phone.

She had woken up at noon but didn't get up until after one in the afternoon. She had helped herself to his coffee and clothes and ended up spending more time in his flat than she meant to.

A large grey jacket from Lothian University and a pair of jeans from the dryer would be enough to keep her warm until she got home. Her clothes from the night before reeked of stale booze and she left them folded in the spare room. She was sure that James wouldn't mind.

She decided to leave once she got a response from him, he even used a smiley face, which he rarely did unless he was in a great mood. Charlotte wasn't so naïve to think that you could accurately gauge someone's mood via a text conversation, but the gesture was enough for her to rest easy for a little while.

The streets outside were quiet and serene, the snow falling gently down was beginning to stay on the ground, carpeting it in what was shaping up to be a pleasant winter sight. A blanket of white that hid the grimy, litter-filled streets was the main thing Charlotte liked about her favourite season, and she knew it was a part that even James enjoyed.

Confidant

James had always complained about winter, how he hated the darkness and the cold. But when they were studying together Charlotte always caught him staring out the window whenever the snow began to fall. He would sit with one arm propping his head up and a pen stopped mid-sentence in a notebook while his attention was caught by the dancing frost.

Charlotte knew that winter held for him a fascination that he could never pursue, he would never be able to stand the temperature or the early dusks, but he would always stand at a window from a warm place and watch the world go by in its subtly shimmering way. He would turn down invitations to go out because he wanted to stay in warm, he would drink too much coffee and barely sleep because he just wanted the excuse of something hot.

James loved winter because he could watch it without interacting with it. He could observe but never touch, and that was just perfect for him. He would be blameless in the drama because he wouldn't be around, he wouldn't leave his flat so everyone always knew where he was and could call on him without needing to feel weird about it.

Winter was when James could be himself, and be alone as often as he needed to without any fake excuses. Charlotte knew that he had been questioning just who he was lately, and such doubt couldn't have come at a better time.

She was worried about him, she was worried about them. Charlotte would give him a call later, already preparing herself to have the phone ring out.

***

'This is so intimidating...' James said as the three of them stepped into the ballroom.

The brightly lit space was gargantuan in size and filled with people mingling and talking quietly amongst themselves. Academics and masters in their fields gathered around the room exchanging ideas and notes, taking part in friendly conversations and light-hearted debates. James thought he recognised a few people within the crowd from dust jackets on books he had read as a student.

James felt comfortable in his suit, though his necktie began to feel a little tight. Dahlia wore a business suit that likely cost more than most educators would make in a year.

Angela had donned a crimson coloured one shoulder dress with a matching purse that she carried with a professional air and posture that James had for some reason not been expecting.

Angela's hair was tied into a tight knot and she was without her glasses, James presumed she was wearing contacts but didn't know whether or not it would be rude to ask.

'Have fun tonight,' Dahlia said, stepping before both of them, 'though not too much,' she winked before vanishing into the crowd.

'I really feel like I don't belong here,' Angela said without losing her composure.

'Tell me about it,' James fidgeted with his tie without loosening it.

'Drink?'

'Oh God yes,' James smiled, wondering if even that would be considered too crass for the undoubtedly high-class gathering that they had found themselves in.

Despite the amount of people mingling around the room, James was served his drinks fairly quickly and even found a seat at the bar for both him and Angela without trouble.

He handed Angela her wine with a smile, the action along with his attire making him feel much more suave than he actually was. He took his own drink, a martini that he couldn't resist ordering, and took a seat beside her on one of the tall stools.

'Expensive,' he said as he took his first sip, pretending to enjoy it more than he did.

'We can probably expense it,' Angela said, sipping at her wine with less feigned enjoyment.

'Seriously?'

'Dahlia's a firm believer in the importance of enjoying life's small pleasures and vices,' she said, resting her hand on her chin as though she wasn't even listening to her own words, 'she believes people should have fun and not worry too much. She thinks people need to relax more.'

'You're one of her patients too, huh?'

'Yeah,' Angela had no problem admitting, 'it's actually written into my contract.'

'Seriously? Mine too!'

'I know,' Angela smirked, 'I wrote it.'

'Really?'

'I was following Dahlia's instructions, like I wasn't creative with it or anything.'

'Still, interesting to know,' James said, not knowing exactly how.

'Are you mad at me?' Angela said, hanging her head slightly.

'For what?'

'Y'know, the questions I asked you in your interview, some of those were mine.'

'I kinda figured.'

'And, that night we slept together,' her body visibly tensed as she spoke.

'Which one?'

'Last week. Wait, you remember?' she looked to James with a shocked expression.

'Not really,' James wasn't proud to admit, 'Charlotte kinda filled me in.'

'Ah,' Angela couldn't help but smile, 'Well, I knew you were gay, but when we got more and more drunk I got ahead of myself and made a move. When you didn't stop me I just kept going. I've been feeling really bad about it.'

'Oh thank fuck,' James let out a relieved sigh, he didn't care if anyone was offended by his language. 'I was so worried. I thought I'd come on to you,' he couldn't hold back a chuckle and another sigh.

'Really?' Angela laughed along with him.

'We were both beating ourselves up for thinking we'd fucked over the other, huh?'

'Seems so. It's so stupid,' Angela was still laughing, 'we work in a psychiatrist's office and we didn't even know to just talk to each other.'

'Yeah,' James pulled himself together too quickly as Angela's words pierced something deep in his mind, something that made the pit in his stomach return and his heart weigh heavily on his chest.

He had been ignoring calls and neglecting to talk to anyone, and for some reason he thought that would make everything okay, better even. He assumed that he would get away for a weekend and get a grip on himself, returning a new and better person in the same way one would return from a spa feeling refreshed.

He realised then how stupid his decision had been, how ridiculous it all felt. Just because he was away didn't mean everyone else went into a paused, suspended state until he came back. In his darkest moments he considered that they wouldn't think about him, that they wouldn't care or notice that he was gone.

But if he was wrong, and if they were going to think and worry, then he was going to lose everything. Or so he told himself.

What he had said to Luke at the shelter, his last encounter with Charlotte, the things Andy said to him that he hadn't even attempted to forgive. No matter who was to blame for any of it, his refusal to talk to any of them would make his inevitable loss completely and inarguably his fault.

'James, are you okay?' Angela looked concerned.

'Yeah,' he snapped back to the bar, to his seat, to the martini he regretted ordering, 'I'm alright. Just, thinking about stuff.'

'You look pale,' Angela said, putting her hand on his shoulder, 'are you sure you're alright?'

'Yeah, don't worry,' James put on his best smile and started fumbling in his pockets. 'Where's my phone?' he asked.

'You left it in your room, I thought you did it deliberately.'

'Maybe I did,' James returned his attention to his drink, 'my mind's been everywhere lately.'

'Well, for all intents and purposes we can treat this weekend as a holiday,' she let go of his shoulder and patted his back, 'let's just relax, yeah?'

'Yeah,' James was glad to feel a real smile return to his face, 'you know, Angela, you just might be the last friend I have left.'

Angela didn't say anything in response, she merely patted James' back twice more and slowly returned to her drink, never dropping the warm look on her face. It was masterful, the perfect response to a deep and difficult thing to say that would make the happiness behind the words remain and the sadness drift away and disperse into nothingness with no more conversation to cling to.

Dahlia would have been proud.

'Excuse me,' Angela said, dismounting the chair carefully. James only noticed then that she was wearing high heels.

Once off the chair, Angela made her way through the crowd towards the restrooms. James watched her until she vanished and returned his attention to his martini with the intention of finishing it quickly and ordering a beer.

He didn't notice that someone had sat beside him until he was spoken to.

'For a gay man you really love to watch women, huh?' James jumped as he heard the voice, and turned around to see someone he had until then completely forgotten about.

Beside him, sitting in Angela's seat, was Dahlia Noore's benefactor, the man who had made James shiver with nothing but a hand on his shoulder.

'It's not that-'

'Relax,' he held up a hand, 'I'm messing with you.'

'You're that man from back then,' James said, realising how dumb the words sounded.

'A bit long winded,' the man grinned, 'I tend to go by Karl these days,' he held out his hand and James shook it, his grip felt as though it would break his fingers.

'Karl,' James thought out loud, 'as in Wisemann?'

'The very same,' Karl beamed, his toothy grin making James a little more uncomfortable than he already was.

'As in Wisemann Industries?'

'Yup.'

'The biggest pharmaceutical company in the world?'

'Yu-huh.'

'Jesus,' James covered his mouth with one hand, 'no wonder you're so intimidating.'

'Am I? Sorry, not my intention.'

A bartender came over and placed a pint in front of Karl, James didn't remember him ordering anything.

'So what are you doing here?' James asked.

'A lot of my company's money goes into what the Noores are researching,' he answered quickly, as though anticipating the question. 'I'm just here to rub shoulders mostly.'

'So why talk to me?'

'A patient who's taken the great See-All's interest? How could I pass up the opportunity?'

James chuckled at the idea that Dahlia's student-given nickname had managed to spread into her professional life as well, the humour he found in that outshining the condescension with which Karl had spoken.

'I should go, however,' Karl stood up, 'I have taken the young lady's seat, after all, and I'm sure I'm not the only one here who wants to see you.'

'What do you mean?' James asked, but Karl had already disappeared into the crowd.

'Sorry,' Angela came up from behind him and took her seat back, 'bathroom took a bit of time to find.'

'Not at all,' James was confused, 'you weren't gone that long.'

'Okay, cool,' Angela took her wine back in her hand and sipped it. The word still didn't seem to suit her.

'To getting away,' James held up his glass. Angela smiled and the two of them clinked, their different glasses making an odd noise as they did so.

James returned to his room several hours later with a pleasant buzz. He and Angela had not mingled at all, and had claimed those bar seats as their own for the entire evening.

He returned to his hotel room alone, and was happy for the opportunity to be by himself for a while. He felt as though his own company would be nice for the first time in what felt like too long.

He grabbed his phone without looking at it and plugged it in to charge at his bedside.

With his suit off and a glass of water filled, drank, and refilled, James got under the soft duvet and felt far too cold for just an instant before the feathery blanket eased around him and he cuddled into himself, feeling a warm comfort in the idea that he would likely get the great night's sleep that hotel rooms often offered to him unconditionally.

As he closed his eyes and began to focus on his breathing, an incoming message disturbed his attempt to meditate himself into unconsciousness. He rolled over with a groan and lifted the phone carefully so as not to let the charger fall out.

The screen lit up with the push of a button, and on it was a message from an unknown number that James initially assumed was from Lorraine before realising that it couldn't have been.

I heard you're in town. xx

***

Luke awoke to his shrieking alarm clock and slammed his fist on the snooze button so hard he felt it might break.

He awoke alone and in his own bed after coming home and retiring early after a few drinks with workmates. He wasn't hungover, though he felt as though he may as well be, as he was still in a bitter mood from the previous morning.

He had not called James as he had intended to, but only because two out of four pints in he came to the conclusion that the bastard owed him an apology and not the other way around. His anger upon waking that morning was a result of him not knowing who was to blame and the fear that he would have to fess up and apologise before James got a chance to so he didn't feel like the inferior friend.

Luke had no idea when friendships got so difficult, or when he became so soft when it came to being mistreated. But it could all wait until later.

As he approached the bus shelter, Luke glanced inconspicuously at the crowd of people who were huddling together like penguins. He kept an eye out for James, though he didn't know why. He told himself that it was curiosity rather than anything else, convincing himself easily whether or not it was actually true.

James was not there, and while Luke felt as though he should be relieved, he instead felt as though an opportunity had passed him by.

The early Saturday morning brought quiet streets and little traffic, giving Luke room to breathe the icy air and collect his thoughts as he made his way to the shop on the corner.

He purchased a jar of ground coffee, milk, eggs, two bottles of wine and enough beer to make the other groceries look like an afterthought or cover for an alcoholic who didn't want the cashiers to know he was an alcoholic.

Luke had no real plan in mind, despite it being a Saturday, but figured he should stock up just in case. It made sense to always have alcohol at the ready in case guests came over.

As he waited in line he thought on how much effort and care James took in keeping his kitchen stocked with booze, teas and coffees just in case a last minute guest came over.

When in James' flat, Luke noticed just how many kinds of tea he had in his kitchen, how many various strengths of coffee he kept despite only ever drinking one kind himself.

He had told James, someone who he had observed to put so much stock in the happiness of others, that no one really cared about him. And with that thought hanging heavily on his head, Luke paid for his shopping and walked quickly home, taking a longer route to avoid passing the bus shelter again.

***

James' mouth still tasted of the tequila that he and Angela had taken before getting on stage. The bartender was taken aback by the order, but both of them were beyond caring what the hotel staff thought of them.

James recognised the look on the workers' faces when they thought no one was looking, the formality and stature that they projected was likely forced upon them by their managers.

They were probably high school students and part time workers who were just trying to save money or earn a modest living, he had no doubt that most of their energy went to keeping up appearances. He didn't know for sure, but James had been in the same boat himself years before and remembered what it was like.

Even behind the shock, there was an obvious look of glee in the bartender's expression while he poured two shots of expensive tequila in front of them. He seemed at least a little delighted to see a hint of delinquency in a sea of sherry glasses and pomegranate seeds in champagne.

James was up before Angela, reading from the page without really taking in a word. He stood up straight and spoke clearly as instructed, grateful for the podium in front of him which hid just how fast his legs were shaking. He was sure that Dahlia was getting a kick out of it.

A round of soft applause sounded throughout the room and James was sure that half of the people he was speaking to weren't really paying attention, a fact he was glad for.

The three of them left the stage and a host who had introduced them took the podium and began speaking far too quietly to the under-enthused masses. It didn't matter to James what volume he spoke at, he wasn't going to listen to a word of it anyway.

The seats at the bar that they had taken the night before were free and James found an extra one and slid it over for Dahlia while Angela ordered the drinks.

'You both did very well,' Dahlia said once they were all sat. She took a napkin from a small stand on the bar and placed it in front of her.

'Yeah, the crowd went mild,' James said, taking a deep breath. His legs were still shaking a little.

'We aren't here to entertain,' Dahlia said, smiling in thanks to the man who brought her a glass of whisky, 'we're here to educate.'

'I'm just glad it's over,' Angela sighed.

'Ditto,' James agreed, lifting his beer to his face, thankful he had learned his lesson about martinis the night before.

'The wine here is nice,' Angela said after taking a sip.

'You get what you pay for,' Dahlia chuckled.

'Speaking of,' James began.

'I'll be covering your alcohol expenses,' Dahlia smiled, 'just don't go too crazy, even my pockets aren't bottomless, you know.'

'Yes ma'am,' James smiled happily.

'You seem more focussed today, James,' Dahlia rested her head on her knuckle, 'did something change?'

'Just a good night's sleep, I guess.'

'I see,' Dahlia didn't sound so sure.

A tall, slender man approached Dahlia then and whispered something in her ear. Her facial expression didn't change as she listened to him speak, neither Angela nor James could make out what was being said.

'I see,' she nodded, 'well, I apologise for this rudeness but my attention is needed elsewhere,' she lifted her whisky from the bar, the napkin beneath it clutched in her little finger. 'Enjoy your night, both of you, you've earned it. And Angela, I'll see you at three o'clock tomorrow for the train.'

Dahlia took her leave immediately, the tall man following close behind her like a bodyguard.

'You're not coming back with us?' Angela sounded concerned.

'Oh, um, nah,' James moved into Dahlia's seat so they were next to each other, 'I have a few friends in the city so I'm staying until Monday.'

'Must be nice to have friends all over.'

'It is,' James said solemnly, 'it comes in handy at least.'

'What do you mean?'

'You know what?' he leaned back as far back as the tall chair would allow, which wasn't very far at all, 'I don't even know myself. Hey, I'm gonna head out for a smoke, do you mind?'

'Not at all.'

'Thanks,' James got up and made his way down the back of the ballroom towards an outdoor exit he noticed while he was on stage and failing to look like he was paying attention.

The rain from the day before was gone, and the tall buildings surrounding the hotel shielded any chilling winds that back home would have made James regret stepping outside.

The back of the hotel was a large car park surrounded by grass patches and flower beds, it was almost too easy to forget that he was in an overpopulated concrete jungle.

James made his way into a small shelter set to the side of the exit with ashtrays set into the red brick walls of what he assumed to be the older parts of the hotel. He lit his cigarette and inhaled deeply, realising that he hadn't had one in some time as the nicotine hit him hard and he had to sit down on a thin wooden bench.

There must have been over two hundred people crowded around that ballroom, and James found it odd that he had the smoking shelter all to himself. He had seen a few people take that exit while he was on stage, but not many. Though when he reminded himself that the room was largely full of medical experts, it made a little more sense that there were so few smokers, but not much.

His teeth began to chatter together as he heard the door open and someone else came into the shelter, he didn't look at them for fear that they would want to start a conversation about the presentation that he had already started to forget.

'I thought you were going to quit?'

James knew that voice.

'Harder to kick than you thought, huh?'

It couldn't be.

'I liked your talk, by the way. You know your stuff.'

'What are you doing here?' James asked quickly.

'Nice to see you too,' there was a sarcastic tone, he was always good at that. James still didn't look up. He sat on the bench, sitting far too close, and lit his own cigarette. 'If you must know, my boss insisted. I was against it but now that I see you here it could be fun after all.'

'I have to go,' James threw his half-finished cigarette on the ground and stood up. He hadn't even taken his first step when a firm, digging grip took his wrist.

'I want to talk more.'

'There you are,' Karl Wisemann seemed to appear out of nowhere and stood before the two of them. 'Stop messing around, you've got elbows to rub.'

'Understood.'

The grasp on James' wrist was released and he was alone before he even had the wherewithal to grab another cigarette from his jacket pocket.

He realised then that he had underestimated just how cold he was.

***

'The bus shelter?' Charlotte asked, unsure of where Luke was going with his questions. 'That can't be right, he takes the tram to work.'

Charlotte had been studying in the university library when her phone flashed noiselessly on the desk with a call from Luke. She would have ignored it if it wasn't the third call in less than an hour.

Wanting to avoid the snow outside, she had taken her phone to the stairwell, where conversations were more easily tolerated than anywhere else in the building.

'I thought it didn't feel right,' Luke said pensively, 'I walk past there every day and have never seen him there before.'

'So what?' Charlotte was getting impatient, 'maybe he wanted to change things up, maybe the tram wasn't running or maybe he just really wanted to take the bus.'

'You're not worried? He's run away before, right?'

'Of course I'm not worried,' Charlotte sighed, 'he wouldn't leave without telling me. Now are you gonna tell me what this is really about? And why aren't you talking to him about this, anyway?'

'He,' Luke paused, 'he said some stuff before he left. Like, really hurtful stuff.'

'You're kidding me, right?'

'What?'

'You essentially tell him that he's worthless and now you feel bad because he hurt your feelings?'

'He told you about that?'

'Of course he did,' Charlotte almost yelled before remembering where she was, 'why don't you give him a ring if you're suddenly so sensitive?'

'I'm worried about him, Charlotte.'

The two remained in silence for a moment before Charlotte let out a heavy sigh and used her free hand to rub between her eyes with her thumb and index finger.

'Look,' she said finally, 'I'll call in on him tonight, okay? I'll let you know if he's in and will talk to him on your behalf. How does that sound?'

'Thanks Charlotte,' he sounded relieved, 'I owe you one.'

'You owe me more than that,' she hung up.

Charlotte wished then that she was a smoker, the excuse to take five minutes to just stand and breathe toxic air for a little while seemed like just what she needed to clear her head.

She was worried, of course she was. Luke had explained that James had his red rucksack, his holiday bag, and had taken the bus that went by the train station instead of taking the tram.

She wouldn't let Luke know that she was starting to feel scared, scared that she had chased James away with her drunken actions on Thursday night. But more than that she was worried that James had once again given up.

She looked at her phone and considered calling him before sending a message that she hoped wouldn't come across as too panicky.

Where are you? x

***

James had spent the remainder of his evening looking over his shoulder, unable to relax or enjoy his drinks. He and Angela had talked and drank for hours, though as he drunkenly shuffled down the warm, bright hallway he couldn't remember a single word.

James had given some awkward excuse for his paranoid behaviour, something about remaining nerves from the talk. Angela hadn't bought it, but James wasn't in the state of mind to care.

He had never felt more pathetic in his life. After nearly seven years he was still unable to move around him, incapable of anything other than rapidly spoken sentences. Were it not the dead of winter, James felt as though he would have sweat through his suit.

To think that nothing but a few simple words would reduce him to a quivering mess in mere seconds disgusted James beyond words. The boiling rage that made him stand up for himself at the bus shelter, albeit in an unhealthy way, was gone. All he had was an emptiness that, after far too many drinks, he was willing to fill with just about anything.

'Had a few, huh?'

James stopped the moment he heard that voice again, the voice that did more to him with four words than an entire lecture from a pissed off superior.

'How did you know where my room was?' it took all his courage just to ask.

'Mine's next door.'

'That doesn't answer my-'

James' sentence was cut off as he was grabbed and thrown against his room door. He yelped in sharp pain but was immediately made silent by a hard kiss on his mouth. He grabbed onto whatever he could and pushed back with little success, though he was granted room to breathe.

'I'm drunk, man,' James said, looking at his feet.

'Me too,' he leaned in and kissed him again, softer this time, and James felt a cold hand reach between the buttons of his shirt and caress his tightening stomach.

James stopped resisting when he realised that he had no real reason to resist. After everything that had happened what was one more regret? Besides, he had no choice anyway. He had danced this dance before. One way or another his body and mind would surrender under his old friend's crushing influence.

He felt his body being released and kept his eyes closed, wondering in the few seconds of nothingness if he had simply imagined the whole thing. He heard an electronic lock beep and his wrist was once again taken in a grip that made his arm ache.

He put up no fight as he was thrown onto a soft hotel bed and pinned to the spot with just enough force to keep him in place, but not enough to hurt too much. It was just like the first time they had met, and James allowed himself to revel in the nostalgia.

The moment one of his hands was free, James grabbed onto a shirt in the dark and pulled him closer. If he was going to allow himself to get lost in the darkness of his old life, he was damn sure going to enjoy the ride.

***

'Come on,' Charlotte tapped her foot quickly after knocking on James' door for the sixth time, wondering if it was time to give up.

It was a Saturday night, he easily could have been out drinking with someone. She called Andy only to find out that he was tied up at the lab. David and Gregg were on a date, though they had informed her that Lorraine was staying at a friend's house.

The only thing keeping Charlotte from total panic was the fact that she didn't have Angela's number, meaning there was still an explanation that she couldn't explore.

She had sent another message to James simply inviting him out for drinks that night, hoping that he would get back to her with whatever plans he was busy with. All she wanted was to know was that he was okay, that he hadn't up and left again.

Throughout the day Charlotte had been hoping to have James answer his door with a happy greeting, or call out for her to enter like he normally did. She had been looking forward to feeling of embarrassment that came with being faced with proof that she had been worrying over nothing.

The feeling didn't come, and Charlotte brought out her phone and called Luke.

'Hey,' he answered, he sounded stressed.

'He's not at home,' Charlotte said plainly, not wanting to hold any real conversation.

'Where do you think he is?'

'I dunno, Luke,' Charlotte couldn't hide her own worry like she had done earlier in the day. 'But yeah, I'm starting to get worried.'

'Drink?' Luke said, he didn't sound like he was in a party mood.

'You-' Charlotte stopped, considering that it was either go out for a drink or go home and slowly panic more and more. 'You know what? Sure.'

'Gimme an hour,' Luke said, some humour returning to his voice, though that may have just been her imagination.

***

James closed his room door behind him, his jacket over his shoulder and his shirt open. He had only just about had the capacity to get his trousers back on before leaving and still wasn't entirely sure if he had remembered to put his underwear back on.

He checked. He hadn't.

He drank a glass of water and looked at himself in the mirror. The right side of his face was red and he had a hickey on the his neck that no collar was going to cover. The left part of his torso felt lightly bruised. He regretted nothing and everything at the same time.

He left the bathroom and turned the main light on. Leaning against the wall he held his head in one hand and clutched his chest in the other. His heart was beating out of his chest and he couldn't think of a way to calm it down. Thoughts, doubts and remorseful dwellings swam through his mind like helpless fish caught in a whirlpool.

Every recent failure came to him at once. Lorraine's divorce, David's relationship, Andy, Luke, Charlotte, even his night with Angela came into his consciousness as yet another reason why he had deserved to hear those awful things that had been said to him. He felt stupid for disagreeing with them, for trying to stand up for himself. He felt like nothing, a salmon fighting against a closing net.

He had always been apprehensive when it came to matters of romance and love, but he couldn't stop his heart from freaking out and could feel that his head wasn't too far off the same mark.

He heard a buzzing then, a sudden and loud sound that made him jump. It took him a few seconds to realise that his phone was ringing. It was still on the dresser where he had left it before going down to the conference that afternoon.

Hesitantly, James checked the screen. It was Luke. He wanted to let it ring out, but knew that the longer he stared at the phone the more likely he was to pick up, and everything inside him was screaming that that was a bad idea.

With a swipe of his finger, he ignored the call, and turned to walk away before it started buzzing again. He didn't look at it this time, and instead turned on the desk lamp and took the envelope that his room key had been in.

He wrote the address as steadily as he could and sealed the envelope tight, there was a post office down the street that he had noted, and there was plenty of time before it opened. This meant that he had the chance to sleep on the fuck-it moment he had just come to.

He would dwell, he would sleep, he would not change his mind.

When the morning came, James was lying under the covers still in his open shirt and suit trousers. He couldn't tell if it had been one hour or eight since he lay down, but figured it didn't matter. At that time of year, the light of the morning meant the day was late enough on.

The shower made his body ache as the water hit him far too harshly. He grit his teeth and bore the mild pain as he washed his face more times than he meant to, he felt as though the sins of the past could wash down the drain along with whatever filth from sweat and semen still clung to him.

It was wishful thinking.

Confidant

His hangover didn't seem to faze him, he considered the possibility that he was still drunk, but felt more that it was a result of his developing numbness. It was ridiculous to think, but he didn't want to question it, he didn't want to question anything anymore.

Dressed and bundled up, he hoisted his heavy bag over his shoulder and stepped outside his room. As he did so he felt the same way as he did when he left his flat on Friday morning, not long before running into Luke.

He felt as though he was leaving not just a room, but a chapter of his life. He felt as though he was saying goodbye to something he would never see again, but this time he knew exactly what he was saying goodbye to.

He passed the room in which he had spent most of the evening and paused without knowing why. He considered knocking, but had no idea what he would say or do. His side still ached and he was sure he was bruised, but he was happy for the pain. Not because he thought he deserved it, but because he had enjoyed receiving it.

The pain wasn't a price to pay or a necessary evil, it was part of the ride. And as much as James fought against the feeling, he couldn't deny that it was the most fun he had had in months.

The hotel staff seemed too happy as he checked out, asking if he'd had a good stay and wishing him a safe trip home. He had thanked them and played along, but knew that they were fully aware of the fact that he didn't want to talk.

Nevertheless, their cheerful dispositions and well-meaning questions were a part of the job, and James wondered then how they managed to keep up the energy for so long.

The day was promising to be a bright one, though the cold still clung to James' exposed skin like wayward strands of tape that just wouldn't come off no matter how much he fought.

He purchased a stamp and double checked the address written shakily with an almost empty pen. Before long he found himself stood before a post box and allowing himself one last moment to think about what he was really doing, one last pause to contemplate the consequences of his actions.

He was overreacting, he was upset, and he knew he would regret everything he was about to do. But at that time it didn't seem to matter, none of it did. He had tried, he had failed, and while he desperately wanted to cling to the life he had built, he felt as though it was all washing away without his control.

The river had flooded, and if he kept going he was sure he would drown and bring everyone down into the depths with him.

He took a deep, chilling breath and posted the letter quickly.

There was no going back anymore. No one back home needed the advice he gave, they didn't need his company or his help, they simply didn't need him.

James felt his pocket vibrate again with another incoming call from Luke. With a heavy heart and an aching head, he ignored it and strode down the street with a feigned sense of purpose.

On his way to Piccadilly Station, James threw his phone into a nearby bin.

10.

Charlotte had only had three drinks with Luke before the two decided to part ways. The majority of their time together had been nothing but an awkward silence with a heavy air of concern that she was sure only she really felt.

Luke had seemed down, but only about what James had said to him. For reasons she couldn't explain, Charlotte had been expecting Luke to be worried about him, too. But she had only seen the self-centred nature that she already assumed to be Luke's dominant trait.

She was biased and overly negative towards him, but she knew that she was. And she held on to that self-awareness with a sense of pride she felt she didn't deserve to feel.

It had been four days since that evening, and Charlotte hadn't left the house since. Every call to James went ignored, every conversation about him ended in an apathetic uncertainty, a casual shrug. Charlotte was starting to think she was the only one who was worried about him at all.

She woke up feeling no more rested than she had done in previous mornings, and even though her eyes were open and her mind was fully awake, her head remained on her pillow for another hour before she could muster the energy to get out of bed.

Her room was well heated in the mornings thanks to some clever timing with the boiler, but it had been off for an hour by the time she got up, making her immediately regret her decision not to get out from under the blankets sooner.

The house she lived in was an old build, the kind with a decommissioned yet draughty fireplace in every room that made the house very expensive to heat. It had been somewhat repurposed several decades ago and turned into student accommodation.

Charlotte lived on the ground floor of the house, something that she didn't appreciate, but it made sense since she was often home later than the five other women who shared the roof.

There were no seminars that morning, and she was ahead in her thesis after having spent the last week diving into it with every waking, sober moment she had. The benefit of having a lot on her mind was that procrastination wasn't going to help, and the only thing that would work as a distraction in any capacity was hard work.

It was the middle of the week, but the directionless feeling in Charlotte's mind made her feel like it was a Sunday. She had made a last minute appointment with Doctor Noore that day, and her mind was put no more at ease when her response ended with a question about whether not she had been in touch with James lately.

Dahlia was the one he spoke to, the one Charlotte spoke to, she connected the two of them in ways they couldn't do themselves. He hadn't revealed too much to his therapist, he hadn't mentioned his internal struggles to Charlotte. But between the two of them they knew everything about James, everything he wanted to share, anyway.

If he really had run away again, then Charlotte knew that she had to resist the urge to look for someone to blame.

Luke had told James that his life was worthless, and unapologetically so. Andy had told him that Luke was right to say it. Angela had made James question himself in a way he probably hadn't done in years. Dahlia pushed James' mental health to a point he had clearly wanted to avoid. Charlotte had pushed herself onto him and revealed years of hurt that she had worked so hard to keep bottled up.

James himself was not without blame. He had allowed such things to hurt him, he had let himself be open and receptive to the drunken ramblings of others as though they were what people really felt. He had fallen into the darkness without putting up much of a fight, weakening himself to the world in a way that must have been at least partially deliberate.

Everyone, including James, was to blame for what had been happening, and Charlotte was as mad at him as she was at everyone else, herself included.

James could sometimes be missing in action, normally because of a particularly bad hangover, but if he had been missing work then something else was up. Charlotte tried her best to be optimistic, that maybe he was just sick or taking a long holiday, but she couldn't convince herself of anything so positive.

She had even taken to avoiding showers until it seemed absolutely necessary, desperate to not spend any time alone with her thoughts. She had purchased a wireless speaker and started listening to music while bathing to distract herself, though even that didn't help as much as she had hoped.

Three sharp knocks sounded at her bedroom door while she was brushing her hair, she called out to say that the door was open.

'Charlotte?' Maggie swung her head round the door. Her bouncing brown locks whipping her in the face as she did so, though she didn't seem to notice. 'Can I come in?'

'Sure,' Charlotte turned round in her stool, 'what's up?'

'There was a letter for you in the kitchen. I think it's been there a while.'

'Oh, sorry. My mind's been kind of all over the place.'

Maggie handed over a small envelope with their address written shakily on the front. It felt like there was something in it, jewellery maybe? There was no return address, though the envelope was marked with the logo of the Hawkside Hotel in Manchester.

'Why would a hotel send you something?' Maggie asked. 'Do you know anyone in Manchester?'

'No,' Charlotte said with uncertainty, 'no one I'd still be in touch with anyway.'

Charlotte thanked her for the delivery, and Maggie smiled and nodded before looking to the envelope. There was an excited glee in her demeanour, Charlotte often forgot how nosey Maggie could get.

With a sigh and a roll of her eyes that wasn't meant to be subtle, Charlotte ripped the envelope open and tipped it over the dresser, its contents clanging onto the wooden surface.

'Keys?' Maggie asked, 'weird way to tell someone you fancy them.'

'It's not that,' Charlotte's lip quivered, tears formed in her eyes.

She brought out her phone and sent the same message to everyone in her contact list she believed the news would even remotely matter to. Her worst fears were true, she had lost him again.

'It's a goodbye,' she said as she sent the message out.

He's gone.

***

Dahlia wasn't surprised to receive an email from Charlotte, though she was surprised that it had taken her so long to do so.

Charlotte was quick to jump to conclusions, easy to worry but difficult to annoy. Dahlia had no doubt that she was feeling a mix of anger, betrayal and fear in equal measures that likely left her frazzled and directionless. While this was completely understandable, it could mean that her university work would suffer, and Dahlia could not abide that.

She had spoken to Karl a lot at the conference, mostly about her nephew's work, but there were some pleasantries that Dahlia sorely missed though rarely got in her line of work.

Given the university he went to and when, as well as his attention constantly being directed to the bar where James sat, something Dahlia presumed he thought went unnoticed, it didn't take her very long to infer exactly who Karl's protégé was.

She had no doubt that Karl himself also knew, and likely arranged for him to come as soon as he found out young James would be in attendance. Karl liked to stir the pot, and his interest in observational field research bordered on the sociopathic. Should they meet again soon, Dahlia would prepare some conversational notes that would chew him out without appearing insulting or presumptuous.

To Dahlia, the social game was to be interfered with, directed, controlled but only slightly, though the observer in question was ethically bound to make their part at least somewhat known. To Karl it was different, he was the kind to set the dominoes in a row and then make someone else flick them down while he watched from a dark corner.

Moreso even than that, he had no problem with playing his games with other people's property. Dahlia was territorial, and she didn't appreciate the game he was playing, though she wouldn't give him the satisfaction of confirming what he no doubt already believed. That she was angry with him taking her own subject from her, knowing full well what it could do to him.

She stood by her main window, sipping at her cortado coffee and seething quietly as she often did when she was faced with the worst possible thing in the world, a complete lack of control.

There was nothing she could do, James was unreachable and unwilling to connect even if he was reachable. He hadn't told anyone, not even Charlotte, where he went when he had walked away from everything years earlier, and he wouldn't have told anyone this time either.

To try to get in touch was a meaningless effort, one that would only solidify Dahlia's feeling of helplessness. She had regained control of her subject after Angela had been unable to contain herself, though the grip was loosening with each thing James had neglected to tell her.

Charlotte had been a valuable resource to gather the information that Dahlia had been thus far unable to extract. She had told her about Luke, the boy who had wondered into James' life and made off with his heart before smashing it on the floor before him. She had told her about Andy, the one James had really tried to form a lasting and meaningful relationship with.

Then there was the other, the one whose name James had never even spoken. The one he had sat in that lounge and waited to see in the hopes that he would get a glance, a smile, a wave, a conversation.

Dahlia was frustrated. James had been the chatty sort, always knowing what to say and often speaking a few sentences more than he should have, but he had been infuriatingly tight-lipped about everything from the moment he re-entered Dahlia's life.

She had initially decided to give James two or three weeks to return before labelling him as a failure and typing up the rest of her notes, but when she received the email from Charlotte an idea came to her.

Dahlia decided that for as long as there was information about James that she could use, where the information came from was of little consequence. While it would be less reliable than she would like, it was better than nothing, and the thrill of having a hopeless situation seem not so hopeless kept her going with an optimism that she was clinging to.

As she looked out over the frozen grass of the university gardens, a smile appeared on her face, a deserved smile that came with the knowledge that she was to rebel against Karl Wisemann's own game and still have a chance at winning.

She remembered then why she had gotten into the game to begin with.

James Steele had been selected because of his unbalanced yet balanced nature. He was of above average, but not of notable intelligence. He was diligent and friendly, but he was also manipulative, overly sensitive and highly hedonistic.

He had fought to get Dahlia as a supervisor, and after reading his file she decided to take him as both student and patient. He had been more than promising, his demeanour often upbeat and jovial, unless he was hungover. Dahlia had seen a lot of potential in him and found his unashamed stories and pieced together recollections of nights and weekends to be oddly enthralling.

Conversations about STD checks and forgetting partners' names came as easily to James as talking about coursework or the weather. Such openness and candour were rare in even the most energetic of people, and Dahlia couldn't help but find his ability to embrace his youth and not let it get in the way of his work fascinating.

But one day he became quiet.

It was a sudden change that came in the winter of his second year. He began missing his lectures, but only lectures on subjects he already seemed to have a grasp on. He had become more reserved in their conversations, his answers to questions were limited to short, stilted sentences. He stopped making eye contact and didn't seem to interact with anyone outside of his own duties.

His duties, of course, included keeping his room door open at all times.

Confidant

Dahlia had a few patients who had a second ear when they needed it, someone whose praises they sang about how helpful he could be. James Steele became known amongst his friends and flatmates as the man to talk to if you were struggling with anything.

He had forsaken his own life and focussed instead on others. A noble lifestyle in theory, but an obviously destructive one.

Dahlia witnessed him becoming more and more meek, less and less outgoing. No amount of prodding or questioning, no matter how subtle, gave her the answers she wanted. It was around then that she began to see him in the psychology lounge, half-heartedly circling words on printed documents and hammering away on his laptop without actually writing anything.

She began to take notes, marking down where she saw him and when. She saw him in the psychology lounge, department cafés and bars, always doing work and always alone. Every location in view of a lecture theatre or seminar room.

With a curiosity she hadn't felt in years, Dahlia began cross-referencing his hangouts and times with timetables of other students. She found a few matches, and narrowed it down to one student who lived in James' dorm.

While this revelation had been expected, it still came as a disappointment. One of the most interesting students she had undertaken in recent years, a student with a unique grasp on the balance of life that most adults struggled to maintain, had lost his way as a result of a low mood and what appeared to be a broken heart.

It was boring, cliché and idiotic. Dahlia had all but lost hope on getting anything for her time spent on James Steele before she received a phone call from one of her subordinates, a social psychology lecturer and deputy head of the department, explaining that James had not attended any lectures at all for over a week.

Dahlia began to check in on his usual haunts at the predictable times. She found nothing. She asked their mutual patients, and found nothing. She phoned his parents and still she found nothing.

James Steele was missing.

Two weeks later, Dahlia met Charlotte Miles, and felt her luck was finally going to change.

Charlotte had been James' best friend since they had met a week into their first year. It was a chance meeting at a university organised event designed to make new students mingle and make friends to ward off the loneliness and mental health issues that often came with over- and under-confident teenagers finding independence for the first time.

Charlotte had fallen in love with him almost instantly, and the two had shared a fling before James began dating, as it were, other people without letting her know. She had realised the kind of man he was far too late into her infatuation, but had remained by his side as both friend and patient ever since. The toll it had taken on her was devastating, and his disappearance had done even more to her already declining state.

And so she was referred to Dahlia by one of her course mates, a student by the name of Angela Hawthorne, and Charlotte was given weekly sessions.

Dahlia had absolutely no idea how, but Karl Wisemann, a man she had only ever known as one of her brother's colleagues, had heard about her practically obsessive research with one young student, and got in touch regarding him.

To the outside world it would appear that Karl was looking to stage some kind of bet, but Dahlia knew that they were about to enter a game that doubled as a piece of psychological research. Should James Steele ever return, then Dahlia was to discover just how his mind worked.

The proposal was that of an observational case study looking at the human capacity to live two or more separate lives concurrently, and the psychological effects of doing so. The research was to take Dahlia's anonymised notes on James before and after his disposition change with his sudden disappearance as an open ending.

With Charlotte's unknowing help, Dahlia and Karl had the study written up and finalised within a year and they were ready to put it through for publication. Though Dahlia found herself hesitating when she realised that she was going to turn a man's life into a part of her legacy, and a relatively miniscule part at that.

Karl showed no such reservations, and pushed Dahlia to do more than she would have had the heart to do on her own. She had not, and dared not, question her partner's interest and stake in what seemed like such a small case. Though she couldn't shake the disturbing feeling that he was having far too much fun with it.

In the late summer, roughly a week before Dahlia finalised her notes, she came face to face with James standing on the other side of her door.

What would be his final year was to start in October, and James said only a few simple words as he walked into her office that day, a look on his face as though he hadn't had a restful sleep in months.

'I'd like to finish my degree, if I may.'

Dahlia could only promise that she would do what she could and took down his up-to-date contact details before welcoming him back and sending him on his way. Her words of encouragement and cheerful disposition did nothing to visibly help his mood, though he looked so tired that she considered referring him to a medical doctor.

She wasted no time in phoning Karl, who was delighted at the news though not altogether surprised. Karl promised to help Dahlia pull some strings and get him reinstated in the university with a pass mark during his largely absent second year to guarantee him a spot in his third year studies. Dahlia had given James the excuse that his attendance and grades were enough to keep him in the course.

He returned to form before Christmas, regaining his love for learning and bringing back more and more energy and smiles with each time she saw him. Though to Dahlia's disappointment, his hedonistic lifestyle had mellowed somewhat.

He still had flings and attempts at relationships, though he spoke about them far less openly than before and with much less gusto.

Charlotte had cancelled her sessions not long after that, though she agreed to stop in every once in a while to let Dahlia know how she was getting on.

A remaining two years passed with little to go on, and Karl seemed willing to take a back seat while Dahlia got along with more important or pressing work. It wasn't until she received the news that James' father had passed away that she got the email asking if she wanted to give their subject a push.

Karl Wisemann was to organise to have James receive a large sum of money under the guise of an inheritance.

The reasons why it would help were obvious, anyone with any kind of disposition towards hedonism would be very easily persuaded to give in to vices if given the opportunity to not have to worry about financial security for a while. All Dahlia had to do was keep quiet and get in touch with him three years later, preferably in the winter, under whatever believable pretence she could think of.

And so, after putting off the study that had proven more longitudinal than anticipated, she encouraged Charlotte to convince James to come to her for an internship.

Dahlia couldn't have foreseen the effect Luke would have on him, nor could she predict that he would still cling to his slightly more prudish life upon receiving the money from Karl. But that was all part of the study, the thrill of being an onlooker came from unpredictable variables changing the subject in unknowable ways.

Karl had overstepped when he brought his subordinate to the conference without telling Dahlia, and he had only dug himself deeper into her bad side by refusing to answer her when she tried to contact him on the matter.

James had once again vanished, but this time he didn't have an unfinished degree to come back to. This time he could be gone for good, if indeed he was still alive.

'Doctor Noore?' Angela peaked around the door, she hadn't knocked.

'Yes?' Dahlia turned from the window.

'Charlotte Miles is here to see you,' she said.

'Thank you, Angela,' Dahlia said with a nod, 'please send her in.'

Angela nodded back and left the room. Dahlia looked into her almost full coffee cup, knowing it had become far too cold to drink.

***

Luke stared at Charlotte's message for a moment without really knowing what to make of it.

He didn't blame himself, at least not entirely, and part of him wanted to laugh though a different part stopped him from doing so.

Storming off was one thing, holding a grudge was another. Running away was an overreaction of cartoonish proportions that made Luke shake his head in embarrassment.

To him it was James' fault for allowing himself to take clearly in the moment words to heart. And the idea that he would take it to such an extreme was enough to make him sit down and hold his head in complete disbelief that someone really would react like that.

Still, something in him burned. He didn't have it in him to either laugh or cry, and his clashing desires to do both left him with a hollow feeling that he knew he wouldn't be able to get rid of any time soon.

Whether or not he was to blame, and in whatever capacity, didn't matter. He wanted to let it go, delete and block him from all possible methods of communication. But James' phone had been switched off for days and he wasn't on any social media, so even the act of purging him from his life was a pleasure Luke had been denied.

He convinced himself that is was a hoax, an overblown huff at the very most. James was probably in his flat, sipping on a whisky and feeling sorry for himself and Luke was going to prove it.

He would give it one more day before he went to James' flat, figuring he'd probably catch him red handed. Then he'd have the right to be mad if he felt like it.

***

'He left you his keys,' Dahlia said after giving Charlotte a moment to collect her thoughts. 'Why do you think he did that?'

'He knows I don't like where I live,' Charlotte spoke monotonously, as though she had shut down to protect herself from becoming overwhelmed by whatever emotion was currently winning out.

'It's cold,' she said, 'overpriced, and my flatmates are all teetotal and nosey.'

'You think he's given you his flat?'

'He's not using it anymore, is he?' Charlotte took a deep breath. She was speaking slowly and without her usual volume, as though she herself wasn't listening to what she was saying.

'Have you tried to get in touch?'

'Of course I have. His phone's been off for days.'

'Have you been to his flat?'

'No, I only got the letter this morning. I mean, it must have arrived before then, but I only got it today.'

'Why is that?' Dahlia crossed her legs.

'I've been working,' Charlotte answered honestly, 'haven't really been around much.'

'Do you feel guilty about admitting your feelings to him?'

'Of course I do,' a bit of colour returned to her voice, 'I should have kept quiet.'

'What would that have helped?' Dahlia cocked her head to the side.

'Huh?'

'What was your plan? Sit back and watch him have fling after fling with the odd relationship mixed in? Have your heart broken over and over until the day you either lose touch or die?'

Charlotte was left speechless for a moment. Such candour and bluntness was expected from any therapist, but Dahlia had her own particular way of speaking that really cut like a knife.

'I don't really know what my plan was,' she admitted eventually, 'I suppose I was happy enough just being close to him.'

'Clearly you weren't.'

'Even I didn't know that.'

'You haven't driven him away, Charlotte. He ran away once, he came back. He'll come back again.'

'I'm not so sure,' Charlotte turned to look out the window. Dahlia was intrigued, she moved and reacted just like James did, whether or not this was coincidence or influence wasn't clear.

'What makes you say that?'

Charlotte took a moment to think, she had tried to convince herself that, whatever was happening to James, he would snap out of it soon and come home. But no matter how hard she tried, she just couldn't convince herself that she would see him anytime soon, if indeed ever again.

'Because this time he's got nothing to come back to,' she said, the beginnings of long overdue tears forming in her eyes.

***

Andy stomped out his cigarette and immediately lit another. Phones weren't allowed in the lab and he didn't get Charlotte's message until his shift was over, it took him a little longer than he'd like to admit to realise exactly what she was talking about.

It wasn't unusual for James to not be in touch for a while, for a man who with an abundance of free time he was always pretty bad at making plans with others. He normally left the job of deciding where and when a night out would be to other people.

He had said some nasty things, but it wasn't like they had never had an argument before. They would fall out maybe once a fortnight when they lived together, but they always made up in the end, usually over a few beers.

Andy had neglected to get in touch because he assumed that before long they would meet for a pint or six, talk it out, both apologise and everything would be forgotten. It hadn't quite sank in that the opportunity to do so was gone for good.

If he had been anticipating such a reaction, Andy would have gotten in touch sooner. He didn't want to think that any of it was his fault, he was just sticking up for his partner, there was nothing wrong with that. Sure, he had been harsh, but James was never so fragile that he'd let something like that get to him. Or, at least, he hadn't been that fragile in a while.

There was something about loss that never sat right with Andy. He didn't really know how to deal with it in others let alone himself. The two of them hadn't been going out long when James' father died, and he had gone to the funeral with him. But he didn't know what to say, how to talk about it, or what to do other than ask James if he was okay over and over again.

Andy had never really faced loss himself, his close family were all alive and in good health, his breakups had always been either his decision or mutual, he didn't know James well enough back in university to really be affected by his disappearance then.

He realised then, somehow only letting it click after over an hour of thought, that James had vanished before, and he had come back. He wasn't gone forever, he was just having a bit of a huff. Most people, when tired or hurt from socialising, would sequester themselves in their homes for a while and focus on work or television while brooding.

But James was rich, for someone in their twenties anyway, so it only made sense that his huffs would be grander, more elaborate, or at least more dramatic.

He put out his third cigarette with a sigh of self-donned relief. James would be back, he just needed time. Andy didn't have to beat himself up about it.

Everyone goes through rough patches, and no one should know that better than James.

Andy convinced himself that there was no one to blame. Sometimes shit just happened. And that was good enough for him.

***

Luke had been intending on waiting until the next day to go to James' flat, but found himself feeling restless and unable to focus on anything other than his desire to find the truth. Like waiting for a reply from a crush, all attempts to distract himself were overshadowed by concern.

In the short walk from his own flat, Luke had managed to hold his head high with a confident stride as he knew he'd find James, get an apology out of him, maybe give one himself, and have everything return to normal.

No more guilt, no more drama. They would talk and it would be the end of things.

By the time he was in front of James' door, the confidence had completely vanished, replaced by a sense of unease that he had been unknowingly fighting since he received Charlotte's message that morning.

He paused without knowing why, and remembered the first time he found himself in front of that door without knowing what to expect.

The decision to go to the flat that day was just as last minute and just as uncertain. He would knock the door and deal with whatever was on the other side. As he reached up to knock on the door, he heard the lift begin to move.

A rush of déjà vu hit him hard, he was beginning to wonder if he really was living that day all over again. This time he wouldn't wimp out.

Luke had gone to the flat that day to see if James really was all Andy seemed to make him out to be. A funny, sarcastic man who seemed to somehow be as jaded as he was caring. When he finally came face to face with him, Luke had wussed out without knowing why, and had felt like an idiot for days. He hadn't told Andy about it, and James respected his unspoken wish to have it go unmentioned.

He stood and listened for the lift, half-expecting it to stop earlier, and froze when he heard it reach the top floor. He had no words prepared in his head, or at least any words he had prepared were lost to him. There was no plan and Luke suddenly felt like he did that first day, with absolutely no idea what he was doing there to begin with.

When Charlotte stepped out of the lift, Luke still didn't feel any more relaxed.

'What are you doing here?' she asked, her confusion and coldness coming through in equal measure.

'You wanted to see him too, huh?' Luke said meekly.

'Of course I did,' Charlotte walked past him as though he was invisible and brought out a set of keys.

'Are they his?'

'Yeah,' she unlocked the door and stepped inside, not holding the door open for him, just like James had done the last time Luke was there.

He went in after her anyway, flicking on the hallway light as Charlotte made her way further into the darkness. The spare keys that Charlotte had posted through the door the previous Friday were still on the floor, having been moved as the front door opened.

Charlotte stood in the middle of the living room and glanced around. James hadn't even been gone a week, but already it felt like it had been the longest time since she had seen him. She felt as though she had walked into a dead man's home, and started to recall things that seemed to happen a lifetime ago.

His rocking chair sat still in the corner by the windows, the ashtray filled with hard, black ash.

The sofa and chairs that they had built together sat, the armchairs unused, the sofa underused. The old grey one sat at the far end, Charlotte had thought before she left the week before that he likely didn't have the heart to simply get rid of it.

He always did cling to the dumbest things.

Luke looked upon the room and its fixtures in a different light. The rocking chair that always looked comfortable, the television James had been watching the mornings after they slept together. The old, ratty sofa that he had made fun of before telling James he wasn't interested in anything but his body.

Luke didn't mean it. At least, he didn't think he did. He hadn't expected James to take it so personally, it was just the ramblings of an alcohol-soaked brain. Luke didn't know what he had wanted to say, but he knew he could have phrased it better.

For Charlotte, it was a room full of memories. For Luke, regrets. For very different reasons, neither of them wanted any of it to be over.

Luke turned his attention to the coffee table, and saw the unopened package that had been there since he first set foot in the flat. He lifted it carefully, turning it in his hands to inspect the box.

'He went to Manchester over the weekend for work,' Charlotte said, 'he didn't tell anyone. He asked his boss for an extra day there, said he was visiting friends.'

'Does he have friends down there?' Luke asked, noting the Manchester return address on the package.

'No,' Charlotte said quickly, 'I think he was either planning this, or he was just keeping it as an option. Buying a day so we wouldn't get worried.'

'Guess that backfired,' Luke said, setting the box down. He remembered all the phone calls he had tried to make, worried he would come across as desperate.

'Guess it did.'

'What happened to him, Charlotte?' Luke asked, turning to her. 'What happened to make him so fragile?'

Charlotte did not meet Luke's eyes for a few seconds as she thought in silence over what to tell him, at least what details she actually knew of, before settling on her answer.

'What do you care?'

'I wouldn't be here if I didn't,' Luke said angrily.

'You're the one who said those awful things to him, you and Andy. You think it was easy for him to hear those things?'

'And what about you?' Luke barked. 'What about your feelings for him? You think *that* was easy for him?'

'How do you know about that?'

'You're not the only talker, Charlotte.' Luke said, his legs began to shake. He didn't want an argument, but he was sick of people telling him that he was so selfish, so unapologetic, so uncaring. Of course he cared, and he wanted people to finally get it through their heads.

'So you're saying this is my fault?' Charlotte raised her eyebrows.

'I'm saying it's yours, mine, Andy's and James'. It's all of ours.'

'I don't see how any of this is any of your business.'

'It became my business the moment I realised he was important,' Luke spoke quickly, his own words surprising him. But if they were true, it would explain a lot.

'What, you're in love with him too? He must give off some pheromone.'

'It's not that,' Luke said, annoyed, 'I just care about him is all.'

'Is all,' Charlotte snorted.

'What happened to him?' Luke asked again, his attention returning to the package on the coffee table.

'Do you know what it's like to give up, Luke?'

'Huh?'

'Giving up, on life. I'm not talking about suicide.'

'I don't know what you-'

'It starts like a feeling of liberation, like every single thing that had ever weighed on you suddenly seems a thousand miles away, in a different galaxy, a different lifetime. But that doesn't last

'Before long you're walking dead. Going through life being able to show enough emotions to prove that you still have them, that you still feel, but no more than that. Every step you make at self-improvement will be the half-stride of a limp man. Everything, even breathing, becomes effort after a while.

'Every conversation, every interaction, every little thing you do will seem pointless, because as far as you know it is. But if you're lucky, and I mean really, really lucky, you'll find a person, or some people, who you can live for. Bringing yourself back from the brink but still there because you get happy just by seeing them happy.

'But you'll still never escape the feeling that as much as they may profess otherwise, you'll never mean as much to them as they do to you, and you'll know it's your fault for taking such meaning and happiness just by seeing them smile and know you had something to do with it.

'They'll be your friends, but you won't be theirs, not really, or at least you'll never feel like it. You're there because you serve a purpose, and you'll live every day in fear of them realising that your purpose will outlive its usefulness, and you'll be alone and hollow again.'

'Jesus,' Luke let out a heavy sigh, 'how do you know all this?'

Charlotte looked to him with tears forming in her eyes. 'Because he told me,' she said, her lip quivering.

It made sense to him then, suddenly it didn't seem like such an overreaction, and Luke hated himself for judging his friend so harshly.

James lived to help others, to see them happy because it was the only thing that kept him going, and collectively they had all snatched that from him with no warning whatsoever.

He had never felt so terrible in his life, and he felt like he deserved to.

'He never wanted that to happen to anyone else,' Charlotte looked to the rocking chair, 'that's why he did what he did. And why he's gone.'

'I didn't know.'

'No, you didn't,' Charlotte sounded as though she wanted to still be mad at Luke but didn't have the energy to keep it up anymore. She blamed herself as much as she blamed him.

'What made him give up?' Luke asked solemnly.

Charlotte didn't answer, instead she went to the rocking chair and nudged it with her hand, watching it sway slightly before turning her attention to the view outside.

In the distance, a cruise ship floated across the water of the North Sea.

***

He arrived home that evening and was already rolling a joint before he got his shoes off. His boss had been working him hard and he needed a holiday soon. The conference had been a fun distraction, though having to spend that much time around Karl really made it difficult to relax.

He lay in bed and thought for a moment about nothing in particular before catching up on the messages of the day. He read them all and set his phone down without replying to a single one, a thought entered his head in the mist of half-hearted attempts at checking in on him and inviting him out for drinks over the weekend.

James Steele was missing.

He always was a runt, a pathetic and over-feeling narcissist who was good in bed but not good for much else. James' friends had seen him as a monster for the way he treated him, his own friends saw him as a martyr for dealing with such a desperate wreck for so long.

Neither group was right. The only real difference was that James had trouble letting go of his feelings, even after he became jaded.

He lit his joint and leant back, propping himself up with a pillow, and spent the next five minutes wondering whether or not he would make it his business to care.

***

Charlotte and Luke stayed in James' flat for a while, even though they had both only really come to see if James really had left. Luke was sure they'd find him in there, sitting in the dark and feeling sorry for himself at worst. But Charlotte knew they wouldn't, she just wanted to be there because she felt she needed to be.

Charlotte was about to make a coffee but realised there was no milk as James had thrown out all perishables from the fridge before leaving, so she settled on a chai tea instead. Luke took his coffee black without complaint, though he drank it in small sips and winced slightly at the bitterness every time.

'Why didn't he tell anyone else?' Luke said, taking a seat one of the red armchairs. It was soft, comfortable, and felt brand new even though it had been built almost two weeks earlier.

'Tell anyone what?' Charlotte sat on the sofa. Both of them had wanted to sit in the rocking chair but neither of them were going to. It wouldn't have felt right, like eating someone else's dinner. It would have felt like the ultimate intrusion into his personal space, the final step past the line that both of them had already crossed.

'What you told me,' Luke sipped and winced, 'about how he felt.'

'I guess,' Charlotte breathed deeply, 'I guess because he thought if he told anyone then they'd stop coming to him, stop trusting him the way they did. It would be the blind leading the blind, and I suppose he was worried that that was his failing anyway. He was offering advice that he himself was never gonna take, or at least didn't think would work in his case.'

'He was overthinking it,' Luke said quietly.

'Would you have come to him if you knew how he felt? How he lived? Would you have spoken to him? Hung out with him? Slept with him knowing he was that damaged?'

Luke had no idea how to answer that. The affirmative would have sounded like a lie, the negative would come across as shallow. He remained silent.

'I thought so,' Charlotte said. Luke still made no attempt to defend himself, if indeed there was anything to defend.

'Do you think it hurt?' Luke asked. He had so many questions, more than he thought, and he found himself asking them before he had really thought about them.

'I think he was happy, at least more than he once thought he could be.'

Luke felt then that the James he knew really had been a lie, a good and arguably beneficial one, but a lie nonetheless. He felt as though they were talking about a completely different person, one Luke was yet to meet, and he was beginning to wonder if Andy had said these things back when they were first going out if he would have bothered to show up that day.

He wished he'd known all this sooner, but in truth he didn't know what he would have done with the information. He knew he probably wouldn't have done anything at all.

It would have mattered when he heard it though, just like it mattered that he was hearing it now. But he wondered then, it what stage of whatever it was he and James had, would it have mattered the most. Because right then, with Charlotte in the unoccupied and echoing flat, it felt far, far too late.

'I don't know if I misjudged you or not,' Charlotte said after some silence, 'I don't know if I actually think this matters to you or if I just need someone to talk to who isn't taking notes.'

'I've done some dickish things,' Luke admitted, 'but they didn't seem dickish to me. I thought of all people you and James would understand.'

'There are lines you don't cross.'

'I know,' Luke didn't raise his voice as much as he wanted to, 'I know I've not been the best friend-'

'Person,' Charlotte glared. Luke didn't want another argument.

'Best person,' he corrected, 'but it's not like I'm a bad guy. I'm just...'

'Selfish,' Charlotte said with a sigh. 'Look, it's not like I think you're so bad either, but I just didn't want another player coming into James' life and forcing him to come to terms with things he's not ready to feel.'

'I know,' Luke said, staring into his coffee. 'At least, I know now.'

He looked around the flat again, at the high ceilings with cobwebs no one would be bothered to remove, the floors that already looked like they needed a clean and the old sofa that would likely sit unused for the rest of its time in one piece.

'What are you gonna do with the place?' he asked.

'I don't know. I'm considering moving in, but only really to keep an eye out for him.'

'Need help moving?'

'I don't have a lot of stuff.'

'Can I come over?'

'It's a free country.'

Charlotte looked tired, Luke didn't take her short answers personally.

'I can keep you company tonight if you want,' he said, 'no funny stuff, that I can guarantee.'

Charlotte smiled at that, Luke was happy to see it.

'I can't believe I'm saying this,' she rubbed the back of her neck, 'but I'd actually like that.'

11.

Angela arrived into work on Thursday morning still half expecting to see James standing outside, smoking his first cigarette of the day like always.

He had only been there a couple of weeks, and they didn't interact much at work, but she still felt as though the office was much emptier without him around. His desk remained set up in the psychology lounge and she had received no order from Dahlia to take him off the payroll.

She felt as though Dahlia knew more than she was letting on, that she somehow knew he'd be back one day. The See-All did not seem the type to do favours or establish lasting social connections on a whim. James had been her student, her patient and her employee, but that didn't make him her friend.

Dahlia had absolutely no reason that Angela could see to keep his position open, and she wondered how long it would be, how long he would have to be gone, before she made his termination official.

Angela did not have feelings for James, she hadn't felt anything for him for years, and she hadn't been hurt by his failure to remember her. She didn't know what had happened that night, but the relief on James' face to see that she hadn't taken anything too personally was welcome.

The feeling that something was indeed very wrong had only hit on the last night of the conference. James had been great company, he had been fun, but then he came back from his cigarette pale and nervous, shaking even. He spent the rest of the night drinking a lot and saying very little.

He had attempted to maintain conversation, seem okay, just like he always did. But Angela knew far too well that people have their limits, and something had happened in that five minute window of absence that had made James reach his.

She had a feeling then, as they drunkenly parted ways, that she may not see him for a while. She didn't voice this concern to James or Dahlia, thinking it was just her worrying too much, but she had to admit that she wasn't surprised when he didn't show up for work on Tuesday. She still wasn't surprised to see that he wasn't outside smoking that morning.

The lounge was empty again, she didn't need to look inside to know that. She went to her desk as usual, greeting Kay with a good morning before turning on her computer without sitting down and going to the staff kitchen to grab a coffee while she waited for it to boot up.

It wasn't worry that was swimming around Angela's head while the cheap coffee machine gurgled and steamed, it wasn't concern or fear. It was anger.

If there was one thing Angela hated, it was being kept out of the loop. Someone knew what had happened to him, and that someone was most likely Dahlia. If asked, she would hide behind confidentiality and expertly feigned ignorance.

Confidant

Angela had seen and processed enough to see that Dahlia enjoyed games, especially ones with human lives, and James' employment and station had the doctor's idea of fun written all over it. And it made Angela mad.

She had tried to be a friend as well as a colleague, but as she walked past that lounge and saw James sitting at his desk doing a lot of not much at all, she felt as though she was walking by a fish tank or hamster cage rather than an office. He was a commodity, something to be observed when bored, a piece of furniture that could walk, talk and provide entertainment.

There were certain kinds of psychologists who took the social aspect way too far in Angela's opinion. Dahlia was one of them. Angela had wanted to show James that he was doing good, that she was happy to see him every day he was in, she had done her best to make him feel like a human being and counterbalance whatever it was Dahlia was doing.

And she thought she had been succeeding until that night.

She was not about to give up her degree, nor was she about to question the doctor openly, but she would spend the remainder of her time there in a state of unforgiving for what was considered an acceptable way to treat a human being.

It didn't matter whether or not Angela and James were friends, it didn't matter that they were colleagues, it only mattered that he was a human person, a reportedly damaged one at that, and he was being used for something Angela wasn't at all comfortable with.

She added milk and one sugar to her coffee, stirring it without looking with a teaspoon she didn't check to see was clean. Dahlia shared her better, more expensive coffee with guests and co-workers when they had meetings, alcohol if it was the late afternoon. Angela didn't know what she would say next time she was in that room, if she would be able to hold back her questions or anger while she sipped on whatever pricey beverage the time of day called for.

She made her way back into her tiny shared office and sat at her desk, she had absolutely no idea what to expect from that day despite the fact that it really shouldn't be different from any other workday.

Angela had made up her mind already. The moment she received the order to remove James from the payroll, she would begin to type up her letter of resignation from the office of Doctor Dahlia Noore.

***

Andy had hoped to wake up in Luke's bed that morning, or wake up in his own beside Luke. Either way, he had not wanted to wake up alone.

They had been messaging the evening before until Andy had gone to bed, but he awoke with no less unease than he had gone to sleep with. Somehow the idea of Charlotte and Luke hanging out together made him more uncomfortable than the idea that Luke had almost definitely been sleeping with James.

He had nothing against either of them, he considered them both friends, but he knew they were at odds with each other, and he didn't like the thought of them bonding over James' disappearance.

Andy had been hoping to keep the two of them more or less separated for as long as he could, at least long enough for them to practically be strangers again before trying to blend the two.

The two of them being at each other's throats over everything, yet bonding over one thing, worried him. If they spent too much time together then the negativity would eventually win out. Andy was afraid that, sooner or later, he would be given an ultimatum and have to choose between the two of them.

He would need to make the decision between one of his best friends and the man he was in love with.

Andy shook his head and got out of bed despite feeling like he could do with some more sleep. He was beginning to think like James, sensitive to what ifs and baseless thoughts that hadn't actually gone anywhere yet.

Two of the most important people in his life seemed to be getting along. This was a good thing and he wouldn't think more of it.

He made his coffee while wearing a dressing gown, his half asleep eyes not really able to focus on anything for too long. He went about his morning routine on autopilot, both out of his fatigue and his want to not really think for a while.

His shift the evening before had been a late one, and he wasn't due back in the lab until noon, so he had a few hours of nothing before he needed to leave.

He considered stopping by James' flat, but knew that doing so would do no one any good, much less himself. If James was there, he would have been told. If he wasn't, he would just let unnecessary worries cloud his mind for the day.

With just a sip of his fresh coffee, Andy was already feeling more alive and happier than he did when he woke up. Fishing a lighter out of his jeans on the living room floor, he lit a cigarette and turned his attention to the window. He wondered if it was going to snow that day, then he wondered if it was snowing where James was.

If it was, then he was probably enjoying it.

***

The tension had been palpable in the office recently. Dahlia had plenty to keep her busy, but Angela had been quieter for the past week and Karl had still shown no interest in returning any of her messages.

Dahlia began to doubt the reasons why she had agreed to such a study to begin with. Ethical limitations on psychological research in recent decades meant that anything along the lines of Milgram or Zimbardo would never be replicated to any notable degree without a hell of a lot of luck and half a lifetime of work.

Even should more up to date studies be successful, the level of ethicality expected meant something of a stagnation was inevitable. One could never hope to prove anything in psychology, one could only back up theories, theories that were either widely accepted already or most likely doomed to fail.

Dahlia had gotten bored of null hypotheses, p-values and findings just under the line of significance long ago. She had a name to live up to, a legacy of her own to build, she was wasting her life in that expensive, new-build office while her own nephew was already making waves in the pharmaceutical business.

Informed consent, debriefings, deception guidelines, right to withdrawal. All things that made Dahlia feel as though she would go to the grave with nothing to show for it but her name on a few dusty books that would rot away in the dark corner of whatever library was unfortunate enough to stock her measly findings.

She would be a footnote.

James' case wasn't a breakthrough, it wasn't particularly unique or special, but it was something. Double lives were easy to carry out, most people did it without even realising. Work and home, spouse and lover, drunk and sober. The case study regarding James Steele was merely a gateway to a grander piece of research so far relatively untouched by the psychological community.

Being able to live multiple lives at once and controlling, to an extent, how often and in what capacity they interacted with each other. James' case would be a foundation upon which she could build her research, make a name for herself outside of that miserable university department.

The reason James was of particular interest was solely due to the fact that, unlike most people, he was aware of the natural dichotomy to his life. He was a bi- or pan-sexual man with a fondness for life and study. He worked, he played, he drank, he fucked, he studied, he learned, he grew.

He was as immature as he was mature, and for a while he had the perfect balance, one which Dahlia could use to get a foothold on the wider research without too much scoffing or doubt from her peers.

She had so many pressing matters, and his case was relatively small in the grander scheme, but she hated leaving work unfinished. She was sick of inconclusive findings and loose threads hanging around her career like a poorly sewn jumper that had been caught on a nail.

She had a name for herself, she was well respected. She was healthy and young enough still to continue making her family proud. But the idea of losing a patient, a research subject, a student and an employee all in one would never sit right with her.

Dahlia was going to find out what happened to James, she would tell herself it was all professional. She had everything she needed for her study. Hell, even with James gone, she had enough to build her case and propose it to her colleagues. With each passing day of James' absence, she considered doing just that.

She had what she needed, she would fight for the funding and go ahead to carry out the research in full. But something still made her hesitate, something that would make her wait a little while longer.

All she needed was a satisfying ending.

***

Luke had already gone to work by the time Charlotte got up. He had taken the sofa and she slept in the spare room, her clothes from the last night she spent there were still folded on the bed.

Neither of them had wanted to take James' bed for the same reason neither of them had sat in the rocking chair the evening before. It simply wouldn't feel right.

Luke had neatly folded the spare blanket and pillow on the side of the sofa and opened the blinds to let in the morning light. Charlotte wondered if he knew to do that from the nights he had spent there or if it was something he had done for himself.

She opened the fridge and saw that Luke had gone to the corner shop to buy a small bottle of milk before he left for the day. She felt bad for thinking he was so selfish, and again considered that she had likely underestimated him before she lifted the milk from the shelf and realised it had already been opened.

He had been wincing at the bitterness of his black coffee the evening before, clearly only really suffering through it for the caffeine rather than anything else. Maybe he was just thinking about himself after all.

As she stirred the milk into her coffee she realised that he had gone to the shop, got the milk and then returned when he easily could have walked to his own place or got a coffee on the way to, or at, his office.

In just under ten seconds, her opinion of Luke had changed three times, and she was beginning to think that her judge of character was not at all reliable, even to her.

Was she wrong or right about Luke? About James? Hell, about anyone?

How many friendships had she terminated prematurely? How many had she clung to when she shouldn't have?

Did James really not realise how selfish he was being?

And there it was, the thought that she had been burying for years but only had to start fighting in recent days.

Just how much more pain was she really willing to put herself through for the sake of someone who would just up and leave without telling her? Had he deliberately set out to Manchester with the intent of never coming back? Or had he simply made the decision then and there?

Did something else happen? And if so then why didn't he tell her? Were they not friends? Was she not here to help him in the same way he helped her and a dozen others?

These were questions Charlotte was angry to have to ask, and she was angry at James for making her ask them. Years of friendship, years of pain he knew he put her through, all ended with a hotel envelope and a set of house keys.

She had felt a lot of things as a result of James, but anger was still a new one, and she wasn't sure she liked it.

Charlotte brought her coffee into the living room and sat in the rocking chair, her attention to the view outside as she sipped and realised she had neglected to add sugar. She didn't care enough, though.

She was angry at James for leaving, and even angrier at him for the way he left. And it was all thanks to an open bottle of milk.

The new furniture was going to go to waste if she didn't do anything, Luke's milk would go off if not drank and Charlotte had been wanting to move out of her draughty ground floor room for a while. She didn't know whether or not she would be able to live there, or even if that was what James had intended when he posted his keys.

He wouldn't have his phone switched off if he was just going away for a while, meaning the keys weren't just an over the top way of asking her to look after the place. She didn't have the legal right or documentation to sell it or rent it out. And if she was to stay, then she could wait for him to come back.

Charlotte couldn't believe her own thoughts.

Wait for him to come back. Like a well trained dog wagging its tail for a master that would rather fuck strangers than give her the time of day.

She knew that wasn't the case, but she was still mad at him.

Yes, she would move in, and she'd start charging him rent the moment he got back. After a good smack on the ear, of course, for leaving in the first place.

She smirked at the thought and rocked gently in the chair while nursing her coffee, but stopped dead in her tracks when a knock sounded at the door.

She set her coffee down and stood up, not knowing why she had suddenly become so tense before realising that if James had come back then he would have no way of opening the locked door. Her body relaxed, though she still didn't know why, when she remembered half way down the hall the Luke similarly had no way of locking the door behind him when he left.

She opened the door without checking the peephole, to see someone she had only met a few times in the past, and even then only briefly.

'Lorraine?'

'Oh, hi,' Lorraine looked confused, 'Charlotte, right?'

'Yeah,' Charlotte almost held out her hand.

'Is James here?'

'No. He's, um, out,' she didn't know why she was lying.

'Oh, do you know when he'll be back?'

'No,' Charlotte said honestly, 'he's on a business trip. Do you want to come in?'

It felt weird to invite someone in to someone else's flat like that. Charlotte stopped for a second to wonder why she had been so tense at the idea that it may have been James behind that door, and why she relaxed upon realising that it most likely wasn't him.

She knew she was mad, but she felt bad about feeling good about not seeing him.

'Uh, No. Thanks. So why are you here?' Lorraine asked.

'He asked me to look after the place while he's gone.'

'Business trip?' Lorraine asked, 'I thought he was unemployed?'

Charlotte paused. Had it really been this long since James had spoken to her?

'He, uh, got a temp position at the uni. I think he was bored,' Charlotte felt uncomfortable.

'Weird, why didn't he ask Andy to look after it, aren't they still together? He does live here, right?'

Charlotte looked to Lorraine for a moment. She knew without a doubt that James had spoken to Lorraine in the last month, long after he and Andy broke up, and Lorraine had definitely been in that flat recently and, for a while, often.

'Uh, no. They broke up.'

'Sucks,' Lorraine said with no emotion at all.

'Jesus,' Charlotte breathed.

'What's up?'

'I just remembered I have an errand to run,' Charlotte said, she had the distinct impression that it didn't matter whether or not her lie was convincing.

'Oh, okay. I'll go. Tell James to message me when he gets back? I need to tell him that Travis and I aren't splitting and I'll still need to talk to him. He's not answering his phone.'

James' phone had been switched off for at least three days.

'Sure, will do.'

'Thanks,' Lorraine didn't look to Charlotte as she walked back towards the lift.

Charlotte didn't get it. Lorraine had been coming to James for sessions for a long time and the two of them had been friends for a while before that, more than that at one point.

She returned to the living room and sat back down on the rocking chair. She lifted her coffee off the window sill and sipped at it, thinking to herself.

Confidant

Lorraine likely considered herself to be James' friend, but she didn't even know about him and Andy, nor did she even know that he was living alone. No one was that inattentive or forgetful, no one was that uncaring about someone who they had been trying to contact.

Only one explanation out of the dozens possible stuck in Charlotte's mind like a squirming fly stuck in a spider's web.

For the entirety of their friendship, Charlotte had believed that James considered his friends to be his patients, that he had seen his role in life as that of an ear. But he hadn't shared any details about his personal life with Lorraine, her and Charlotte had only ever met by coincidental timing and she was never out drinking with them.

Come to think of it, David was often nowhere to be seen either. He would occasionally show up to parties and the pub but rarely stayed long and he and James didn't talk much if at all.

To Charlotte, this meant that James had a divide that he had never told anyone about. There were those who were friends, those who were patients, and those who were both.

It was a leap, but Charlotte felt as though it was right. He wasn't cold and unfeeling, he wasn't just bouncing from day to day. He had friends, he had people he felt he could count on when he needed them, people who would be there for him the way he was for them.

And they had taken that away from him.

Charlotte suddenly felt uncomfortable sitting in that chair, and she got up and moved to one of the armchairs.

It was all so confusing. Was he overreacting, or should they have seen it coming? What was it that tipped him over the edge? Who was to blame, if anyone?

Charlotte sighed deeply, she decided she wasn't going to leave the flat that day. She would sleep there, but only in the spare room. She would keep the flat clean, but not personalise it in any way.

She would live in that flat, but it would forever belong to James, even if he never came back. And the possibility that he wouldn't was looking more and more likely by the minute.

Charlotte sank into the seat. Why did he leave? Was he going to come back?

And if so, why?

***

'Charlotte said that?' Andy asked before taking a gulp of his pint, reducing the glass to half full.

'Yeah, I mean, he never told you? You did live with him,' Luke was only a few sips into his own drink, having spent the last few minutes quoting what Charlotte had told him to the best of his recollection.

'We didn't talk much about that kind of thing,' Andy leant back, 'at least *he* didn't.'

'He never told you about before he vanished? The first time, I mean.'

'Not really, I didn't know him that well back then and Charlotte always warned me not to pry. I tried a few times, sure, but he just kept saying it was ancient history.'

'To think,' Luke sighed, 'he was hiding that much pain all this time.'

'Oh, fuck off,' Andy barked, making Luke jump. 'It's not like he's alone in that. Everyone's hiding something like that, no one's ever really as happy as they make themselves out to be. And those who are are all miserable fuckers who just being everybody down.'

'You don't really think that?'

'Of course I do,' Andy leant forward and lifted his pint again, 'why do you think therapists are a thing, why Dahlia's in business or why people, including me, ever went to James in the first place?'

'Someone to talk to?'

'Exactly,' Andy took another heavy swig, 'everyone has someone they go to to unload all their shit, even if they don't want advice for it, just so they can be fun around other people.'

'It's not just about that,' Luke said defensively, 'people want to be happy for themselves. They wanna sleep well at night and enjoy the lives they have.'

'Well, yeah,' Andy said, 'but that normally comes from others. Self-worth, good memories, confidence. It's all because of how others see us.'

'What's gotten into you?' Luke lifted his own drink and took a heavy swig of his own, he wanted to keep pace.

'I don't know,' Andy sighed, 'I'm pissed off.'

'At James?'

'Him, me, my boss, Charlotte. How is she, by the way?'

'Coping,' Luke turned his attention to his drink and wished he'd gotten something lighter, easier to rush. 'She'll be fine.'

'I'll call her tomorrow,' Andy said, calming down. 'Sorry, it's been a long week.'

'Don't worry about it,' Luke said sadly.

'Do you think she'll move into the flat?'

'I don't know, maybe she'll stick around to see if he comes back.'

'Lucky her,' Andy smirked, 'it's a nice place.'

'Yeah,' Luke sighed again, 'why didn't he leave it to you, anyway?' he hoped he wasn't brining up any harsh feelings.

'He's known Charlotte longer,' Andy said with a shrug, 'he knows she doesn't like her house and, to be honest, I did complain about the place a lot when I lived there. It gets cold in winter, and it's too out of the way.'

'So's my flat,' Luke said awkwardly.

'Yeah, but I don't live there,' Andy said warmly.

'Been a while since I've been here,' Luke admired The Regal, realising a little too late that it hadn't been a long time since he's been there, it had just been a long time since he and Andy drank together.

They both realised it then. For boyfriends, the two of them almost never hung out.

'Would you rather be out drinking with him?' Andy asked after a silence neither of them found comfortable.

'What?'

'He's good to drink with, always seems to know how to make people laugh. I'm just being a downer.'

'Hey,' Luke leant forward and touched Andy's hand, 'of course not. I miss him, sure, more than I ought to in fact, but I like being with you.'

'Like, huh?' Andy sighed and moved his hand away and lifted his glass back up to his lips. He paused just before taking a sip. 'You did sleep with him, didn't you?'

'Yeah,' he saw no reason to keep it a secret, not anymore.

'Thanks,' Andy said with a small smile, 'for telling me, I mean.'

'You're not mad?'

"Course not,' he said, holding up his glass, 'next round's yours, though.'

Luke couldn't help but chuckle and hold up his still mostly full glass. Andy could be stressed, he could be a downer. But he was easy to talk to, he was there for Luke and stood up for him when he felt down or fragile. They were a good fit, and he knew it.

The reason they didn't hang out so much was because they didn't have to. They were there for each other no matter what. They both knew it but both worried, still. They would take comfort in what they had, and what they had was each other.

***

'You know,' Maggie began with a mouthful of apple, 'I never took you for the sugar daddy type.'

'What?' Charlotte was just about finished packing up the last of three boxes of her stuff.

'He gave you a flat, Honey,' Maggie raised an eyebrow, 'what else do you call that?'

'He's just a mate,' Charlotte said, managing to not sound defensive, 'and he didn't *give* me the flat, I'm just looking after it for him. Besides, he's younger than me.'

'Mate, right, the gay guy?'

'He also goes by James.'

'Goes or went?'

'No, Maggie,' Charlotte pointed to her, 'not now.'

'Sorry, sorry,' she held up both her arms. 'This is just pretty sudden, Pet. Do you have to leave tonight?'

'No, but if I don't I'll freeze. Sorry to leave you hanging like this.'

'You're paid up and bills are included. No skin off my nose. But I am gonna miss you, Honey,' she held out her arms and Charlotte hugged her tight.

'Hey,' she said, patting Maggie softly on the back, 'I'm not moving away, I'm just moving out, and probably not forever. Come visit, okay?'

'Come visit your new penthouse? Yeah, I think I will,' she said dramatically.

'I think that's the last of it,' Charlotte said, looking at the small beer boxes that contained everything she owned, or at least everything she could be bothered to bring with her. 'I could have sworn I owned more stuff than this.'

'Yeah,' Maggie agreed, 'but it's not like you're moving in to your own place, right?'

'Right,' Charlotte really was beginning to convince herself.

'Want me to keep the room free for you?'

'I'll have to get back to you on that,' she said, hoping it was a satisfactory answer. 'Is Franny about?'

'No, she's out with her new boyfriend, why?'

'Good,' Charlotte let out a relieved sigh, 'was hoping to not have to see her.'

'Meow,' Maggie acted surprised, 'she's not that bad.'

'She put my towel in the toilet because she didn't like the colour.'

'She was in a mood!'

'She's *always* in a mood,' Charlotte rolled her eyes. 'Anyway, it's old news. Let me know if she moves out and I'll come right back, okay?'

'I know you're joking,' Maggie snickered, 'but I will.'

'That'll be the cab,' Charlotte said as she saw a car pull up outside, 'drinks tomorrow?'

'On you,' Maggie insisted, 'now that you're rent free.'

'Of course,' Charlotte smiled and hugged her friend. She didn't feel as sad as she thought she would, and she didn't know whether or not to feel bad about that.

12.

It would be two weeks before Charlotte felt at all comfortable in that flat, at least for more than an hour or so at a time.

She had gone through every channel she thought she should. There had been a missing persons report filed, though the police didn't seem to prioritise the situation at all, which to her was fair enough.

James had checked out of his hotel and posted the keys himself. The only recent finger prints had been from the hotel staff, Dahlia Noore and James himself. His was being treated as a runaway case and, being in his mid-twenties, the police did not dance around the fact that, other than an official post on their social media sites which they urged her to share as much as she could, there would be little to no action taken on their part.

She had thanked them and given her contact details, knowing she would likely never hear from them again. She had done all she could, but still felt as though she hadn't done nearly enough.

She bought a Christmas tree, something she never thought she would see in that flat, a small plastic one that somehow still shed needles everywhere.

The callers had stopped coming, Lorraine never came back and David seemed to profess more concern than Charlotte suspected actually felt. Charlotte had no idea just what James was going through, he must have known that some of the people he had devoted time, attention and caffeine to wouldn't give him the time of day or a single worried thought should he disappear, but he stayed and helped them anyway, even though he didn't have to.

She considered putting waiting room back up, just to make the place feel right again, but realised that would invite the idea that he had come back to the visitors and wouldn't be fair on those who did call round to see if he was back.

A few of the callers Charlotte didn't recognise, even their names were new to her. She began to wonder just how much there was that James hadn't told her, and just how much she would probably never learn.

With the exception of the Christmas tree and the wardrobe half filled with Charlotte's clothes, the flat was more or less the same as it was when James left. She had stuck to her decision to preserve it as best she could, making herself only at home enough to be comfortable living there, but not so comfortable that it stopped being his flat and became hers. Though her stance on that had begun to waver.

James' phone was still off, and Charlotte doubted that he even had it on him anymore. As time went by she started to feel less concerned. Her worry was gradually being replaced with unease, which itself was dulling over time. She tried to hold on to it, because to let go of it would be to let go of James, to give up.

She missed him dearly, as did Andy and Luke, who made sure she was never alone for too long.

On digging around for wrapping paper she knew she had seen around before, Charlotte came across the landline phone that had come with James' Wi-Fi modem. She plugged it in and checked the number, deciding to leave it there just in case he had no other way of getting in touch.

It was a meaningless and empty effort, but one that gave her comfort nonetheless. The first few times it rang she leapt to it immediately before hanging up on the cold caller of the day, understanding why James had unplugged and hidden the thing to begin with.

By the fifth day of the phone's new life, Charlotte had become much more numb to its ring, though she still answered it every time just in case.

It was a week before Christmas when Charlotte left the university library for the last time before she took a break. Even though it wasn't that long until January would rear its ugly head with its false promises and return to form after a week's worth of binge drinking and eating, to Charlotte it felt like it was too far in the future to worry about. And that suited her just fine.

The central plaza that housed the library was wet and slick as the snowfall had just begun. Charlotte stepped out and lit a cigarette. She had picked up the habit because of Andy, who had drunkenly convinced her that the slight hint of tobacco scent was part of the flat's aesthetic and should be kept. She still wasn't quite used to it, and smoked very rarely, but she had definitely come to appreciate the five minutes outside to take stock of whatever had gone on in whatever building she happened to be exiting.

It hadn't been snowing when Charlotte entered the library early that afternoon, and the graceful white specks dancing in the glow of the buildings that evening seemed to be the stuff of fairy tales.

'Charlotte?' Angela approached her, 'is that you?'

'Angie,' she smiled.

'I didn't know you smoked?'

'Recent habit,' she admitted, 'it's dumb, I know. But it does help.'

'I get that,' Angela said, though Charlotte imagined she didn't get it at all.

'Just out of work?'

'Uh, yeah,' Angela fixed her glasses for some reason, 'just finished up my last day.'

'Last?'

'Yeah, handed in my notice. I got all the credit I need for my degree and need to focus more on my studies, y'know?' Angela spoke awkwardly, hesitantly and without making eye contact. Charlotte got the impression that there was more to it, but didn't want to pry.

'Hey,' Charlotte said warmly, sensing that Angela wasn't in the mood to be on her own, 'you hungry? I haven't eaten all day and would kill for a burger.'

'That'd be nice, if you don't mind?'

'Not at all,' Charlotte smiled, 'I could use the company.'

Most of the undergraduates had already gone home for the Christmas break, but the cafés were all full of youngsters holding mugs of hot chocolate and mochas with both hands as the heating systems and crowded rooms seemed to do nothing to fight the cold chill of the increasingly snowy evening.

The upside of this was obvious to both of them, and they each grabbed a pasty from the campus bakery just before it closed and headed to Omega for drinks.

'I don't know why I didn't take you for a wine person,' Charlotte began as they both sat down.

'I didn't think you were into beer,' Angela said, looking at Charlotte's stomach.

'Luck of my genes, I assure you,' Charlotte smiled, 'I should be a blimp by now.'

'You can worry yourself thin, you know,' Angela said. Charlotte wasn't sure who of the two of them she was speaking to more.

'So why did you leave?' Charlotte asked, 'I have to admit I don't know a lot about what you do, but James always said you seemed passionate.'

'He did?' she blushed, 'I don't know if passionate is the word but I enjoyed it.'

'So what's the story? Too much work?'

'Nah, I made up my mind to leave when James was taken off the payroll.'

'He's been getting paid this whole time?'

'Yeah, Dahlia was convinced he'd come back, as we all were, and she's keeping his desk where it is,' she took a deep breath, 'but as far as the department is concerned, James doesn't work there anymore.'

'Makes sense,' Charlotte said quietly, 'but why did that make you quit? I didn't realise you were that close.'

'We weren't, really,' she admitted, lifting her wine, 'but I sort of got uncomfortable with what Dahlia's been doing. Seemed like I needed a change of company.'

'What do you mean what she's been doing?' Charlotte asked, the concern in her voice was obvious.

'It's not important,' Angela sipped her wine, 'it was just time to move on.'

'So what are you gonna do now?'

'I don't know,' she sighed, 'I've got a lot of uni work to do, and a reference from Doctor Noore carries a lot of weight, so I'm not worried.'

'Lucky you, I've got no idea what I want to do,' Charlotte said, realising it was the first time she had ever admitted it out loud.

'Whatever pays the rent,' Angela said, trying not to make it sound too depressing.

'Not like I have that to worry about either,' Charlotte tried to sound aloof.

'Oh?'

'Yeah, I'm living in James' old,' she stopped herself, 'James' flat.'

'Ah,' Angela sighed deeply, 'you haven't heard from him either, huh?'

'No,' Charlotte said, it didn't hurt as much to admit it. 'When you think about it, he's just doing what we did to him, just a bit more dramatically.'

'What do you mean?'

'It's not important,' Charlotte sipped her beer, 'not anymore.'

'How about we focus on something less depressing?'

'Hell yes,' Charlotte laughed, 'I'd say we're overdue for a catch up.'

'I'll say,' Angela said happily. She made the decision to not bring up what Charlotte had said to her in the office the last time they ran into each other, it seemed like so long ago and she had a point, it didn't matter anymore.

***

Dahlia sat in her office with nothing but the monitor and a desk lamp providing her light. She could see the snow hitting the window and imagined how cold it must be outside. She had a whisky to in her left hand and a mouse in her right.

It had been over an hour since she finished typing, and she had reread what she written more times than she cared to count. Her eyes were starting to ache and her heart was getting no lighter.

Before her, preceding the blinking curser, was James Steele's case study. A long-term observational look into the human capability of leading a double or triple life and its adverse effects. In a separate window she had an email regarding the potential to build on the study with many volunteers and how such a lifestyle, or lifestyles, could be affected by individual differences.

The proposal had been thought out, her arguments as clearly presented as she could make them. The case had been attached to the email along with various notes, citations, appendices, her and Karl Wisemann's contact details and a scanned Missing Person's Report she felt ethically obliged to include, though she wasn't entirely sure why.

Everything was ready, and she knew she would go on with the research whether or not she gained approval. She knew the ethical limitations and how to get around them when she could, she had enough sway to nudge the correct authorities and funding wouldn't be a problem if she was denied it by the greater community.

She had given up on waiting for the ending she wanted, on waiting for James to return. Angela's resignation upon the order to have him officially removed did not come as a surprise. She had seen and likely heard too much at that conference, and while her future in the field was bright. she was never going to be a protégé of Dahlia's. Or, at least, she'd never be comfortable as one.

All that was left was to hit send, then the real work would begin. The fun work, the work she had been looking forward to for a long time.

But with it came a hesitation. To send off what she had written would prove James to be a pawn and nothing more. If he were to return then he would never trust her again, there would be no more data, there would be nothing more to build on with her proverbial patient zero.

No matter how well she had anonymised the research, she would lose him.

'Fuck it,' she said, the seldom-used word feeling salty in her mouth.

She drank the remainder of her whisky in one swig, switched tabs, and sent the email.

She leant back then, realising for the first time that what had amounted to seven years of curiosity and intrigue was about to become a very big part of her career, indeed her life.

All there was to do now was wait, both for replies from her peers, and Karl's undoubtedly smug retort.

Her time with James was done, and she would miss it. She might even miss him. Without him she had no doubt that things would get interesting for those he had surrounded himself with.

But she wondered, would the lost little fish flap helplessly upon the banks of their tributary, never to find their way back to the current they struggled yet yearned to follow? Or would they thrive in their new and unexpected home? Perhaps someday evolving legs with which to walk upon the shore and discover that the river from which they crawled ran to nowhere in particular after all?

She wondered if she would ever get those answers, and if indeed they would still be relevant when she did.

***

'Come on, man,' Andy called from the living room, 'we're gonna be late!'

'It's a Christmas party,' Luke said, wondering in to the room with his shirt only half buttoned, 'not a business meeting. I think we can afford to be fashionably late.'

'We were on track to be fashionably late twenty minutes ago,' Andy fixed his tie with his reflection in a picture frame.

'Are you absolutely sure this is a formal thing?' Luke said, buttoning his shirt and grimacing at the tie Andy had left for him on the sofa.

'Positive,' Andy started fixing his hair, 'apparently Karl Wisemann will even be there.'

'Whoop-dee-doo,' Luke lifted the tie.

'He's my boss's boss's boss's boss's boss, man. I make a good impression and I'm in.'

'Then why am I coming?' Luke sighed, 'since when am I known for good impressions?'

'People like the gays,' Andy shrugged, 'we get, I dunno, leeway or whatever.'

'Kind of a shitty attitude,' Luke grimaced.

'Play your strengths.'

'Being gay is a strength?'

'It is when you work in an inclusive twenty first century company.'

'I guess?'

'Great, we gotta go.' Andy kissed Luke on the cheek and made his way to the door to put his shoes on.

Luke took a moment to smile to himself. Andy was overthinking things, they were going to a party, Christmas was coming up and the world seemed to be in balance again.

Everything was returning to normal, and even though that was a touch boring for Luke's tastes, at least it was safe.

'You coming or not?' Andy called from the hallway.

'Be right there!' Luke looked to the sofa. He remembered how startled he had been when James had leant down out of nowhere and kissed him for the first time. He remembered leaning into it, even dragging James closer. He remembered how good it would feel, and he knew that even though it would take him a little while longer to accept that it would never happen again, he was happy that it had happened to begin with.

'Taxi here in five!' Andy called out.

'Okay,' Luke finished tying his tie and put his hand on the light switch.

He would feel ridiculous saying goodbye to a one-time occupied spot, but he had already taken to thinking of James' flat as Charlotte's, at least he was trying to. He smiled without knowing why, and switched off the light.

***

Angela was in the mood to celebrate by the time her and Charlotte arrived at the penthouse.

There had been some hesitation, but Charlotte's news that Luke had left an unopened bottle of wine in the kitchen was enough to convince Angela to keep the night going, though she had successfully argued against going to a club beforehand.

'Only one wine glass,' Angela was looking through the cupboard.

'Suits me fine,' Charlotte said, opening a beer. Angela had somehow forgotten that her friend was not a wine drinker.

Charlotte was glad for the company, but more than anything she was happy to have someone over who would actually think of the flat as hers. Angela had never set foot in that flat, no memories, good or otherwise, to taint their mood or conversation. It was perfect.

'Wow,' Angela said as she stepped inside the living room, craning her head to look at the high ceilings before seeing the distant lights across the water in the distance.

'Nice, huh?' Charlotte said smugly, 'wish I could take credit.'

'It's gorgeous,' she admired the sofa.

'Now that I can take credit for,' Charlotte took a seat in one of the armchairs while Angela got comfortable on the sofa.

'Good colour,' she said, 'suits me,' she lifted her glass of wine. 'Though I'll do my best not to spill a drop.'

'Relax,' Charlotte said warmly, 'don't worry about a thing.'

'Thanks,' Angela smiled.

'You know,' Charlotte began, 'I remember thinking we'd be really good friends back then.'

'Back then?'

'First year, criminology. We hung out all the time, remember?'

'Yeah,' Angela recalled, 'you helped me with forensics.'

'God, yeah,' Charlotte groaned, 'I remember thinking that was gonna be so much more fun than it was.'

'I thought it was alright,' Angela shrugged, 'difficult, but alright.'

'I think it was that module that made me say fuck it,' Charlotte said, wondering just how she had come to the decision to leave that minor.

'You left, too?'

'Yeah, bollocks to it,' she waved her hand in the air.

'We'll be graduating together won't we?'

'I reckon so,' Charlotte drank.

'I can't get over how nice this place is,' Angela turned her attention back to the ceiling, then the window, then briefly over the old grey sofa for returning to admire the new, comfier sofa she was sitting on.

'It is nice, huh?' Charlotte smiled, 'what's your gaff like, then?'

The slang from her teenage years was returning to her, a sure sign that she was drunk and in a good mood.

'Same place,' Angela said with a distinct lack of pride, 'haven't budged an inch.'

'Wait,' Charlotte sat forward awkwardly, 'you're still in halls?'

'Yup,' Angela said, the word coming out of her mouth like a bark. 'I kept asking and they kept giving it to me, don't know how but it's kind of depressing watching everyone around me stay the same age while I just get older.'

'Now you fuck off with that shite right now,' Charlotte pointed at nothing in particular, 'Twenty six, wait, how old are you? Whatever. Twenty whatever ain't old.'

'I know,' Angela laughed, 'I'm just at the end of my-'

'Move in here,' Charlotte leant back in her chair and started swirling her beer in her hand.

'What?'

'Move in here, it's not like I'm paying rent and I could use the company.'

'But isn't this-'

'None of that,' Charlotte sat up again, unsure as to what was the best way to sit to make her seem more sober. 'I've been meaning to take the main bedroom anyway and, to be honest, I don't like how much this place echoes.'

Charlotte paused for a moment, suddenly she felt the alcohol ware off, even though she knew that couldn't have been the case. Her thoughts seemed to be sobering her up, she felt as though she needed it even as she took another heavy swig of her beer.

'I mean this is just drunk talk, right?' Angela laughed awkwardly, 'We don't really know each other.'

'You never really know someone until you get shitfaced with them.'

'Good logic.'

'Always been my motto,' Charlotte held up her bottle, 'so let's assume it's not drunk talk. What do you say?'

Angela looked to the ceiling for a third time, she imagined her own room then, the room she had lived in for the last seven years. It was tiny, the bathroom was communal. She could brush her teeth from her bed and the undergrads were driving her nuts as the old brick walls blocked absolutely no sound.

She could afford better, but she didn't like the idea of moving. At least her tiny room was something she was familiar with, she knew what to expect and hadn't really considered risking ending up somewhere worse.

'I'd like that,' Angela said eventually, 'I'm paid up for next term already, so I can always go back if it doesn't work out. But maybe we should talk about this when it's not,' she checked her phone, 'half one in the morning.'

'Count on it,' Charlotte beamed.

'You going home for Christmas?' Angela wanted to change the subject. While the offer had touched her, and she had already chosen to accept it, she didn't want to finalise any important decisions with so much wine in her head.

'Nah, my family isn't the festive type. You?'

'Probably,' Angela said quietly, 'they live in Manchester and I hate it there, but at least there'll be plenty of food.'

'And booze.'

Charlotte looked to the Christmas tree that she had bought, the erratically decorated little thing sat in the corner with a few presents underneath it that Charlotte herself had wrapped with the elegance of a blind tyrannosaurus.

She had no idea what she was going to do for Christmas, and had imagined spending it alone with no real thought to the holiday. She made up her mind then to ask around, maybe even learn how to cook a turkey.

She would celebrate the winter one way or another.

'It's snowing,' Angela said with a childish glee. Together they looked to the window.

'Yeah,' Charlotte said solemnly, 'it's pretty.'

'You reckon you'll be here a while, then?' Angela asked.

'I reckon so, yeah,' Charlotte didn't take her eyes off the window.

'It's a really nice place,' Angela said, knowing she had likely complimented the flat a bit too much. 'Hey, Charlotte?'

'Yeah?'

'Thanks for tonight, I don't normally have the time for nights like these, I've missed them.'

'Plenty of time now, right?' Charlotte smiled.

'I guess so,' she returned her attention to the window, 'still, thanks.'

'It's been great, Angie.'

***

Luke and Andy arrived back at Luke's flat drunkenly singing Christmas songs that they both hated and laughing at nothing. The Christmas party had been a success to their drunken minds, and any embarrassing or low moments were left to the side for their hangovers to worry too much over.

'I think I left the wine at Ja-' Luke hiccupped, 'at Charlotte's. Beer okay?'

'You know it,' Andy allowed himself to fall onto sofa.

'Sweet,' Luke sang as he opened the fridge and grabbed two cans. 'Glass?'

His question went unanswered, he was about to ask again when he heard snoring come from the sofa. Andy had fallen asleep earlier than Luke had anticipated, but he had been expecting it to happen at some point, Andy couldn't hold his drink as well as most of his friends.

He put one of the beers back in the fridge and sat cross-legged on the living room floor. He grabbed his tablet and set a random playlist.

Luke didn't know why he didn't go to bed, the moment he opened his beer he realised that the correct move was likely to wake Andy up, get him into bed and then go to sleep. Something in his head, most likely the alcohol, told him he needed another drink, even if he had no one to drink it with.

The party had been fun, though he didn't really know anyone. He had forgotten the names of just about everyone he had been introduced to. Andy hadn't spoken to Karl Wisemann after all, and he wasn't about to look too desperate by trying.

So they mingled and drank, then drank some more, then danced. Luke had wanted to dance more, but no one else seemed to be as interested in it as he was.

He missed dancing, going to clubs and leaving at an unknown time with an unknown person. He wasn't willing to part with that life, but he knew Andy would never be okay with it.

Andy didn't like clubs, and even if he did he could never stay awake or hold his drink long enough to make the evening fun. Luke missed his old friends, but they had all moved away. He had been alone since graduation, with nothing but casual acquaintances and colleagues to fill his free time with.

Everything changed when he met Andy, they had hooked up casually once but stayed in touch, something Luke normally found to be a fruitless effort that was doomed to fail. But after a few dates they had become quite close, and Luke had really seen something in their relationship.

But it wasn't enough, he could be with Andy for the rest of his life, but he still needed friends. Andy talked about James a lot, but never brought up how they knew each other or even how well. When Luke mentioned that he had been having some doubts about his life, Andy had given him James' address without hesitation, insisting that he was the one to talk to.

Luke hadn't wanted to simply latch on to Andy's friends, but found himself wanting to. There was a divide in his life then. He wanted to live free and single, no plans or responsibility to keep anyone but himself happy, but he also wanted to keep the security and happiness that his time with Andy had given him.

And so he turned to James.

The kiss that evening in his flat had come out of nowhere, and Luke had played into it. From then on Luke had seen James as the balance he needed, he would have Andy to be there for him, look after him and be looked after by him. Andy would be the tether that kept him from slipping too far while James would be the drink and fuck buddy that would keep the fun of bachelorhood alive and well.

When James unknowingly crossed that line by getting serious with their conversation, something inside Luke had snapped. He was there for fun, good times and sex, not heavy conversation and therapy.

He had gotten mad, hurtful. But he didn't know how to explain to James that he wanted to forget about the bad shit with him and just enjoy himself. He had heard about James' promiscuous past from everyone, and had hoped he'd find something of the wild party animal he was hoping for in him. But he had no way of getting it across without looking like a user.

But in avoiding this explanation, he instead just looked like a complete bastard, and he was beginning to realise that that would be how James thought of him until the day he died.

He had been given no chance to ignore or forget what had happened. He wasn't going to get the James he wanted back, indeed he wasn't going to get James back at all.

Sipping his beer, he relaxed and let the music sink in for a while. He had wanted a fuck buddy, he had wanted fun, but instead he only got hurt. More than anything he wanted to explain what had happened and get an explanation himself.

He wanted to see James again, he wanted to drink with him though he didn't know what he would say if given the chance. He wanted to fuck again, but didn't know how he'd feel about it.

Andy snored on the sofa, and Luke turned to him. He wanted to smile, to be happy seeing him, but he was too worried, too regretful. It had been weeks, but still he checked his phone expecting to see James' name, he opened his messenger apps again and again, hoping to discover a bug or glitch that had stopped notifications.

Charlotte seemed to be coping well, or better at least, and he didn't know why he couldn't move on as easily. What was a lost toy? A broken plaything?

He had wanted to think of James as something he could use for laughs when Andy fell short, but hearing what was said to him at that bus shelter, being hurt so much by words that came from someone he didn't want to get emotionlessly close to, he knew that he had made a mistake.

Exactly where that mistake had been made eluded him, and his deep remorse that wouldn't go away remained without specific explanation, without form. But that didn't stop it from keeping him up at night.

Now that he was gone, the balance had shifted. Everything was off and Luke found himself faking more smiles and forcing more laughs than any healthy person should.

It all started with Andy, but it had all ended with James. And Luke had no idea if he could suffer one without the other.

***

Charlotte stayed in her new bed until the early afternoon, only getting up because she decided that she couldn't go another minute without eating something.

Had she been sober, Charlotte was sure that she would have never been able to get to sleep in that bed. She had washed and changed the sheets since moving in, but the room had gone unoccupied for weeks. It began to feel a bit silly to her, as though preserving the room in memoriam or dedication to a lost friend.

It was time to move on, to claim it as her own, but she needed an excuse to do it. Angela was nice, friendly, easy to talk to and could hold her alcohol. She ticked all the boxes and made the perfect choice for a roommate.

In truth, Charlotte hadn't considered inviting anyone else to come and live with her, and her suggestion the night before had surprised her at the time. But once she had asked and saw Angela's reaction, she knew she had made the right decision.

More than anything, having both bedrooms occupied was the final confirmation she needed, the final step in accepting that James was never coming back. Though it wasn't at all the final step, it still felt like a good start.

Angela was already up and was nursing her hangover in the living room with a glass of ice water when Charlotte walked in with oven-heated pasties she had purchased and frozen for just such an occasion.

'Want some?' she asked with half a mouth full of food.

'No thanks,' Angela waved, Charlotte took her as the kind of person who couldn't eat after a rough night.

'Did you think about what I said?' Charlotte took a seat on the sofa.

'About me moving in?'

'Yeah,' Charlotte took another bite, she didn't care how much it burned her mouth.

'I think I will,' Angela smiled, 'when can I move in?'

'How about today?' Charlotte said quickly, covering her mouth with her hand while she ate. 'You have to go home to get a change of clothes anyway, so why not just pack up while you're there?' she swallowed, 'hell, I'll help if you want.'

'You sure?' Angela sat forward.

'Of course, roomie!' Charlotte beamed. Her head hurt.

***

Luke was awoken by something other than his shrieking alarm clock and thanked the heavens that he had the mind to switch it off before he went to sleep, even though he didn't remember doing so.

His bedroom was windowless, so he had no light to wake him up naturally, instead he had been awoken by the faint sound of a tone deaf attempt to sing a song that Luke didn't recognise. Andy was singing in the shower, meaning he was unsurprisingly hungover.

Luke had not missed it.

He got up and reached for the painkillers by his bed, swallowing them dry as his water glass stood empty. He was ravenously hungry but knew that Andy wouldn't be, which made the smell of bacon wafting into the room all that more unexpected.

With a dressing gown on and slippers on his feet, Luke went into the kitchen to see a bacon and fried egg sandwich sitting on the counter next to a bottle of barbeque sauce.

Andy never ate while he was hungover, and he wouldn't have made a sandwich for himself before getting into the shower. Luke shook his head and smiled. Andy had made him breakfast despite what Luke imagined was some intense suffering, and he had done so before even tending to himself. Or had he known that his singing would wake Luke up?

Either way, Luke felt loved.

He ate his sandwich with gusto, deciding against barbeque sauce once he noticed that Andy had fried the egg runny.

'Thanks for this,' he said when Andy emerged from the bathroom with a groan. It seemed as though the singing had made him feel worse. Luke wondered then if Andy even noticed himself that he was doing it.

'Hey, no worries, I know what you're like when you're hungover,' he lifted a small towel from the radiator and began drying his hair.

'What time is it?' Luke asked, setting the plate on the drying rack.

'Beats me,' Andy threw the towel back onto the radiator, 'oh, by the way, did you get Charlotte's message?'

'No, haven't checked my phone yet, why? What's up?' Luke sounded more expectant than he meant to.

'She's asking us about Christmas plans.'

'Does she not have any of her own?' Luke put the kettle on and lifted the coffee jar towards Andy, who shook his head and winced at the idea.

'She tends to stick around, I don't think she's very close to her family.'

'Huh,' Luke said, realising Christmas was less than a week away. He had just expected to hop on the first train out of town to his parents' house, he hadn't considered any one of his friends, even Andy, wanting to spend Christmas with him.

'Do you have any plans?' Luke asked, suddenly aware of the fact that he should have asked a lot sooner.

'Nah,' Andy said, 'they'll want us in the lab over the holidays, I'm only getting the three big ones off.'

'You gonna take her up on it?'

'Yeah,' he said with a smile, 'yeah, I reckon so.'

13.

'Hey!' Charlotte answered the door to see Andy's smiling face. He carried a shopping bag filled with bottles, knowing full well that the traditional gift of wine would go unappreciated.

Charlotte wore a nice blouse that Andy assumed was purchased for the occasion and a green and red apron that matched the Santa hat she wore on her head.

Andy wore a blue shirt that he saved for special occasions and a black silk tie that he would say the same about were it not the only one he owned. Above it, a thick jacket he believed was too expensive given he could only wear it comfortably for two months out of the year, three if he was lucky.

'May I come in?' he asked.

'Since when do you ask?' Charlotte laughed, stepping aside to welcome him in.

'That smells good,' he said once inside.

'That *sounds* good,' Charlotte motioned to the clinking bag.

'Gammon?'

'Slow cooked in cola,' she said smugly.

'Very nice,' Andy put the carrier bag on the counter and loaded its contents into the fridge, leaving two bottles out.

'Stout or IPA?'

'Oh, stout please,' Charlotte said, 'could use a warm up.'

'It's boiling in here,' Andy joked.

'I'm still a cold bitch,' she got the bottle opener out of the top drawer.

'And one bottle of stout's gonna change that?'

'It's a start,' she opened both beers and passed Andy his, 'cheers.'

'Cheers, so when's dinner?'

'Impatient.'

'I haven't eaten all day!'

'Good, 'cause I made a lot,' she checked the timer on her phone, 'another hour.'

'Dangerous,' he said, 'we might be too drunk to enjoy the food.'

'You, maybe,' Charlotte patted his shoulder, 'I can actually hold my alcohol.'

'Ouch,' Andy laughed.

They made their way into the living room. Even though Andy had visited Charlotte a lot in the last month, he still expected to see the old grey sofa where it belonged, in the middle of the room and not pushed to the back.

The Christmas tree still seemed out of place to him, not because of its placement or decoration, but purely because it was a Christmas tree.

A small dining table that Andy didn't recognise had been set between the sofas, four wooden folding chairs sat at it.

'Table's on loan from a neighbour,' Charlotte said, 'I never realised just how rarely James cooked for people until I noticed he didn't have one.'

'He always used other people's kitchens to cook,' Andy corrected, 'said it made it more personal.'

'He never cooked for me like that,' Charlotte said, leaning over one of the chairs and admiring the table. Four heart shaped coasters were placed on it, Andy assumed they were also on loan.

'Because he couldn't stand your housemates,' Andy smirked, 'what was her name? Fanny?'

'Franny, Christ,' Charlotte rolled her eyes and groaned, 'I'd finally managed to forget about her. Thanks for the reminder.'

'Apologies,' Andy laughed. He looked around the room, the room he had been in many times, and he reflected on a thought that he had reflected on every time he set foot in the space.

Charlotte went to sit on one of the armchairs, walking around the red sofa to do so. For a moment Andy believed she was going to sit in the rocking chair and almost called out for her not to, as though if she did then it would set off some horrific chain reaction.

Andy knew then, as he had known before, that this was not the flat he had lived in, the flat he had shared. Even though very little had changed, it was not James' flat anymore. It was Charlotte's.

'Angela not here?' he asked, taking off his jacket and draping it over one of the dining chairs.

'Nah,' Charlotte said with a fake sigh, 'she has this ridiculous thing where she likes to spend Christmas with her family. What about Luke?'

'Same.'

'Freaks, am I right?'

'You're right,' Andy took a seat in the other armchair and looked again to the dining table. 'Why four place settings?'

'Four chairs, four coasters,' Charlotte waved her hand in front of her, 'seemed like the aesthetic choice, that and it would make it feel like less of a date.'

'Like it was gonna feel like one anyway,' Andy laughed. He knew it was a joke, but wanted to play along.

'Besides,' Charlotte spoke quieter, 'Christmas was James' busiest time for, y'know, guests. And I still don't know how many people came to see him. I figured if they wanted to come then they'd have a place. No one should be a alone this time of year.'

'Nice of you,' Andy said, making his tone serious so she knew he wasn't joking.

'Not to mention a whole night alone with you and I might just kill myself,' she laughed.

'Only after killing me,' Andy lifted his beer and they clinked their bottles together.

'Of course,' she said. Humour returned to her voice, Andy could tell that she really wasn't faking it anymore, or at least not as much.

The solemnity was still there, but it didn't come up as often. It was being replaced with a quiet acceptance which, over time, would become a buried feeling in her mind, only ever brought up in the darkest and most silent of nights alone.

Charlotte was a master at burying her feelings, at making people think she was on top of the world when she was suffering more than any one person ought to. Andy had discovered far too late that she had unknowingly learned from the best.

But something in her had changed recently, something good. She had been more open, more talkative, more willing to speak about things than before. It was because of that that Andy was able to trust that her smile and laughter were genuine, it was because of that that he asked his next question.

'Do you,' he paused, 'do you think he left because he felt like there was no more he could do?'

'What do you mean?'

'I mean. Look at us. He knew his presence was hurting you, he knew that Luke's feelings about him, or his for Luke, would drive us apart,' he paused for a moment, Charlotte didn't interrupt. 'I think,' he said eventually, 'I think in a way he believed his work here was done, and if he stayed then he'd just start undoing everything.'

Charlotte breathed deeply but did not lose face, she had considered the possibility before and accepted it as a possible explanation. She was only slightly rattled to have the words spoken to her, the message behind them was nothing new.

'Maybe,' she said at last, 'and maybe he was right. It's not like we can ask him, though. I just, I just wish...' she stopped speaking while she gathered her thoughts.

'You just wish you got a chance to say goodbye,' Andy finished for her.

Charlotte nodded in response.

'Me too,' Andy said. Looking out the window, he expected to see snow, but instead only saw the glittering lights of a cruise ship out on the North Sea, no doubt filled with formally dressed, childless drunks ringing in Christmas Eve.

'Delicious,' Andy set down his fork and leant back in his chair, worried his belt was going to snap.

'Thanks, can't beat a classic,' Charlotte let out a satisfied sigh and sipped her beer.

'I think turkey is the classic.'

'Well I make my own classics, then.'

'When does a trend become a tradition?' Andy asked without knowing why.

'When it becomes popular, I guess.'

'Then I think we have found our new tradition.'

No one had come to the door to make use of the extra settings or food, though neither of them really expected anyone to. The two had eaten their fill, though they had room for more alcohol.

They barely spoke while they ate, Charlotte was a talker even over food, but took Andy's silence as a compliment to her cooking and respected his focus on eating.

'Sofa?' Charlotte asked.

'Oh Christ yes,' Andy said, groaning as he stood.

The two fell, more than sat, on the sofa, and curled up their legs to make room for each other. Andy had loosened his tie and Charlotte had removed her apron, though the hat stayed where it was.

'Reckon you'll do New Year's?' Andy asked, 'this place was always the best for it.'

He was right, the spacious living room made for a comfortable gathering and the many windows offered views of fireworks displays courtesy of particularly festive neighbours.

'Probably,' Charlotte said, 'it was always fun here, and it's not like I've got anywhere else to go.'

'Luke's is a ground floor flat and my living room can barely fit one,' Andy said, 'looks like you've got no choice anyway.'

'I'll make it small,' Charlotte decided, letting out a small belch, 'just you guys and Angie probably. Maybe David and Gregg.'

'Good luck,' Andy chuckled, 'the two only have time for each other now. Romantic twats.'

'I always thought you were the romantic type?'

'I have my limits,' Andy smirked, 'there's being romantic, and then there's 'where for art thou' sickening.'

'Yuck, I see your point.'

'They're insufferable,' he sighed.

'At least they're happy.'

'True. What about you?'

'Huh?'

'Are you happy?' Andy asked genuinely.

Charlotte didn't need as much time to think about that as she thought she would, when an answer entered her head she didn't fight it, she didn't look for reasons to argue or defend it.

'Yeah,' she said quickly, 'I am. Are you?'

'Yeah,' Andy said just as quickly.

'It's weird,' Charlotte said, 'this last month has felt like a whole new life. Like everything that happened before, everything that I thought *was* my life, was just a phase.'

'Things change, I guess,' Andy said, knowing exactly what she meant.

'But do they have to change so quickly?'

'I know what you mean,' Andy sighed, 'I wish we could just pause sometimes, y'know? Like, keep things the way they are.'

'Maybe that was his final piece of advice,' Charlotte said, looking to the rocking chair. 'You don't always get to say goodbye to the things you love.'

'Sometimes things are just gone, huh?' Andy snickered a little, 'if you ask me, that's a pretty shitty lesson.'

'I'm empty,' Charlotte held up her bottle.

'One sec,' Andy downed the remainder of his own, forgetting how strong it was, 'me too,' he said, barely holding in a belch.

He got up and went into the kitchen, grabbing their plates on the way and leaving them by the sink. In a more sober and less full state he likely would have offered to do the dishes, but knew he couldn't be bothered and would likely make a hash job of it anyway.

Andy was a firm believer of the idea that a beer or two made housework more tolerable, but he was far beyond that state.

Instead he left the dishes where they were and made his way to the fridge. They had drank all the beers that he had brought, but Charlotte had stocked up as well. Andy smiled as he read the labels of the bottles he grabbed, Charlotte always did have good taste.

'Do you still sing in the shower when you're hungover?' Charlotte asked when he came back into the room.

'Yes,' Andy said warily, 'how do you know about that?'

'James used to complain about it all the time,' Charlotte chuckled.

'Why do you ask?'

'I assume you're sleeping here tonight, and I want a lie in tomorrow.'

'I'm not gonna wake you up,' Andy said.

'See that you don't.'

Andy hadn't considered whether or not he was going to spend the night there, he had expected to get drunk and catch a taxi home in the early hours like always. He had forgotten far too easily that it was Christmas Eve, that getting a taxi would likely be impossible and Charlotte probably wouldn't want to be alone.

He was grateful that he had already snuck her present under the tree the last time he was over.

'So how's Luke?' Charlotte asked.

'He's good, yeah,' Andy nodded, 'he's been quiet lately, I think winter's hard for him. But he seems fine, can still hold his drink better than I can.'

'Oh, Honey,' Charlotte patted his shoulder and gave him a condescending look, 'most people can.'

'He's,' Andy paused, 'we're doing good. Yeah, really good.'

'Glad to hear it,' Charlotte smiled, 'it's strange,' she paused. 'I can't believe how long it's been since everything's just been, I dunno, fine.'

'I get that,' Andy said, 'everything was so dramatic for years. Who was fucking who, who got drunk and embarrassed themselves, who was cutting, who was in therapy. It's been a long time since everything was just okay.'

'I'm not sure I like it, it seems boring.'

'Either we'll get used to it,' Andy repositioned himself on the sofa to accommodate his full stomach, 'or something will fuck up. I'd say it's just a matter of time, so let's just enjoy the calm.'

'You're right,' Charlotte said, 'but if it goes on too long I may just rock the boat myself.'

'Gimme a heads up before giving in to that urge, okay?'

'No promises.'

'Damn.'

'I'll send out invites for New Year's tomorrow,' Charlotte yawned, 'I cannot be bothered right now.'

'Here here,' Andy yawned as well.

'Don't go pussin' out on me,' Charlotte gave him a playful tap on the arm, 'I'm not goin' to bed with beer in the fridge.'

***

Andy awoke on what he initially suspected to be the sofa, the expectation coming from nothing but past experience. He was pleasantly surprised when he rolled over and found that he was lying in a bed, a familiar bed in a less familiar room.

It was the bed he and James shared when he lived there. Same mattress, same frame that squeaked too much and needed to be tightened every now and then with the Alan wrench on the window sill.

Andy realised then that he was in the spare room, Angela's room.

James must have bought a new bed in recent months and moved the old one into the extra room, replacing the air mattress that they used for overnight guests.

The bed hadn't been tightened in a while, maybe Angela didn't mind the squeaking or she just didn't know how to make it stop, and Andy made a mental note to let her know next time he saw her if he didn't find the energy to do it himself beforehand.

He heard movement in the kitchen, a clanking of cups together and what he thought was the faint sound of a boiling kettle. He could sing in the shower all he wanted if Charlotte was up, as he only gave his word that he wouldn't wake her.

Andy didn't know where that particular hungover habit had come from, and he often didn't realise he was doing it himself until he had already started. But something about being conscious of his intention to sing made him feel odd, uncomfortable, so he decided then that he would refrain as best he could.

He got up and was relieved to discover that he hadn't been sleeping naked in someone else's bed. He was wearing underwear and a t-shirt he imagined Charlotte had given him to sleep in. It was about his size, if not a little smaller, and he presumed it belonged to her before recognising the logo on the side.

It was James' shirt, an old one from his days behind a bar, one he commonly wore as pyjamas. Andy found it strange that he didn't feel weird wearing it.

Without getting dressed any further, he got up and went to join Charlotte in the kitchen.

'Mornin'' she greeted, pouring herself a coffee, 'want one?'

'Christ no,' Andy said, 'it dehydrates you.'

'It also wakes you up,' Charlotte said.

Something about their conversation made Andy pause, though his pounding headache made it impossible to think too hard about why.

'I'm still good,' he said with a groan.

'Suit yourself,' Charlotte seemed tired, 'pass me the milk, wouldya?'

Andy opened the fridge and saw immediately that there were four beers left on the bottom shelf, meaning it wasn't just him who had failed to live up to Charlotte's goal. He lifted the milk and checked the date.

'It's a couple of days out,' he said.

'I'll live,' Charlotte held out her hand and took it from him, 'not like any shops are open.'

'Not a fan of black coffee?'

'I'd rather die,' Charlotte said, sniffing the milk before adding it to her cup.

'I know the feeling,' Andy groaned, 'got any painkillers?'

'Try the left cupboard.'

Andy opened it and found a blue box of exactly what he needed. He grabbed the pills and took two without water, only realising how dehydrated he was as he did so.

'You seen your phone?' Charlotte asked after taking a sip.

'Nah, why?'

'Luke sent out a message to everyone this morning, like seven o'clock, I think he was still drunk.'

'Sounds about right,' Andy chuckled, 'from what I can gather his family are nuts for booze.'

'No wonder he fits in with us so well.'

'Well, you.'

'Awk, Pet,' Charlotte said with a cheeky grin, 'you're still learning.'

'Bite me.'

'Breakfast?' Charlotte walked around Andy and opened the freezer, 'I've got some pasties.'

'Ooft, no.'

'No coffee *and* no food?' Charlotte looked to him with what might have been disgust. 'So, what? You just wait for your hangover to go away?'

'Pretty much.'

'Yikes,' she got out a packet of two pasties and set them on the counter before preheating the oven, 'no wonder you can't keep up.'

'And how does that make sense?'

'I dunno,' she yawned, 'it just does in my head.'

'Most things do to the hungover mind.'

'True enough,' Charlotte decided that she couldn't be bothered waiting for the oven to preheat, she wrapped a tray in tin foil and put the pasties in before grabbing her coffee and going in to the living room. Andy followed behind once he poured himself a glass of water from the tap.

The dining table was gone, Andy didn't know if Charlotte had given it back to the neighbours or stored it in the old waiting room for space. He recalled vaguely being woken up by someone at the door and some scraping noises, and figured that must have been it.

Charlotte hadn't thought to wake him and was up far earlier than she claimed she would be, Andy didn't question why.

'Some people swear by hair of the dog, you know,' Charlotte sat down in her favourite of the two identical armchairs.

'Never understood that,' Andy sat in the rocking chair without thinking about it, he realised too late how uncomfortable he was in it but decided to stick with his decision. He didn't want to appear too sentimental or bring anything up unnecessarily.

'Me neither,' Charlotte said, 'but I've tried it. Have you?'

'Don't have the stomach for it,' Andy rubbed his torso, 'put a beer in front of me now and we'll both regret it.'

'Fair enough,' Charlotte said. 'Oh!' she got up suddenly, managing somehow to keep her coffee from spilling. Her sudden exclamation hurt Andy's head.

'What's up?' Andy said, rubbing his temple.

'I completely fuckin' forgot,' Charlotte walked around the sofa and to the tree. 'It's Christmas Day.'

She was right, and Andy had no idea how both of them had managed to forget. The reason he had come over the night before was for Christmas dinner, the reason he had spent the night in that bed was so he and Charlotte could spend Christmas together.

And somehow, in the haze of food, conversation, alcohol and its ramifications, they had both completely forgotten.

Charlotte handed Andy a haphazardly wrapped box and smiled widely.

'Thanks,' he took it from her, 'but shouldn't we wait 'til the others are here? Like on New Year's or something?'

'Fuck 'em,' Charlotte shrugged, 'we can always do more presents later. One now couldn't hurt.'

'If you're sure,' Andy said, standing up and setting the box on the chair. He made his way to the tree and lifted the present he had hidden behind it as best he could.

'You're shitting me,' Charlotte chuckled, 'you sneaky little bastard.'

'Not gonna let this slide,' he said, 'tit for tat, that's how it works.'

Charlotte took the present from Andy and opened it with gusto, tossing the wrapping paper onto the sofa without a care. She unveiled the massive blue dressing gown.

'Wow,' she said with a smile, 'unexpected.'

'I got it for you before you moved,' Andy admitted, 'you always complained that your house was too cold.'

'I love it,' she beamed, tearing off the thin plastic wrapping and putting it on without stopping to remove the tags. 'Comfy,' she said as she felt the sleeves.

Andy opened his present with less abandon and laughed when he saw the shot roulette wheel he had been given.

'I see,' he smirked, 'you wanted to play this at New Year's before we open our presents.'

'Damn right,' she said, 'your other present goes with it, but that's all I'll say.'

'I think I can guess,' he cocked his head to the side.

'I'm looking forward to it,' Charlotte sat back down and lifted her coffee from the floor, 'it's gonna be a fun night.'

***

Luke stepped off the train at Waverley Station and made his way through the crowds of homeward bound masses, likely grateful for the end of the holiday that they had likely been looking forward to for weeks.

He went to the taxi rank on the north side of the station and waited for an opportunity. It was snowing then, it was far too cold and the footpaths were far too icy to make the twenty minute walk comfortable, even if he did have the energy.

Instead, Luke got in a taxi after a ten minute wait in the freezing streets and gave his address with a shivering and tired voice.

It was only three in the afternoon and his journey had been less than two hours, but he felt as though he had just stepped off a long haul flight that he had spent the majority of drunk.

It was the day before New Year's Eve, and he knew that if he was going to be any fun at all for Charlotte's party he would need food, a long shower and an even longer sleep, though maybe not necessarily in that order.

Andy would be at work that day, but Luke didn't really want to see him. He wouldn't make good company in his state, nor would he be able to tolerate the company of others. In his time away he had had plenty of time to think about where his relationship was going, though had reached no real conclusions. He decided to stick it out, make it work. He was deep enough in that it wouldn't matter if they broke up in a day, a week or a month.

There was no reason to make any real decisions in a hurry, nor was there any reason to trust his well-pickled brain at that point in time.

The taxi driver attempted conversation, about how Christmas had gone and if he was with family or friends, but Luke wasn't in the mood to answer and instead redirected the questions back in the hopes that he could tune him out and watch the streets go by.

He always missed the city when he was away, and found a comfort in coming back. He would enjoy seeing his flat again and hoped Andy had turned the heating on the day before like he had promised to.

The snowfall was thin, it likely wouldn't lie even though Luke hoped it would.

His flat was warm, meaning Andy had indeed kept his promise, and thankfully empty. Luke had kept his arrival time a secret so he would be free of a surprise visit. If his doorbell rang he would ignore it, if Andy let himself in he would be shooed away in as polite a manner as Luke could conjure, though he presumed it would still not be all that polite.

There was no food in the fridge, so Luke called up the first takeaway he found online that could deliver within forty minutes. Once he hung up he sat on his sofa and sighed, feeling his stomach grumble as he did so.

He realised his mistake, he had ordered food before taking a shower, and he wouldn't risk missing it. Forty minutes wouldn't have been such a gamble were Luke not so sure that he would stand under the hot water for as long as his body would allow.

It wasn't about temperature, it was about comfort.

He considered opening a beer, but only briefly, before rejecting the idea and going instead for water. He still had no wine, though he didn't want any, and realised he would have to hit a shop early the next day before going to Charlotte's.

That was tomorrow's problem, though, and he could barely focus on anything in the present as it was, so he put it to the back of his mind.

The doorbell rang just over half an hour later, and Luke considered ignoring it before remembering that he had ordered food.

On any other day, and in any other state of hunger, the bog standard Chinese platter he was faced with would have been decent enough for a lazy night in, but nothing to sing about. In that moment it was like Luke was eating food that he had tasted as a child and spent his entire adult life trying to rediscover.

He didn't care how unhealthy it was or how fat it would make him feel. It was exactly what he needed then and there.

By six o'clock he was fed, showered and had given in to the temptation of beer, promising himself he would only have the one to help him sleep.

Even though he had regained some energy by the early evening, the amount of food he had eaten and the beer he drank had him prepared for sleep as he went to bed before nine o'clock. He plugged in his phone and noticed several messages, likely asking how his journey was and if he got home safe. He ignored them and tucked himself under the covers.

It had been hours since he said a word to anyone, even with the delivery guy he had communicated only in grunts and noises. Had he been more bothered he would have worried that he came across as rude.

But right then nothing mattered other than his own comfort. He didn't care about letting Andy know he had gotten home safe, he didn't think to thank his family for the fun Christmas, he didn't think to explain to anyone how he was, well or not, even if he really knew himself.

For that one day he would think only of himself, he would allow a selfish evening before giving himself completely to the gods of socialising the next day. No one was going to assume he was hurt or dead, no one would think he wasn't okay or had run off like some selfish asshole.

Luke knew people cared about him, even if he rarely cared about himself, and it was that knowledge that had haunted him for the past month.

He stuck around because he felt loved, and he knew that the only reason someone would run off is if they felt the exact opposite. Or worse, nothing at all.

But it wasn't the time for that, that afternoon, evening and night were all his to spend with himself. Luke had been putting all of his effort into making himself comfortable, loving himself as much as he felt others loved him. Caring.

It took more effort than he was okay with, and he wasn't okay with that.

As much as he wanted to be alone for no more reason that simply because he did, he wished desperately that he still had someone to talk to. Someone who wouldn't overreact, judge, prescribe anything or talk back.

He wished he had an ear, and knew that at one point he did.

Luke didn't know what he would say, just like he hadn't really known what to say to James whenever he asked him what was on his mind, but it had been enough just knowing that he had an ear, a shoulder, or more if he wanted it.

He still hadn't come to terms with the loss that meant more to him than he felt it should. Despite how briefly they had known each other, he missed James just as much as anyone else. Maybe more.

And it was with that thought at the front of his mind that he slid into a deep and dreamless sleep.

***

'Thirty four!' Charlotte called out once the ball stopped rolling. It was Luke's turn, and he took the shot with gusto.

Andy's second present from Charlotte, an expensive bottle of tequila, went well with his first. Though he recognised that it wasn't really a gift for him.

The evening had gone well, and as a surprise to everyone David and Gregg did show up, and it was not as difficult to pry their attention away from each other as Andy had professed.

Angela did not know Andy or Luke too well, and she had never met David or Gregg. She had been dreading the party as much as she had been looking forward to it, unsure if she would really be able to relax in her own home while surrounded by virtual, and actual, strangers.

She was more comfortable than she thought she would be, and even found herself laughing at in jokes thanks to Charlotte's startlingly detailed brief of everyone who was going to be in attendance.

Every now and then Angela would stop and consider just how empty she felt her life had been before that winter. She had woken up, gone to work, gone home, studied and slept. That had been her routine almost every day for as long as she cared to remember.

She would drink with people sometimes, often with students who had stopped to chat in the office after sessions with Dahlia or had questions about their course. She drank with Dahlia, too. Sometimes in her office and sometimes in a campus bar, but she never really had anyone stay in her life for all the long, either by lack of convenience or the simple fact that they just didn't click.

That evening, the evening she had been dreading, she felt as though she really had good friends in this world, friends she could count on, friends who would stay. She was happier than she had been in a long time, and she owed all of it to Charlotte and their chance encounter outside of the office. All of it going back to when they first met in that criminology seminar seven years before.

They had considered inviting Dahlia to the celebrations, but figured that she was likely either not the type to get drunk with people half her age. That, and she likely had already accepted an invitation to some fancy gala in a rooftop ballroom somewhere exotic.

Angela had sent an invitation anyway, a simple email asking if she wanted to come, but received no reply. She wasn't sure if she was grateful for the lack of response, but she was able to go on without feeling bad knowing that she had at least tried.

'You're up,' Andy nudged Angela, who only just noticed that she had been too deep in thought.

'Sorry,' she smiled and spun the roulette wheel while Charlotte refilled the shot glass Luke had just emptied. 'Twenty seven.'

'Get it in ya!' Charlotte was far too enthusiastic, whether the booze was hitting her harder than normal or she was just happy was hard to tell. Angela took the shot and winced, she really did shots, much less tequila, but she knew what to expect from the shot she had before getting up on stage in Manchester.

'Can we take a break?' Gregg said with a sigh, 'I don't wanna black out before the bell.'

'Speaking of,' Andy brought out his phone and checked the time, 'we got twenty minutes.'

'Enough for a game,' Charlotte leant back.

'Or some good conversation,' Angela said, somehow feeling as though she was speaking out of turn.

'Or a decent wank,' Luke said with a smirk.

Angela laughed at the joke that she never thought she would find funny. She felt it wasn't just the tequila, nor was it the relaxed feeling of being around friends after a day of mild panic. It wasn't the sudden and welcome loss of anxiety either.

Angela was changing. She felt as though she had been wrapped in a cocoon for years, a blanket or shield that she didn't remember trapping herself in, but had chosen to stay inside. It was safe, it was warm, but it wasn't freedom, not in any real sense.

When she invited James out for drinks that first week she didn't for a moment expect to expose herself to a new kind of life, a new way of living and thinking. She went from comfortable loneliness to being part of a group, a tiny room to a penthouse, a state of static being to a real, normal life.

And she couldn't have been happier or more grateful to anyone who had anything to do with it.

'Happy New Year!' they all called out in unison as the television showed the countdown end. Fireworks were set off outside the building and they all gathered around to watch them, the large windows allowed for all of them to have a decent view.

They each took another shot at midnight, even though none of them really wanted to. It just felt like the right thing to do and none of them thought to disagree or argue in case someone else felt strongly. It was easier to take a shot and deal with it than have someone argue that you should take a shot.

The fireworks were set off by people who lived nearby, the empty street outside made for a great spot and they all enjoyed the show.

In the distance, and from large boats across the water, even more fireworks were being released. Some were close enough to still be heard seconds later, others looked like colourful stars shining brightly for mere seconds out in deep space. Beautiful displays that offered nothing but a brief and pleasantly startling experience before vanishing into embers that went out before they touched the snow dusted streets below.

There was a sadness to the spectacle that each of them felt but none of them would mention, a deep and too stubborn notion of just how temporary everything was. Friendships, relationships, jobs, homes, family. All of these things were fleeting even when they were still there.

With the exception of David and Gregg, everyone then realised that, once and for all, they were saying their own goodbyes to a friend they would from then on consider departed, gone for good. And while they would be thankful for everything he had done, they would not mourn him anymore.

All of them pretended not to notice the tears that Charlotte had begun to shed.

14.

The days grew longer at last, and the pavements were no longer as treacherous as they had been. The darkness of night receded back to what felt like normal, acceptable times. No longer did anyone have to get up for work and then return home under the glow of streetlamps.

The sun seemed to shine brighter as the days warmed. Jackets were still a must, but it was possible to get away with just two layers if only walking to the corner shop.

It was already beginning to feel like springtime in mid February, and everyone seemed to agree.

Luke was still not used to how bright the mornings were again, he squinted his eyes as he walked into the living room and grabbed some leftover pizza from the fridge before he even thought about coffee.

It was a Saturday, no one was at work and Charlotte and Angela were far ahead on their studies. There was time yet before Gregg and David's wedding and a brunch had been organised, though it was thankfully optional. Luke had already decided that he would not shower or get dressed until just before he had to leave.

His suit was cleaned, pressed and ironed the night before and was placed gently on the sofa so as not to crease it. Luke didn't really know why he had put so much effort into making it look nice, for obvious reasons no one ever really paid attention to guests at a wedding.

He supposed he did it to show Andy up. Andy had never ironed anything correctly in his life and often looked scruffy even at the best of times. Luke would get some mischievous enjoyment in wearing an immaculate suit next to him, that and his own self esteem could use the confidence that wearing a well prepared suit often provided.

He didn't bother microwaving the pizza. Holding a slice in his mouth, he switched on the kettle and poured instant coffee into the biggest mug he had without using a spoon. He was out of milk, but he didn't care, he had recently come to enjoy the bitter taste of a black cup, especially in the mornings. Though only if it had a little bit of sugar.

His phone buzzed on the counter top and he checked it to see a message from Charlotte, asking him to confirm if he would be over for some pre-wedding champagne. He had forgotten about that invitation, he looked to his suit and wondered if he'd risk putting it on early if he could be bothered going at all.

He realised that, like Charlotte, he didn't want to turn up to the wedding without a drink in him. And since she only lived around the corner, it wouldn't make sense to not go, and he wanted to see people anyway. Besides, if he didn't then he would end up arriving at the ceremony alone, and he didn't like the idea of swimming through a sea of well dressed strangers to find his friends, especially if he was to arrive at them a few drinks behind.

He messaged back to say he'd be there and set his phone down. He still had a few hours to kill, and he was going to kill them by doing absolutely nothing. He would enjoy acting like a slob before dressing up and attending a formal event, where he would most likely get drunk and act like a slob again.

The cycles of a hedonistic twenty-something were as cruel as they were kind, the hangover he was sure to suffer the next day would be physical evidence of that.

Andy wasn't sure what to expect when he opened his wardrobe and saw that all of his white shirts were creased to hell and back. He didn't own an iron, at least he didn't think he did, and even *if* he did, he had no idea where it would be.

He decided to suck it up and hoped that wherever the ceremony was going to be held wasn't so warm that he'd need to take off his jacket. He knew he should have given Luke a shirt, he was always ironing even when he didn't need to.

By the time the reception began no one would care anymore and he could take off his jacket and show his shirt all he wanted. Hell, he'd probably even get some laughs out of it from anyone who cared enough to comment.

That was his plan, and he was okay with it.

With a yawn and a stretch, he closed his wardrobe and went to his bedside where his phone had fallen off the charger once again. He cursed under his breath as he checked the message from Charlotte and confirmed that he shared her opinion on never turning up to a wedding sober.

It seemed to him like it had been a decade ago since he and Gregg had their brief attempt at what could be called a relationship. Andy had been on the rebound and had wanted some fun before trying to settle down, Gregg had wanted to settle down immediately.

He was happy that they both got what they wanted in the end, though it being with David was something of a surprise.

A season ago, David had been attempting to experiment with his sexuality, with varying levels of success. He even tried hitting on Andy once, though Andy refused the offer as it made him far too uncomfortable.

Life went in mysterious ways sometimes. To someone who had only met David in passing or on occasion, it would be apparent that he had no idea what he wanted. But behind the neurotic, self-loathing veil there had clearly been a lot of introspection and thought.

As long as David was happy, Andy didn't see how any of it was anyone's business but his own.

He went into his small kitchen and prepared the cafetiere his parents had bought him for Christmas, though it didn't arrive until a week into the new year. A filter coffee would be just what he needed, he wouldn't think about putting his suit on until the moment before he left, and he would do his best to keep it on until he was sure no one would notice the state of his shirt.

He realised then that he had left his tie at Luke's, and sent a message asking him to bring it to Charlotte's if he was going.

In truth, Andy barely knew David, and he didn't know as much about Gregg as their history suggested. The invitation had some as something of a surprise, albeit not much of one, and he wondered if the night was going to fun, boring, or some uncertain area in between.

Either way, it wouldn't matter. He'd have people there to party with, drink with and potentially ditch early. His best friends would be there. All of them, as far as he was willing to be concerned.

Angela liked to portray herself as someone who didn't really enjoy wearing dresses. She had avoided the tomboy archetype as much as she was able, but only because she didn't feel as though it suited her.

In truth she simply wore whatever clothes she felt were comfortable and only acted and spoke as she felt was appropriate for whatever situation she was in. She was malleable that way, adaptable, though she still felt as though she were a touch too fragile for someone her age.

She loved wearing dresses, but only if the occasion called for it, and as a result had developed an affinity for formal functions and events.

She had not been expecting an invitation to the wedding of two people she had only met once, but was delighted to RSVP with a yes as soon as she did. She had not been shopping for a new dress like Charlotte had been, as she knew no one in attendance had seen any of the ones she had worn before.

She had narrowed it down to three of the six she owned, each one laid out on her bed. She stood over them, pondering. In the end she realised it was an easy decision, and she lifted her favourite crimson one shoulder outfit and brushed it down with her palm.

She had bought it for her undergrad graduation, and had felt uncomfortable when she wore her gown over it. She had only been seen in it a few times in the past, often at events that didn't call for anything quite as nice.

She would wear that dress and whatever hat Charlotte had picked out for her, she didn't mind if they clashed. Angela had no problem with standing out, not anymore.

She put the others back in the wardrobe and closed it. She had a pair of heels that matched the colour, but she had always hated wearing heels. Instead, after receiving the invitation, she had ordered flat-soles that she felt would be much better. The only problem she saw with that was that she wouldn't have an excuse to get out of dancing, and considered instead wearing the heels that she told herself she'd get rid of ages ago.

She sat on the bed as she thought, the comfortable bed that was twice the size of the one in her old room. Andy had shown her how to tighten it and the squeaking no longer kept her up. When the bed did squeak, she had kept quiet, as she was already living rent and bill free at the behest of someone she didn't really know. Complaining about a noisy bed would have been the height of rudeness.

Besides, the bed could blast rock music at three in the morning for all she cared, it would still be an overall step up in life.

In time, even Andy had stopped referring to it as a spare room, and knew it as hers. Angela had to admit that it took her longer than she wanted, too.

It was her room, it was her life, those were her dresses in her wardrobe. And nothing could take it away from her. For her new accommodation, friends and outlooks, she would keep her head held high no matter what.

Dahlia sat in her favourite robe at her breakfast bar. It was the early afternoon, but it being her first day off in months she couldn't help but indulge a lazier attitude.

The sunlight she had sorely missed flooded her living room and the wet grass on her lawn shone in it like many sparkling diamonds in a clean jeweller's display case.

She sipped at her cortado coffee, enjoying its taste as well as its effect. The coffee machine in her office was not as good as the one in her home, though it had far more use. She considered swapping the two, but decided it would be in some way unethical to spoil her patients too much or lord her status and affluence over the other staff members more than she already did.

Through the various grapevines she had received the answers to her questions, but found herself no more fulfilled by them. She had expected changes, yes, but ones so sudden and so positive were as boring to hear as they were elating.

She was happy everyone was doing well, but she knew it was time to distance herself from the lives of those who had nothing to do with her or her research anymore.

It was a fun and interesting chapter in her life, albeit an ultimately small one.

She lamented never meeting some of the characters of the stories she had heard. Andy and Luke would have been interesting to talk to, even if only once, and the confused David must have had some intriguing inner workings to turn his life, indeed his way of life, around so suddenly and with seemingly no help or influence.

Indeed one could never expect to be privy to all facets and workings of anything, unless they were to build something themselves. This was the curse of the psychologist. No matter how clear a degree of significance or how apparent the evidence, it was impossible to know everything. There was always something out of reach, out of sight and out of control that would manipulate findings in ways even the most gifted of minds would struggle to anticipate.

Charlotte did not call to see Dahlia anymore, and she was not at all surprised. Though it did limit what she heard somewhat. Angela had sent the odd message, which Dahlia had chosen to either ignore or only respond to formally, as though she still thought of her former employee as just that, a former employee.

It was a shame, to be sure, but Dahlia knew that the potential and aptitude Angela had shown, and continued to show, in her work would not go to waste. She had faith that they would meet again, even then she had faith that she hadn't seen the last of young James Steele, though she knew not to hold her breath.

The next time they met, if indeed they ever did again, it would be a chance to connect as friends, mentor and mentee, not as researcher and subject.

Though, of course, to James there would be no obvious difference.

Charlotte walked into the hall after fumbling for too long to get the front door open, in one hand she held the cheapest dress she could find, and in the other a double bag of three bottles of champagne.

She went into the kitchen and set the bag on the floor, lifting out the bottles one by one before checking the time on her phone. Andy and Luke would be there in about an hour, meaning she had overestimated how much time she would take out.

She threw the dress over the kitchen door, it was a dark blue thing that fitted her and didn't seem like a rip off, which was all she needed to be happy with it.

She had picked out some hats for her and Angela based only on the assumption that people still wore hats to weddings. The last one Charlotte had worn, and the only one she owned, was the Santa hat she had on when Andy had spent Christmas Eve with her.

Charlotte opened the fridge and groaned at its contents. Angela's resolution to go vegetarian was going very well, Charlotte's to cut down on booze had lasted all of three days.

Nonetheless, it meant that half the fridge was full of food that Charlotte wouldn't touch, and the other half was full of beer. She looked to the champagne bottles and realised there was absolutely no way they were all going to fit.

She opened the vegetable crisper, which had always been her beer storage, to find it full of leeks, lettuce and spinach, the other one was full of green, yellow and white things she didn't recognise.

Cursing under her breath, she closed the drawers and inspected the rest of the fridge. It took some careful and creative manoeuvring, as well as the disposal of things long since out of date, but eventually she managed to get two of the bottles in, leaving the third out.

She was tempted to put it in the freezer, but didn't know whether or not it was safe to do so and left it be. If it came to it, and Charlotte had forgotten to replace the bottles, then they would have warm champagne and be happy with it.

On that thought, Charlotte wondered whether or not champagne was even supposed to be served cold.

Of course it was. Right?

She groaned again. Formal events were not her thing, and she hoped they'd get through all three bottles before leaving. If she arrived without being at least a little tipsy then she knew she would be uncomfortable beyond imagination.

She would have preferred beer to champagne, but was occasionally a stickler for tradition. That, and the dress only just fit her and she didn't fancy taking any chances.

She went into the living room and sat on the sofa, suddenly happy for the fact that she still had an hour to spare.

The sun had stopped shining into the living room, the position of the flat only made it so it got the most natural lighting in the morning, but Charlotte was okay with that. It was nicer to wake up to the sunlight than have to deal with it blinding you in the middle of the day or have it glaring off the television screen towards the evening.

She couldn't imagine living anywhere else, and had absolutely no plans to move either before or after graduation.

She could hear Angela shuffle coat hangers in her room, and figured she was still picking out what to wear. Neither of them had showered yet to her knowledge, and Charlotte figured it was the perfect time to do so.

Grabbing her dress from the kitchen, she made her way into the bathroom and turned the shower on, recognising as it heated up that Angela must have been in while she was out as the water was set to an impossibly high temperature.

She threw her towel over the partition so she wouldn't have to step out of the warm cubicle to dry off. As she washed herself she felt the urge to sing, something she had never thought to do in the past.

'Hey!' Luke smiled widely as Angela answered the door. 'You look lovely!'

'Thanks,' Angela blushed.

'Didn't think you were the dress type,' he said as he walked in.

'Didn't take you for the suit type,' she replied.

'Only when I have the occasion.'

'Ditto.'

'Is Andy here already?'

'Yo!' Andy called from the living room.

'Go on in,' Angela gestured towards the living room.

'Hey,' Andy turned round in the sofa as Luke walked in, 'did you bring m-'

'Yes,' Luke took the necktie out of his pocket and threw it at Andy. 'I swear, you are hopeless.'

'Do you even know how to tie that thing?' Charlotte joked from the rocking chair.

'Piss off,' Andy laughed, fastening his top button.

'I was told there would be champagne?' Luke asked.

'Kitchen,' Charlotte pointed, 'there's a glass set out for you.

'You have my thanks,' he left the room, nearly bumping into Angela as he did so.

'Wedding, huh?' Angela rounded the sofa and sat on one of the armchairs, 'this'll be a first.'

'Ditto,' Andy straightened his tie.

'Same,' Charlotte shrugged.

'Not me!' Luke called from the kitchen.

'Step dad,' Andy clarified. Charlotte and Angela nodded.

'So what's the plan, anyway?' Luke walked back into the living room with a flute in his hand. It was plastic, something Charlotte had bought hastily when she realised that they only had one wine glass in the flat.

'Ceremony's at five,' Charlotte checked her phone, 'reception's at seven. I take it all of us skipped out on the pre-wedding brunch?'

Everyone nodded.

'Cool. David's parents are Quakers or something, so I don't know how much booze there'll be.'

'Ditch out early if we sober up?' Andy asked.

'Fuck. Yes.' Charlotte nodded intensely, she was not joking.

'Wait, and they're okay with,' Luke paused, 'y'know?'

'Religious types aren't necessarily homophobic,' Angela pointed out, 'even if they were literally Quakers, I think they're pretty open about it.'

'Yup,' Charlotte said, 'but David's parents are tight asses with alcohol, so getting drunk is a no no, but we can just do that on our own later.'

'Is it bad that we're prioritising this over the couple?' Angela chuckled.

'Nah, this is a priority.' Charlotte winked.

'No open bar, no deal,' Luke chimed in, 'that's normally my number one rule.'

'Prepare to make an exception,' Andy smirked.

The champagne went down easy, and they all joked and laughed like they had done their whole lives. Angela and Luke no longer felt like newcomers, like additions to an already thriving group. They were all part of the same herd, they were best friends and felt like they always would be.

There was nothing to argue about anymore, no reason to get angry and nothing cry over. Everything they wanted was right there.

It was a strange new world to them, and none of them really knew why. They were adults, making adult decisions and living grown up lives, but they had their youth, their healthy lives and healthier livers.

They could skip the wedding if they wanted and go to a bar or a club, they could talk about whatever they wanted and do whatever they liked. The past didn't matter and the future was too far away to think about.

It was a first for all of them, and none of them said it, but only the present mattered to them then. The here and now of the day, the evening, even the parts of the night that would be forgotten come the next morning.

They were alive, living between the good and bad, only doing what they knew was right when it was needed, wrong when it seemed like fun, and neither if they just couldn't be bothered.

The world was their own, as were their lives, and it all revolved around that that flat, that room, that rocking chair that anyone could sit on and not feel weird anymore.

'Right, we better get a move on,' Charlotte said once the last bottle was done. Everyone stood up and began shuffling to get their things in order, checking pockets and putting on jackets.

'Gonna pee,' Luke said, excusing himself.

'I'll get a taxi,' Angela said, leaving the room after him.

'Reckon this'll be fun?' Charlotte asked once Andy was done with his inventory of himself.

'I think so, and if not we can bail anytime after 'I do', right?'

'Good point.'

Andy's attention was drawn to the coffee table then, to the unopened package that stayed in exactly the same place every time he was in that room. He had never asked about it before, not since James, but he found that, with enough fizzy wine in his head, it suddenly mattered a lot more to him than it had before.

'You've never been curious?' he said, gesturing to the box.

'Of course,' Charlotte said, folding her arms, 'but he must have left it unopened for a reason. Besides, it's the only thing left in this flat that you could really say is still his.'

'You threw out his clothes?'

'No, well, I,' Charlotte stammered, 'okay, so the *only* thing is dramatic. I just don't wanna open it. We both know who it's from. Whatever it is, it can't be good news.'

'Agreed,' Andy said, still not entirely sure exactly what Charlotte meant. 'Why not just throw it out?'

'Can't bring myself to,' Charlotte shrugged, 'it's part of the furniture now.'

'Ten minutes!' Angela said as she walked back in to the room. 'Everything okay?'

'Yeah,' Charlotte smiled, 'we all ready for this?'

'Yup yup,' Andy answered.

Luke came back from the bathroom, still shaking his damp hands.

'Ten minutes,' Angela said, 'more like nine now.'

'Got it,' Luke said shakily, the bathroom had been cold.

'Enough time to smoke,' Andy got out a cigarette.

'Outside, if that's okay?' Angela said while Charlotte took one from Andy's pack without asking.

'Cool,' Charlotte nodded, 'let's get a move o-'

Charlotte stopped speaking as three sharp knocks sounded at the front door.

END

Confidant

About The Author

Scott Edward Hamill is a graduate of Lancaster University currently living in Edinburgh. He began writing at a young age and has released books such as *Robert Did It*, *Save my Soul* and *Absence*, as well as short stories and poetry across the internet and several anthologies.

He is currently working as a full time author and freelancer in creative writing, copywriting and translation.

Printed in Great Britain
by Amazon